LAUREN CONRAD

L.A. Candy

HARPER

An Imprint of HarperCollinsPublishers

L.A. Candy
Copyright © 2009 by Lauren Conrad
All rights reserved. Printed in the United States of America.
No part of this book may be used or reproduced in any manner what-
soever without written permission except in the case of brief quota-
tions embodied in critical articles and reviews. For information address
HarperCollins Children's Books, a division of HarperCollins Publishers,
10 East 53rd Street, New York, NY 10022.
www.harperteen.com

Library of Congress Cataloging-in-Publication Data
Conrad, Lauren.
  L.A. Candy / Lauren Conrad. — 1st ed.
  p. cm.
  Summary: When nineteen-year-old Jane Roberts is cast in a new
reality show, she discovers that the fame and fortune of her new life
come at a high price to herself and her friendships.
  ISBN 978-0-06-176759-3
  [1. Reality television programs—Fiction. 2. Interpersonal relations—
Fiction. 3. Self-perception—Fiction. 4. Friendship—Fiction. 5. Con-
duct of life—Fiction. 6. Los Angeles (Calif.)—Fiction.] I. Title.
PZ7.C76472Laag 2009   2009007285
[Fic]—dc22   CIP
                                                        AC

Typography by Andrea Vandergrift
10   11   12   13   CG/BVG   10
❖
First paperback edition, 2010

To my mom and dad,
who have always supported me.
I love you.

GOSSIP

YOUR #1 SOURCE FOR ALL THE HOLLYWOOD DIRT THAT'S FIT TO SLING

Which up-and-coming reality starlet is in for a rude awakening? She may star in the hottest show on PopTV, but rumors are swirling about her off-camera behavior. Does L.A.'s newest darling have a sweet tooth for trouble? Well, she won't be able to keep her secrets from viewers for long. Cameras are following her every move . . . even when PopTV is not filming. Welcome to Hollywood!

A few months earlier . . .

1

ALWAYS LOOK ON THE CLOSET FLOOR FIRST

Jane Roberts leaned against her dresser, studying the way her white silk nightie looked against her sun-kissed skin. Her loose blond curls cascaded softly over her shoulders as she pretended not to be interested in the guy in her bed.

"Come over here—or am I going to have to come get you?"

Jane smiled mischievously at the ground, then raised her face to him, staring into his chocolate brown eyes.

She slinked back to the bed, slid onto the white silk sheets, and nestled next to him.

"Janie, you're the most amazing girl I've ever met. I'm so in love with you, it's crazy," he said, gazing into her eyes.

"Really, Caleb?" Jane smiled, and reached for him . . .

. . . and woke up to find herself lying next to some strange, sweaty guy. Some strange, sweaty, *half-naked* guy. He smelled like bad cologne and armpits and pot.

He rolled over sleepily in her direction. "Cassandra?"

Jane yanked the sheet (not silk) around herself as she sat up—which was not entirely necessary, since she was wearing her favorite faded baby blue Gap jammies that covered . . . well, everything.

"Who the hell are *you*?" she yelled.

The guy flinched at the decibel level of her voice. He rubbed his bloodshot eyes and stared at her. "Your hair was, like, black or brown last night," he said, confused. "And really long. It kept swishing against my face when we—"

"Okay, that's enough," Jane cut him off.

Soooo.

This was one of Scarlett's friends. Or, more accurately, one of Scarlett's here-today, gone-tomorrow hookups. Jane's BFF (and, as of a week ago, roommate), Scarlett Harp, was famous for giving guys the wrong name, or the wrong phone number, or both—deliberately, so she wouldn't have to see them again. If it turned out the next morning that she actually *liked* the guy and wanted to see him again, she'd tell him she'd been too wasted the night before to get her contact info straight—*so sorry!*

But this rarely happened. When it came to long-term relationships, Scarlett had Commitment Issues (according to Jane) and High Standards (according to Scarlett).

In any case, WTF was this guy doing in her bed?

"*Cassandra* is in the next room," Jane informed him curtly.

The guy grinned sheepishly. "Oh! Sorry, dude. I got

up to take a leak, and—"

"I don't need the details." Jane gave him a gentle shove. "Bye!" She turned away as he pushed himself from her bed, but not before catching an eyeful of the snake tatt that slithered creepily across his back. *Ew.*

Jane jumped out of bed and slammed the door behind him. She had to take a shower, like, *immediately.* Who knew how long he had been in her bed, polluting it with Old Spice and man sweat?

In the glass bowl on her nightstand, her goldfish, Penny, zipped through the water, her tail swishing excitedly. "Breakfast in two seconds, Pen," Jane promised. She hoped she wasn't out of fish food. Could goldfish eat granola—or maybe English muffin crumbs? What was in fish food, anyway? And, more important, *where* was the fish food?

First things first. Shower. Her eyes scanned the floor for her bathrobe. She headed for her closet, stepping over a couple of cardboard boxes that she hadn't gotten around to unpacking yet. The boxes were marked JANE'S BEDROOM STUFF in plum eye pencil, because she hadn't been able to find a Sharpie during her marathon packing spree back home in Santa Barbara.

She and Scarlett had moved to L.A. less than seven days ago, and she still had a lot of settling in to do. In fact, she'd been living under what her father called "battlefield conditions": ripping open boxes at the last minute when she needed something, like her favorite blue bikini or her blender for making strawberry-banana smoothies. Every day she promised herself that she would finish unpacking soon. Maybe tomorrow. Or maybe next month. Whenever.

Jane's procrastination was something her new roomie was familiar with. There was very little the two friends didn't know about each other. Jane had first met Scarlett fourteen years ago, in kindergarten. Back then, Jane loved to raid the costume trunk and dress up her classmates in feather boas, silk scarves, velvet capes, and strings of plastic beads. Then she'd organize tea parties, pouring pretend tea into tiny plastic teacups. But five-year-old Scarlett wouldn't play along, saying that dress-up and tea parties were "shallow games for shallow people." Jane had no idea what the word *shallow* meant then, but Scarlett had intrigued her with her rebellious personality and above-grade-level vocab.

They had been best friends ever since. Scarlett was still the same old Scarlett: a rebel with off-the-charts SAT scores who never hesitated to say whatever was on her mind. And despite the fact that she refused to brush her hair or wear anything fancier than jeans, she was gorgeous.

And Jane was still the same old Jane: wanting to dress everybody up and organize parties. In fact, that's why she had moved to L.A., after doing the backpacking-around-Europe-after-high-school thing with Scar—to intern for event planner Fiona Chen, who specialized in celebrity weddings and parties. Since Scarlett was starting her first semester at the "University of Spoiled Children," better known as the University of Southern California, or U.S.C., the two had found an apartment together in Hollywood. It wasn't the fanciest place in the world. Or the biggest. Or the quietest—Jane's bedroom window was about twenty feet away from the entrance to the 101 freeway. This may have been a blessing in disguise though, because she shared a thin wall with Scarlett, and Scarlett had her, um, boy habit. So the steady hum of traffic was kind of like a white noise machine. Kind of.

She might not have fully unpacked yet, but Jane already had ideas for how to decorate their humble new home. With a little paint (she was thinking turquoise, tangerine, cream), some plants (bromeliads, cactus, a ficus tree with tiny Christmas lights), and some goodies from Target (silk pillows, velvet throws, faux vintage lamps), it could be a palace. (Optimism was another known Jane personality trait.)

In her head, Jane was always planning, imagining, simmering with creativity. Even now, standing in front of her closet door, she was distracted by a magazine clipping that she had taped up—a photo of an antique purple fan with tiny glass beads. Flipping through *Elle, Vogue, Dwell,* and other magazines, she was constantly inspired, thinking about what would go with an Oscar after-party or a beachy wedding or a black-tie-at-midnight birthday bash. (A lot of her friends lived to party, whereas Jane lived to *plan* parties.) She had papered her beige, or cappuccino, walls (or were they just dirty?) with clippings of gorgeous venues and locations, flower arrangements, clever center-pieces, random pretty objects.

Jane spotted her fuzzy blue bathrobe on the closet floor, right next to Penny's fish food. *Always look on the closet floor first,* she told herself. She was really excited about her internship. She was really excited about being in L.A., period. She couldn't wait to begin enjoying her new job, new boys, new adventures, new everything. She and Scarlett were going to have so much fun.

Jane's life had always (well, almost always) been pleasant, predictable. She wasn't sure when or how, exactly, but all that was about to change. Moving to L.A., putting off college for the Fiona Chen internship . . . all of it was meant to shake things up, to make room for something new and amazing in her life.

Jane's happy fantasy was interrupted by the sound of a loud burp, then a toilet flushing. A moment later, there was a knock on her door. "Cassandra?" a guy's voice called out.

"One door down!" Jane shouted back.

Ugh. Her new and amazing life would have to wait until she and Scarlett settled on some house rules. Like . . . Scarlett was not allowed to bring home guys who were too stupid or too baked to find their way back to her room.

On second thought, maybe Jane would just invest in a lock for her bedroom door.

2

YOU'RE NOT A **TOTAL** BITCH

Scarlett poured a cup of coffee, black, into her favorite mug, which said: COGITO, ERGO SUM, her favorite saying by her favorite philosopher, René Descartes. It was Latin for "I think, therefore, I am," but she liked to tell anyone who bothered to ask that it was Swahili for "I'm shallow, but you're ugly," although she actually thought of herself as the opposite of shallow, and she considered beauty—or at least what passed for beauty in Southern California—to be highly overrated.

Scarlett knew that she had a strange sense of humor. It made people a little wary of her. But she liked it that way.

The midmorning sun slanted through the grimy windows and lit up the urine-colored kitchen walls. Outside, palm fronds swayed against the black-and-white backdrop of this week's billboard: some random teen modeling a thong. Noises rose up from the street: cars honking, rap blaring from someone's apartment, the guy from the ground-floor bodega swearing in Spanish. (Scarlett spoke four languages passably, including Spanish, and recognized *mierda* and *caray*.) The window fans whirred silently, stirring up the thick air without actually cooling anything. The cracked white thermometer with the smiley face on it registered 92 degrees.

Sipping her Coffee Bean and Tea Leaf French Roast, Scarlett caught a glimpse of her reflection in the garage-sale mirror Jane had propped next to the fridge to "make the room look bigger." (Although who wanted to make a urine-colored room look bigger?) Wearing only a faded black tank and American Apparel boy briefs, Scarlett recalled the dozens of times guys had told her how hot she looked in this particular ensemble. But her appearance was not a quality she thought much about. In fact, her attractiveness sometimes got in the way of what she really wanted. It made other girls jealous of her and, consequently, they snubbed her (at best) or acted like sabotaging, PMS-plagued, psycho bitches from hell (at worst). It made guys unable to see past her super-long, wavy black hair, olive skin, and piercing green eyes to actually connect with her brain, which she worked hard to cultivate and was actually quite proud of. This made hookups easy, but friendships with guys nearly impossible. Her good looks made her parents—Mom was a shrink, *gag*, and Dad was a cosmetic surgeon, *double gag*—lecture her frequently and patronizingly about the risks of teen sex, as if only hot girls got pregnant or contracted STDs.

Scarlett had read in some book that Descartes was thought to have had sex only once in his life. Poor Descartes! Maybe Mr. "I think, therefore, I am" should've spent a little more time thinking about sex. Scarlett believed passionately in a life of the mind *and* the body— that is, to be brilliant and to hook up as often as possible. It was a good life, as far as she was concerned. Even though it sometimes led to mistakes, like the one she had brought home last night.

"Morning."

Scarlett glanced up. Jane was standing in the doorway, stifling a yawn. She was wearing her blue robe that made her look about ten years old, and her long blond hair was wet. There was a spot of white moisturizer on her lightly freckled nose, and she smelled like strawberry shampoo. She was, as always, an adorable little mess. She looked like the girl next door, and had the innocence to match. That innocence made some people (like Scarlett) fiercely protective of her. It made other people (like all the assholes of the world) try to take advantage of her.

Scarlett smiled. "Hey. You want some breakfast? Or is it lunch already?"

"Hmm. What do we have?" Jane asked.

Scarlett opened the fridge. Half a questionable-looking lime, one peach soy yogurt with an expiration date of yesterday, and a pizza box containing a few slices from a couple nights ago.

"Hmm. Maybe we should go out," Scarlett suggested,

frowning at the contents of the fridge.

Jane joined her. Her five-foot, five-inch frame was four inches shy of Scarlett's. "Well . . . I wouldn't want to tear you away from your hunky new boyfriend," she teased.

Scarlett laughed.

"I had the pleasure of meeting him this morning," Jane went on. "In bed."

"Excuse me?"

"He wandered into my room by accident. I don't know, Scar. He wasn't up to your usual standards." Jane grinned.

Scarlett grinned back. "Yeah, well, what can I say? I met him a couple nights ago at that used bookstore around the corner. He was in the literature aisle, reading James Joyce. I thought he might be interesting so when he asked me out I said yes." She added, "Anyway, he's gone. Which, as you know, is how I like my men."

Jane reached into the fridge, opened the pizza box, and grabbed a slice. She leaned up against the counter and bit into it. "One of these days, you're going to fall in love with some guy, and you're not going to know what to do with yourself."

Scarlett took another sip of her coffee and considered this. Love . . . who needed love? As long as she had her books and her friends and an occasional hookup, she was perfectly content. Real relationships—the kind that were supposed to last but never did—were more trouble than they were worth. What, was she going to be like her mother, who taught her patients how to get in touch with their feelings but who never said "I love you" to her own husband? Or like her father, who chiseled women into perfect SoCal goddesses but who never told his own wife that she was beautiful? Besides, life was too short to be stuck with one guy and one guy only. There was an entire *universe* full of them.

"You want to do something today?" Jane asked her, offering her some pizza.

Scarlett took a bite. It didn't taste *too* old. "Sure. Like what?"

"It's Saturday. We should do something fun. We're in L.A., and we haven't done much since we got here." Jane paused and stared out the window. "Maybe we could go shopping on Melrose? And tonight we could go out to dinner and maybe go to a club?"

Scarlett arched her eyebrows skeptically. "It's funny how you say that, like you actually know what clubs to go to in L.A."

"I'm sure we can figure it out." Jane shrugged as she tossed the pizza crust into the empty sink. Then she narrowed her eyes at Scarlett. "But you have to promise me one thing," she said very seriously.

"What?"

Jane smiled. "No picking up guys with snake tattoos or an offensive amount of Old Spice."

"Is there an *in*offensive amount of Old Spice?" Scarlett asked drily. "At least I'm getting some action. Unlike some

people in this room, who haven't been with a boy since—"
Scarlett stopped short.

Jane's smile vanished. Her blue eyes widened with hurt. Scarlett was mortified. *You idiot,* she scolded herself. *Shut up.*

Jane had been in love once in her life, with Caleb, her high school boyfriend. Caleb, who had left the year before to go to college out of state, broke up with Jane a few months ago. They had tried long distance for a while, but a relationship consisting solely of phone calls, emails, and occasional visits hadn't been enough for him. He had finally ended it, saying that it wasn't working and that he didn't want to ruin something that had once been great. In actuality, Scarlett thought it was his way of saying, "I can't keep cheating on you without you eventually finding out," but she would never tell Jane that. Jane had been devastated, and she hadn't been with another guy since.

"Sorry, Janie," Scarlett said. Besides Caleb, she was the only other person in the world who called her that. She reached over and hugged Jane. "I'm really sorry. I'm a total bitch."

"You're not a *total* bitch," Jane replied. She faked a smile.

"Seriously, I'm sorry. That was really lame. How about I buy the drinks tonight at whatever amazing place you find for us to go?"

"You're *definitely* buying," Jane told her.

Jane started leafing through a magazine. Scarlett noticed

that the magazine was upside down, although Jane seemed oblivious. Jane sometimes got quiet when she was upset—unlike Scarlett, who had no problems saying whatever was on her mind, and *loudly*. She wished, not for the first time, that Jane would forget about Caleb already. He may have started out as Mr. Perfect, but he had ended up breaking her heart. He wasn't good enough for Jane—not nearly.

Of course, the best way to forget about a guy was to meet another one. Maybe Jane would get lucky in L.A.—maybe even tonight? There had to be thousands of cute, available guys in such a big city, right?

3

LET'S GO SPEND SOME MONEY

Melrose Avenue was lined on both sides with small, funky-looking boutiques with names like Too Cute! and Wasteland and Red Balls. Jane loved the crazy, colorful facades: a Day-Glo pink storefront next to a lime-green-and-purple one followed by a store with an all-black window display studded with different-sized silver spheres. One boutique had a mural of two French poodles French kissing. Another featured a window display of mannequins in goth makeup and straitjackets.

Jane took her phone out of her hobo bag and started snapping pictures. You never knew where inspiration might come from.

"What are you doing? You're making us look like total tourists," Scarlett complained, adjusting her black Ray Bans.

"Relax, Scarlett. You can walk ahead of me if it's that

embarrassing. Hey, is that Jared Walsh across the street? Oh. My. God!"

Scarlett groaned. "Now, you're *really* making us look like tourists."

Jane knew her best friend better than that. Scarlett may *act* unimpressed by celebrities. But behind her shades, she was definitely watching Jared and feeling the small rush an A-list celeb sighting gave. In person, he looked a little shorter than he seemed. They watched the actor as he hurried into a parked black Jag. Jane had read a cover story about him in *Gossip* magazine recently. She wondered if it was really true that he had a coke habit, and that he was cheating on his pregnant wife (whose twins were due any day now) with a seventeen-year-old model.

The August sky was a bright, cloudless blue, and the air shimmered with heat. Jane was eager to do some shopping before trying one of the fun restaurants she'd found online. It might take the edge off the mood she'd been in since this morning. Jane kept remembering her dream about Caleb . . . and then Scarlett bringing him up. Jane hadn't been thinking about him as much lately. She hated being reminded.

"Hey. You still with us, Jane?" Scarlett said, cutting into Jane's private little self-pity session.

"Huh? Oh. I was just wondering which store we should try first."

Scarlett glanced around. "I don't know. There's the

S&M place over there with the dog collars and whips. Or the Sluts-R-Us place with the dresses with the nipples cut out. Or—"

Jane rolled her eyes. "Stop it, Scar," she begged. "I'm serious."

"I'm serious, too. I just want a pair of jeans," Scarlett said.

"Because you don't have enough of those? Maybe it's time to branch out, sweetie."

But even as Jane said this, a scruffy-looking guy passed them, stopped on the sidewalk, and glanced appreciatively at Scarlett's denim-covered behind. He was about the fiftieth person to do that today. Scarlett always got a lot of attention wherever she went. She never even had to try.

Jane and Scarlett continued down the street. It was Saturday afternoon, and Melrose was mobbed. Jane loved to people-watch, and she checked out everyone they passed. There were couples holding hands (guys with girls, guys with guys, girls with girls), teens, tweens, middle-aged gawkers with money belts and brand-new white sneakers, and cute Japanese girls traveling in packs. There were dozens of women who all had the same look. Jane was beginning to realize they were an L.A. cliché: bleached blond hair, plumped lips, fake tan, boob job. It was like being in the land of the blond clones.

Jane also noticed a few homeless people. One of the men had a sign attached to an empty Marc Jacobs shoebox that said WILL WRITE SCREENPLAY FOR FOOD. Jane stared wistfully at the man's German Shepherd puppy—it was curled up at his feet, looking at her with its sad eyes—and impulsively dropped a crumpled five into the shoebox. She hoped they wouldn't run into more homeless people with puppies, or she would go broke very quickly.

"That puppy's homeless," Jane whispered to her friend. "I wish we could adopt it."

Scarlett frowned. "That *man* is homeless. Do you want to adopt him, too?"

Jane sighed and shook her head. She had always wanted a puppy (her mom was allergic, which, growing up, meant no dogs), and had settled for a series of hamsters, guinea pigs, and goldfish as puppy substitutes. At home, she had volunteered down at the local animal shelter on weekends. She had wished she could rescue them all.

Jane felt Scarlett's arm around her shoulders. Scarlett always knew when she got into a mood about animals. "Come on, sweetie. Let's go spend some money."

"Hmm."

Scarlett dragged her away from the puppy and after a while the shops started looking less pop art and more subdued, minimalist. Jane pointed to an elegant white storefront across the street. "That place looks nice. Wanna look inside?"

"Sure," Scarlett agreed.

They made their way across Melrose, past a sleek yellow

Ferrari and a couple of Harleys that had stopped at a red light. The two biker dudes made a point of calling out to Jane and Scarlett; it sounded like an invitation to do something obscene on the backs of their bikes. Scarlett grabbed Jane's elbow, and the two of them hurried into the store, laughing and pretending to gag.

The inside of the store was as white as the outside. White Japanese rice paper covered the walls and the floors were a rough, unpolished white marble. A dozen or so white outfits hung on sleek white racks. At the white mod counter stood a saleswoman—wearing white, what else?—and a single customer: a short (about five-foot-four) guy with spiky black hair and Asian-looking features who was dressed in tight jeans, a black muscle tee, and red sneakers.

"She needs that dress by tonight," the guy was explaining to the sales clerk in a loud, dramatic voice. "If she doesn't have it by then . . . well, you know." He raised a hand to his neck and made a violent slicing motion.

"Of course," the sales clerk replied apologetically. "I'll call our other store and see if they have it in her size. She's a four, right?"

The guy gasped. "A four? Eeeeek! Don't ever, *ever* let her hear you say that. She's a two. Write that down—two, two, two!"

Jane tried not to look so obvious about the fact that she was eavesdropping.

Scarlett leaned over to Jane. "Can we get out of here?"

she whispered. "This place is a little, um, *white* for my taste."

Jane grinned. "I know what you mean. Wait a sec, though. I want to look at that cami over there."

She headed to one of the racks near the counter and the gorgeous white cami. It was made of some airy, gossamer fabric that looked impossibly soft, like angel wings. Jane reached out to feel it.

"Please don't touch that!"

Jane practically jumped at the sharp tone of the sales clerk's voice. "Excuse me?"

"I said, please don't touch that," the woman repeated, narrowing her eyes at Jane.

Jane could feel heat rising in her cheeks. "Sorry, I was just looking for the price tag," she mumbled.

The sales clerk raised her eyebrows. "It's twelve hundred dollars."

Jane flinched—not just at the woman's rudeness, but also the insane price tag. Twelve hundred dollars? For a cami? She started twirling a lock of her hair, winding it around her index finger. It was a nervous habit she'd had since she was little. *Nice attitude for someone working retail,* Jane thought.

Scarlett opened her mouth to say something—probably a sentence beginning with the words "Listen, bitch!"— but Jane spun around and shook her head quickly, silencing her.

The guy in the black tee glared at the sales clerk. Then

he turned to Jane and put a hand on her arm. "You don't want to shop here, hon," he whispered. "It's overpriced, overrated, and"—he raised his voice a notch—"the hired help needs to learn some manners so she can keep her day job. Otherwise, how else will she pay for her Botox treatments, her leased Lexus that she pretends to own, and her sad Louboutin knock-offs?"

The sales clerk looked shocked. "I heard that!" she snapped. "And you can forget about that dress for your boss. You can tell her that—"

"—the clothes here look almost as cheap as the help, and that she should take her business elsewhere?" The guy smiled at her. "Consider it done. Have a nice day!"

As Jane and Scarlett were both trying not to laugh, the guy turned to them and said, "Come on, girls. Let's go to the store across the street. It's way better than this place."

"Now *this* would look amazing on you," Diego told Jane. He held up a teal silk minidress. Rows of tiny, delicate gold beads accented the low (but not too low) neckline. "And for you," he added, turning to Scarlett, "well, why don't we talk about that purple blouse? Not very many people can pull off that color, but it would look sick on you."

The guy in the black tee—he had introduced himself as Diego—had escorted Jane and Scarlett to a small but stylish boutique called Madison, where the clothes were fun, fabulous, and beautiful (and they came in colors other than white). Jane spotted trendy, classic, and everything in between.

"How do you know so much about fashion, Diego?" Jane asked him as she sorted through a rack.

"Call me D," he insisted. "Everyone calls me D. As for fashion—well, I know a little about everything, Miss Jane. Including the fact that you're a natural blonde, which makes you practically an extinct species in L.A."

Scarlett fingered a black silk blouse that was hanging on a mannequin. "So, Diego . . . D . . . what was that about just now? Across the street? Who were you buying the dress for?"

D fluttered his hands in the air. "Oh, that's *so* not important. The boss lady wanted a dress. She sent me over there to get it; she's not going to. End of story. What about you two? Wait, wait, let me guess! *You*"—he scanned Scarlett up and down—"moved to L.A. to be a model. Well, I can assure you that Ford and all the rest of them are going to be clawing each other's eyes out to sign you first. I'm sure you've seen the competition. Not many exotic girls like you. Just a sea of underfed blondes. And as for you"—he turned to Jane—"you're hoping to be the next Drew or Reese, aren't you? You're like the perfect California golden girl, and there's not an ounce of silicone or acrylic in you."

Jane and Scarlett glanced at each other and laughed.

"We just moved to L.A., like, a week ago," Jane explained to D. "Scarlett's a freshman at U.S.C. I'm going to intern for an event planner."

D's eyes widened. "Oh! You girls actually *do* something! Well, good for you! So you're new to L.A.? Do you just love it?"

"We're still kinda getting settled," Jane replied. "Do you know of any good places to go out? We're a little clueless. I heard there's a great place on Las Palmas. I forget what it's called. My cousin used to go there last year and—"

"Last year? Well, then, you can't go there," D interrupted. "For the most part, club life in L.A. is six months, max. It's probably overrun with cheap extensions, midriffs, and Ed Hardy by now."

"Club life?" Scar said skeptically. "Last time I checked, vodka didn't expire after six months."

"Well, in L.A., the clubs do. They're only hot till they're not, ya know? I'm sure the place was fabulous for the first couple months, but most places are in and out faster than Juicy track suits. When they open, you're fighting to get a table. A few months later, you wouldn't be caught dead there. They keep the places open as long as people show up. Then they paint the walls, change the interior, and pick a new name." He added, "Okay, so maybe some of them *do* last longer than one of Jared Walsh's marriages." He smiled mischievously.

"Well, we were thinking of going out tonight," Jane said. "Any suggestions?"

"Hmmm . . . I don't really go out on weekends. It's a little desperate. Hyde just got a new promoter though. That could be fun."

D's comment was cut off by a loud, insistent buzzing. "Oh, F," he muttered, reaching into his shirt pocket for his BlackBerry. He glanced at the screen. "Oh, double F. It's the boss lady. I've gotta bail, sweets, or she's going to serve my private parts on a sushi platter at her dinner party tonight."

Jane giggled. D was one of the funniest guys she'd ever met. He was quick and sassy, but friendly. "Okay, well, it was really nice meeting you," she told him.

She was about to ask D for his number, but he was already on his way out the door, punching buttons. "Take care of my friends, okay, Sabrina?" he called out to one of the sales clerks. He held his BlackBerry up to his ear. "Hi, Veronica. Yes, yes, I'm so, so sorry. She said what . . . ?"

And then he was gone.

4

HOW DO YOU KNOW
SHE'S HIS GIRLFRIEND?

"What about this place?" Scarlett asked Jane.

The two girls paused in front of a divey-looking bar on North Cahuenga not far from their apartment. The neon blue sign read BIG WANGS. Through the windows, Scarlett could see two pool tables and a tiny stage, possibly for karaoke. Small blue leather booths and worn wooden tables lined the walls. At every corner, large-screen TVs hung from the ceiling. The place looked pleasantly busy, with some of the twenty-something Saturday-night crowd spilling out onto the sidewalk, smoking cigarettes.

Jane studied the sign. "Big Wangs? Sounds classy."

Scarlett laughed. "Come on, Janie. Don't be a drag. There are cute guys in there." She put her hands on Jane's shoulders and shook her playfully. "Live a little, woman."

"Yeah, okay."

"And they probably don't card here." Not that Scarlett

was worried about that, but she knew Jane would be.

Scarlett grabbed Jane's hand and pulled her along. They pushed their way through the crowd and looked for a table.

"You're right. There *are* lots of cute boys here," Jane remarked.

"Yeah, you gotta trust me on this stuff," Scarlett said, looking around. "I don't see any tables. Bar?"

Jane's eyes darted around the room. "Yeah, I guess that's our only option."

"I don't know if this is one of the fabulous places you were imagining, but if I remember correctly, you've never been one to turn down a Dirty Shirley," Scarlett called out cheerfully to Jane. "Should I order two?"

"Aw, you know me so well," Jane joked.

They walked up to the bar and squeezed into an empty space. The bartender—a big guy with a buzzed head and a black tee with SIZE MATTERS written across the front— eyed them and smiled. "What can I get you lovely ladies?" he said.

"Two Dirty Shirleys, please?" Scarlett smiled at him, leaned over the bar, and reached for a cherry. The guy was cute. She had always had a soft spot for bartenders. For one thing, they had good social skills because they talked to so many different people every day. More important, they knew how to make drinks. And most important of all, they had the power to ignore the whole annoying "checking ID" business.

"For you, anything," the bartender said smoothly.

He reached for two plastic cups, then nodded at someone. "Another one for you, Braden?"

Scarlett followed the bartender's gaze. Leaning up against the bar to the left of her was a young guy: supertall, slender, disheveled dirty-blond hair, hazel eyes behind black-rimmed glasses, just the right amount of sexy stubble. Dressed in faded Levi's and a soft-looking gray tee with a hole in the shoulder, he was finishing off a Guinness and reading some sort of manuscript. *Hmm, forget the bartender,* Scarlett thought.

Scarlett turned to the guy. "You always bring reading material with you to sports bars?" She had to raise her voice to be heard above a loud group of girls behind them.

The guy stared at her. "Well, how would I know that I would meet someone as sweet and charming as you to keep me company?"

Scarlett blushed. Very few people ever sassed her back. "Touché."

He studied her and Jane for a second, then extended his hand. "Braden."

Scarlett shook it, hard. "I'm Scarlett."

The bartender slid two large plastic cups toward the girls. "That'll be fourteen," he said. Scarlett reached for her purse.

"I'm so sorry, but I don't think your money's any good

here. Drinks are on me," Braden said, pulling out his wallet.

"Actually, I'm buying," Scarlett started to say, then decided to drop it. How could she explain to this stranger, Braden, that she had promised these drinks to Jane? That she had been an ignorant jerk this morning and teased Jane about her ex, Caleb? She could buy those drinks for Jane anytime. Besides, either way, Jane wasn't paying.

Oh right—*Jane!* Jane was standing next to her at the bar, entertaining herself with a bent straw. "This is my friend, Jane," Scarlett said to Braden.

Jane reached across Scarlett and shook Braden's hand. "In case you didn't notice me, I'm the less attractive friend to the right," Jane said with a little wave.

Scarlett mentally cringed. Why did Jane always do that? Scarlett loved her to pieces, but the self-deprecating crap had to go. Jane was often putting herself down. Anyone could see how pretty Jane was—except, sadly, Jane herself.

Braden smiled. "I noticed you. And I think you're selling yourself short."

Now it was Jane's turn to blush. This guy was good.

While Braden paid for the drinks, Jane leaned over to Scarlett. "Okay, so I guess I'm gonna be playing unnecessary wingman to you *again*," she whispered.

"Oh, please—"

"What'd I miss?" Braden interrupted, slipping his wallet into his pocket.

Scarlett turned to Jane. "Jane was just wondering if you come here often."

Jane smiled awkwardly. "Uh, yeah. Do you frequent Big Wangs, Braden?"

Braden laughed.

Scarlett fished the cherry out of her drink and watched Jane twist a lock of hair around her index finger. Wow, was Jane flirting? It wasn't good—*did she really just say "frequent Big Wangs"?*—but it *was* flirting. It had been too long since Jane had shown any interest in a guy, and she was long overdue for some quality male attention. Now all Scarlett had to do was get Jane to trade spots with her without seeming too obvious, like some sort of matchmaker-slash-pimp. She didn't mind letting Jane have Braden. There were plenty of other possibilities here tonight.

"Big Wangs? Yeah, I work nearby from time to time, and I like to walk over here to meet up with friends."

"You work around here?" Scarlett asked. She glanced at the manuscript he'd shoved into his back pocket. "Starving writer?"

Braden chuckled. "Close. Starving actor. I've got a big audition next week."

"What kind of audition?" Jane asked.

"It's a sci-fi pilot. It would be so cool to get the part. I love sci-fi. I was one of those *Star Trek* geeks in high school—you know, the kind that girls like you probably avoided like the plague?"

"It's not that we were avoiding you, it's that we were

shy about our bad Klingon accents," Jane joked.

Go, Jane! Scarlett mentally cheered. "So have we seen you in anything?" she asked Braden. She leaned back as a guy wedged himself between her and Jane to get another drink from the bartender.

Braden shook his head. "I just signed with an agent, like, six months ago. I did a walk-on for this Sundance Channel drama that kind of never went anywhere. And a play you've never heard of, and you never will, because it closed after two nights. My agent's been trying to persuade me to get into commercials. But I just don't see myself selling cough syrup or life insurance, you know? I'm one of those 'principled' actors who holds out for low-paying, high-prestige indie jobs. My agent's ready to kill me. I think I've made him, like, twelve dollars in commissions."

"Maybe you'd better let me buy those drinks, after all," Scarlett offered.

"Next time. By the way, I think I just turned into one of those people who start every sentence with the words 'my agent.' Ugh."

"Forgiven," Jane assured him.

"So what do *you* two do in L.A.?" Braden said. "And you have my permission to use the words 'my agent.' I promise I won't leave."

"Scar and I don't have any agents," Jane said before giving them the brief summary of their L.A. life.

Braden nodded. "An event planner, huh? Cool. And U.S.C., that's awesome." He took a sip of his refreshed

Guinness. "Santa Barbara is one of my favorite places in the world. My friend has a beach house there. It's beautiful."

"Did you grow up in California?" Scarlett asked him.

"Yup. Pacific Palisades, born and raised. I thought about moving out to New York City after high school. Maybe someday."

"Scar and I went to New York City with our school, senior year," Jane said. "Remember, Scar? We got separated from the group and ended up in Times Square."

Scarlett smiled. "We didn't get *separated,* Janie. That bitch Jenn Nussbaum offered to hold our backpacks for us while we went to the bathroom at Toys 'R Us, then she took off and left us there without our cells and wallets. She was getting back at us . . . well, *me,* actually . . . for that little incident involving her boyfriend, Doug, at his birthday party. Anyway, we were stuck in Times Square without our phones, and, like, three dollars for dinner."

"We split a pretzel," Jane recalled. "I was *so* hungry. It was the best meal I'd ever had! And it was Dave, not Doug, you slut."

"Whatever. Then we rode the Marriott Marquis elevators up and down about a hundred times," Scarlett went on.

"That was so much fun," Jane murmured. In the dim light of the bar, Scarlett could see the smile on Jane's face, as though she were lost in the happy memory of New York City. Or in the happy moment right here and now, basking in the attention of a new boy. "New York City is so awesome. We have to go back sometime," Jane went on.

"Well, if I ever end up moving out there, you can come visit me," Braden said. "I won't leave you stranded in Times Square."

Scarlett listened to the long, loaded pause as Braden's words hung in the air, sizzling and simmering between him and Jane. *Maybe this would be a good time to pretend that I need to pee,* she thought.

She stepped back from the bar and was about to excuse herself when she saw a red-haired girl walking toward them. The girl was short, curvy, pretty. She was wearing a flowered sundress and flip-flops. Her gaze was fixed on . . . *them.* Her, Jane, and Braden. Or more specifically, Braden, who didn't see her coming because he was busy talking to Jane about puppies or something.

"Hey, you," the girl said, touching Braden's shoulder. "Sorry I'm late."

Braden glanced up sharply. "Oh! Hey!"

He kissed the girl on the cheek. She leaned back slightly and went back in for another kiss—on the lips.

Braden broke away from the kiss, looking flustered. "Hey, guys! Um, this is—"

"Willow." She smiled at Scarlett and Jane.

Scarlett instinctively moved closer to Jane. Jane tugged at the lock of her hair stuck around her index finger. Her happy, mellow, I'm-in-a-bar-and-I-just-met-an-awesome-new-guy vibe had totally died.

"I'm Scarlett, and this is Jane," Scarlett said quickly.

"We were just on our way to a party," she fibbed. "Do you two want to come with us?"

Being the actor he was, Braden knew his line well. "Actually, it's kinda late. I have that audition next week, and I need to get up early to rehearse. Maybe next time?"

"Sure," Scarlett said cheerfully. "Nice to meet you, Willow. Bye!"

"Bye!" Willow said, leaning possessively into Braden.

"Bye," Jane said with a small wave. Scarlett noticed that she avoided Braden's eyes.

Scarlett linked her arm through Jane's as they made their way out of the packed bar. Outside, the air felt warm and velvety, and the city glittered against the dark sky. A guy and a girl were making out under a streetlamp.

Jane stared wistfully at the couple for a moment. Then she turned to Scarlett. "What was up with that?" she demanded.

Scarlett rolled her eyes. "I was saving you. Do you really want to hang out with that guy and his girlfriend?"

"How do you know she's his girlfriend?" Jane snapped back. "He said he likes to meet friends here. Maybe she's just a friend," she added, studying her nails.

Scarlett shook her head.

"Okay, so, *fine*. Maybe she *is* his girlfriend," Jane conceded. "He seems like a really nice guy, though. After all, it's not like we know a lot of people in L.A. Maybe we could be friends with him." She glanced over her shoulder at the door. "Maybe we should go back and ask for his number—"

Scarlett grabbed Jane by the shoulders, spun her around, and pushed her gently in the opposite direction. "We'll run into him again, I'm sure. He's in this neighborhood a lot, it sounds like. Besides, I promised I'd buy you drinks. Why don't we find another bar?"

Jane glanced over her shoulder again. "What did you say?"

She hadn't heard a single word. "Another bar," Scarlett said firmly. "*This* way."

5

IT'S ALWAYS BETTER TO BE THE DUMPER THAN THE DUMPEE

"Mom, I gotta go! I love you but I'm sooo late! Bye!" Jane said, snapping her cell shut. She glanced at the clock on her dashboard as she pulled into the parking lot: 9:05 a.m. It was her first day on her new job, and she was already five minutes late.

She caught a glimpse of herself in the rearview mirror and saw that her hair was—well, "windblown" would be a kind way to put it. Because it was such a beautiful, balmy morning, she had rolled down all the windows of her VW Jetta and had driven just a little over the speed limit to make up for the fact that her alarm had failed to go off. Now a windblown mess lived on top of her head.

Jane reached into her enormous orange leather tote bag and dumped its contents onto the passenger seat: wallet, two lip glosses, pen, sketchbook, notebook, protein bar, bottle of water, rolled-up *Women's Wear Daily* (better known as *WWD*), apple, another pen, breath mints, tube of stain remover, eye pencil, another pen, and two movie ticket stubs. Aha, there it was—her favorite tortoiseshell hair clip. She quickly twisted her hair into a knot, secured it with the clip, and checked her reflection again. Perfect . . . *ish.*

After stuffing everything back into her bag, Jane ran out of the car, barely remembering to lock it, and raced into the building. Inside the modern lobby, she signed in with the security guard and then headed up to the fifth floor.

Fiona Chen Events reminded Jane of a fancy spa. The reception area had dark gold walls, soft lighting, and a miniature Zen garden with a trickling waterfall. Soothing New Age-y music hummed over invisible speakers. The air smelled like lavender, clean and comforting.

Behind a long gold desk, a petite blond receptionist spoke softly into a headset. She peered at Jane from behind a massive arrangement of purplish black calla lilies and bamboo leaves and whispered, "Can I help you?"

Jane gave her a little wave. "Um, hi! I'm Jane Roberts. I'm the new intern." Her voice sounded really loud to her.

"I'll let Fiona know you're here. Please have a seat."

Jane started to thank her but was stopped short by the sound of exotic birds singing. No, it wasn't birds; it was the receptionist's phone. Jane had never heard a ringtone like that. "Good morning, Fiona Chen Events, Naomi speaking," the receptionist whispered.

Jane noticed a sleek brown leather couch and sat down. She reached to twirl a lock of her hair, then remembered that she was wearing it up. She drummed her fingers on the couch and tapped her foot. *Calm down,* she told herself. *Relax. Breathe in and out with the trickling waterfall.*

She had a good reason to be nervous though. After all, this was her first real job. The only other jobs she'd had were the usual high school gigs: babysitting, lifeguarding, waitressing. She had even worked behind the counter of an El Pollo Loco—"The Crazy Chicken"—although the only crazy thing there had been her boss, Dwayne, who carried a photo of his dead parakeet in a locket around his neck and yelled nonstop. Jane had quit after two weeks.

And this was her first time meeting Fiona Chen face-to-face. Her interview back in June had been over the phone because Fiona was too busy to meet in person.

Jane knew that she was lucky to have this internship, even though it barely paid anything so she would have to live off her savings and help from her parents. She owed it all to her mother, who had arranged the interview; she and Fiona had been sorority sisters back in their Berkeley days.

"Jane?"

Jane's head jerked up. Standing in the doorway was a strikingly beautiful woman dressed head to toe in black, her black hair in a tight ponytail. The only makeup she wore was flawless black eyeliner that winged out at the edges.

"Fiona Chen," the woman said brusquely. Jane noticed

that she didn't smile. "Please come in."

"Thanks, it's nice to meet you," Jane said. She jumped to her feet and extended her hand.

Fiona shook it quickly. Her hands were cold. She turned to the receptionist. "Naomi. Hold my calls for the next ten minutes, unless it's our September twelfth birthday girl. She's having some sort of existential crisis about her step-daughter's dress, and I need to intervene personally. Also, call around to our usual rental places and see who can give us four sixty-by-sixty white silk tents for this Saturday's wedding. Yes, I mean Saturday. Our bride decided to change venues at the last minute. Also, see if you can find us a thousand robin's-egg-blue balloons for Sunday's baby shower. Robin's egg blue, not any other kind of blue. Also, reschedule my oxygen facial from six to seven. Oh, and call Anthony over at Sublime Stems and tell him to replace these dreadful calla lilies. They look like death. Please."

"Yes, Fiona," Naomi whispered, writing frantically.

Fiona turned and walked through the doorway. *Am I supposed to follow her?* Jane wondered. *I guess I'm supposed to follow her.* She picked up her bag and rushed to catch up.

Jane trailed after Fiona through a maze of hallways. There were more dark gold walls and more New Age-y music and more lavender smells. They passed half a dozen people whom Jane assumed were employees (one of them was thumbing through a rack of tuxedoes; another was inspecting bolts of pale pink fabric; the rest were busy at their desks), but Fiona didn't introduce her to any of them.

37

Jane wasn't sure, but she thought that a few people gave her looks of pity.

They ended up in a magnificent corner office with floor-to-ceiling windows that overlooked downtown L.A. There were no dark gold walls, no New Age-y music, and no lavender smells. Instead, there was a sleek silver desk (with one perfectly straight, neat pile of papers), some 1950s-style chairs (they reminded Jane of funky old diners . . . which reminded her that she had forgotten to eat breakfast), and a shelf full of books with titles like *Your Party, Your Way!* and *Unforgettable Celebrations.*

Fiona sat down behind the desk and waved to one of the chairs. "Let me start by explaining our philosophy at Fiona Chen Events," she began without waiting for Jane to sit down. "We have worked diligently to create a calm, stress-free atmosphere for our clients. Hosting a party is a huge undertaking. That's where we come in. We take the burden off the client's shoulders. We take care of the client. We take on all the details, big and small, so the client can just enjoy the party. That being said, you will be answering to me and only me. I am, at the moment, between assistants. But as soon as I hire a new one, which should be very shortly, you will be answering to that person as well. As far as your duties are concerned . . . I like my coffee half-caf, half-decaf, with just a touch of soy milk . . ."

She stopped abruptly and glared at Jane. "Why aren't you writing this down?"

"Oh! I'm sorry!" Jane pulled a blue Mead notebook out of her purse. Now, all she needed was a pen. She felt Fiona's eyes burning through her skin as she rummaged through her purse. Where the hell was a pen? She had, like, three in there. Pen! Crap, it was her Winnie the Pooh pen. It was the most unfortunate option of the three, but it did write. She glanced up at Fiona with an "I'm ready to go!" expression.

Fiona continued. "A touch of soy milk and a level, not heaped, teaspoon of raw organic honey. I believe in hard copies of absolutely everything, so you will need to learn our filing system, which is not alphabetical but chrono-logical, and by type of event, with a separate area for filing research on vendors and locations for future refer-ence. Until I get a new assistant, you will need to answer my phone, screen my calls, and take messages as necessary. In order to ensure that my clients receive my utmost per-sonalized attention, I take on only one event per day, up to three hundred sixty-five per year. Which means that on any given day, I might have up to three hundred sixty-five clients calling me, along with each and every one of their caterers, florists, stylists, photographers, mothers, mothers-in-law, et cetera, et cetera. I am, as you can see, an extremely busy woman."

As Jane listened to Fiona go through her list of duties, she felt a frisson of disappointment. Fetching coffee? (With raw honey? Did people cook honey?) Filing? Answering the phone? When she first got this job, she had envisioned long but satisfying days of helping anxious celebrities, selecting gourmet menus, and scouting fabulous venues.

But every career had to start somewhere, right? And "somewhere" usually meant fetching coffee, filing, and answering the phone. Jane reminded herself yet again that she was fortunate just to be here, even if she was basically the office bitch. So many girls would kill for her job. After all, Fiona Chen *was* one of the biggest event planners in L.A. And most of her clients were super-famous. It really was a big deal.

Fiona's voice cut into her thoughts. "Do you have any questions for me?"

Jane began tapping her foot. Fiona narrowed her eyes at Jane's silver ballet flat moving furiously on her pristine white carpet.

Jane willed her foot to stop and plastered on her most enthusiastic, positive, worker-bee smile. "I think I got it," she said brightly. "I just wanted to say again how happy I am to be here. This is what I've always wanted to do. So thanks again for having me."

Fiona smiled back—except that her smile was absolutely cold, arctic. "Well, why don't you start on phones and we'll go from there. I'll get one of the girls to show them to you." She added, "Oh, and Jane? I forgot to mention one thing. Here at Fiona Chen Events, you are not Maryanne's daughter. You are just Jane. Do we understand each other?"

Jane gulped. "Yes."

"Good. And please don't be late again."

OMG, Jane thought as she struggled to keep her enthusiastic, positive, worker-bee smile plastered on her face. *I'm so screwed.*

At noon, Jane sequestered herself in one of the ladies' room stalls and speed-dialed Scarlett on her cell.

Scarlett answered after one ring. "Well, hello there, Ms. Big-Shot Event Planner. Hey, can I hire you when Snake Tatt and I get married? I was thinking Vegas, Mardi Gras costumes, live reptiles—"

"Oh my God! She's gonna fire me," Jane interrupted, choking up. "I can't do anything right. I filed all the things that were supposed to be filed under 'Accounts Payable' under 'Accounts Receivable.' Or was it the other way around? And then I accidentally hung up on Miranda Vargas when she called about this charity fashion show."

"You talked to Miranda Vargas?" Scarlett said, sounding impressed. "Did you tell her we're huge fans of *Vice Squad*?"

"No, I didn't *talk* to her, Scar, I *hung up* on her. And then I went to Trader Joe's and bought regular old honey-honey instead of raw honey, and Fiona noticed that her coffee tasted different, and she started yelling at me, even though we're all supposed to speak in soft, peaceful voices around the office so we can maintain a stress-free environment for our clients—"

"What the fuck is raw honey?" Scarlett interrupted.

"I don't know. The point is, Fiona hates me."

Jane heard someone come into the ladies' room. High heels clicked against the black tile floors. A stall door opened and closed.

"I've gotta go," Jane whispered.

"Janie, wait," Scarlett said firmly. "Listen to me. You are *not* going to get fired. This is only your first day. First days always suck. Remember our first day at Café Mexicana three summers ago? I got in trouble for correcting the manager's Spanish too many times. And you accidentally mixed up the salsas and almost gave the guy a heart attack. At the end of the day, we went back to my house and swiped a bottle of Ketel One from the parents' liquor cabinet. Nobody got fired. Everything turned out okay."

"No, Scar. Everything *didn't* turn out okay. That vodka was evil. I was sick for the next two days. And didn't we both quit that job?"

"Yeah, we *quit*. We weren't *fired*. Never forget, it's always better to be the dumper than the dumpee."

The person in the other stall started peeing. Jane pressed her phone tightly against her left ear and covered her right ear with her hand. This was really bizarre, talking to Scar and listening to someone pee at the same time.

"Are you peeing, Jane? I told you not to do that when you're on the phone with me. It's weird," Scarlett scolded her. "I'm at U.S.C. dealing with registration. I'll see you later, okay? We'll do something fun. Love you."

Jane cracked a smile. "Thanks. I now feel slightly better about my boss hating me. I'll see you tonight."

Jane said good-bye to Scarlett and tucked her phone back in her bag. The person in the other stall flushed. It was not a gentle, peaceful flushing sound but a loud, gurgly, explosive flushing sound. Jane thought, *Down the toilet. Just like my future.*

Jane emerged from the stall and dropped her bag onto the slick black countertop. She studied herself in the mirror. She was a mess. She took a deep breath and pulled a small comb out of her bag. She undid the clip in her hair and attempted to smooth her blond waves into a more polished updo.

"Don't worry. She hates everyone," a voice behind her said.

Jane looked over her shoulder. Coming out of the stall next to the one she had been in was a frail-looking blond girl—the one from the front desk. She was wearing a neat black wrap dress and black patent leather peep-toed heels. She looked very put together.

"Naomi, right?" Jane said.

The girl nodded. She studied her reflection in the mirror and swept a strand of hair out of her face. "It was probably your bag."

"Excuse me?" Jane said, confused.

"No, it's totally cute. Fiona just isn't a fan of color. She prefers neutral. Black, white, cream, beige, gray. That way, we don't clash with whatever color scheme we're working with that day. It's silly, but she thinks it distracts."

Jane turned back to her reflection and examined her not-too-neutral outfit. She had chosen a peach top with ruffles down the center, tucked into a red, high-waisted chiffon skirt that ended just above her knees.

Jane couldn't help but laugh at herself. "I don't think it was just the bag."

Naomi smiled. "Tomorrow will be better."

6

THE ONLY WAY TO BELONG
IS TO ACT LIKE YOU BELONG

"Is this the right place?" Scarlett asked as Jane pulled the Jetta up to a long, vine-covered building on Las Palmas. It was next to a large parking lot filled with Hummers, Mercedes, and a few Range Rovers. Scarlett couldn't care less about being outclassed in the transportation department, but was concerned that finding a spot might be a problem. The place was a mob scene, and she didn't feel like having Jane drive around for half an hour searching for an empty spot. She wanted to get inside and get a drink before midnight. It was a school night after all.

"Yup. Les Deux. I Googled the address this morning. A girl from work told me about it," Jane said.

"It's kind of a zoo."

"I don't care. It'll be fun! And you promised we'd do something fun tonight."

"Indeed I did," Scarlett said.

Her first day on campus had been uneventful—she

picked up her ID and registration packet—but she was happy to blow off some steam with Jane, who'd had a crappy first day at work. How crazy that their lives were about to be so different. Scarlett would be studying at night while Jane would be recovering from her workday.

Jane managed to find parking down the street in a different lot, but when they got back to Les Deux, they found another obstacle waiting for them: a line, not of cars, but of people waiting to get in—young, dressed up, drunk, semi-drunk guys and girls gabbing, flirting, checking their phones, texting, smoking—that extended down the block. One group of girls (probably drunk) was swaying arm in arm and singing "Gimme More." Another group (definitely drunk) was pulling down the straps of their tighter-than-tight dresses and flashing people passing by. Manning the front door to the coveted club was a huge brute of a guy wearing an all-black suit and a beanie. He stood next to a red velvet rope that he unhooked to let a few people through at a time.

"I am *not* waiting in some lame line to get in," Scarlett declared. "Come on, let's just go somewhere else."

Jane grabbed her arm. "We came all this way. I'm sure it'll just be a few minutes. It's a Monday night—how crowded could it be in there?"

Scarlett rolled her eyes.

She and Jane joined the seemingly endless line behind two guys with bleached tips and Day-Glo tans. At least she and Jane had a better chance of getting in than those two. Did one of them actually have flames on his shirt? Poor guy.

Five minutes passed, then fifteen, then thirty. She and Jane texted some friends from high school and made catty remarks about the other people in line, and texted some more as they slowly made their way to the front. They had been standing in sight of the door for about twenty minutes when a sleek black Mercedes glided up to the curb. Seemingly out of nowhere, a wave of photographers appeared, their cameras swinging and bouncing. The door to the Benz opened, and a long, bare, perfectly shaped leg emerged, sporting a five-inch silver heel (how did women walk in those, anyway?). Then came the other leg, then a flash of a white miniskirt. The rest of the package poured out of the car to a burst of flashbulbs and excited shouts: "Anna! Anna! *Anna!* Over here, Anna!"

"Ohmigod, that's Anna Payne," Jane whispered. "She's sooo gorgeous!"

Anna stopped in the middle of the sidewalk and posed for the cameras. Scar had to admit that the actress *was* stunning. Flashbulbs continued popping, and the photographers continued shouting her name, until one meticulously timed moment later some generically handsome guy slid out of the Mercedes, took Anna's arm, and steered her past the screaming, awestruck line of drunk and semi-drunk partiers to the front door, where the huge brute in the beanie whooshed them inside with dizzying speed.

"That was *crazy*," Jane said breathlessly. "Do you think there are other celebrities inside?"

Scarlett checked her watch. "We might never find out. We've been in this line forever. If we don't get in by midnight, we should bail. You don't want to be late tomorrow. You might miss an important raw-honey lecture."

"Scar, no! I wanna have some fun. I had a bad day at work."

"Oh my G! What are you girls doing standing out here?" Scarlett heard someone squeal. She felt a hand grip her arm and spun around. It was Diego—D! He was wearing loud purple pumps, fitted jeans, and a black fedora. *Yay, someone we know!* "What's a guy like you doing on a line like this?" she teased him.

"Nothing. And neither are you." He grabbed her and Jane's hands and began walking. "Don't you know pretty girls don't wait in lines? Come with me!"

"Wait! We're gonna lose our spot. We've been waiting forever!" Jane pleaded.

Ignoring Jane's comment, D pulled them right up to the front of the line and waved to the big guy manning the door, who automatically unhooked the thick rope so D, Jane, and Scarlett could pass.

"Thanks!" D said to the guy.

"Who the hell are they?" somebody in line whined.

"Seriously!" someone else piped up.

Amazed, Scarlett and Jane followed D inside. They

walked into a large courtyard enclosed with vine-covered stone walls. There was a massive illuminated fountain in the center with greenery spilling over the edges. Booths made up of low glass-top tables surrounded by tufted black leather sofas filled the place. It was dramatic and stunning, easily the coolest club Scarlett had ever been to.

Seemingly unaffected by the scene, D led the two girls across the cobblestone courtyard toward a wide doorway and into the main room, which was plastered with vintage red wallpaper and dimly lit by the chandeliers mounted above each booth. Scarlett could tell that Jane was taking in the decor as much as the scene. She just hoped Jane wasn't about to pull out a tiny notebook from her tiny clutch and start taking notes. Scarlett watched clusters of beautiful people dancing and sitting around candlelit tables, pouring themselves glasses of Grey Goose, Bombay Sapphire, and Patrón straight from the bottle. What was up with that? she wondered. Wasn't that the bartender's job?

Most of the girls were wearing dresses and heels. The guys sported dress shirts. It occurred to Scarlett (not that she gave a damn) that she was probably way underdressed in her jeans and black racer-back tank.

Scarlett knew she was kind of out of her element in the midst of all this fabulousness. Still, she had to admit that it was kind of cool being in an impossible-to-get-into L.A. club, hanging out with the likes of Anna Payne. (Well, not hanging out *with*, she corrected herself, but hanging out *near*!)

Scarlett spotted a cute blond DJ spinning an eclectic mix of music in a booth in the corner. Aretha Franklin turned into Britney Spears, then into MGMT. The decibel level was kind of intense. She squeezed D's shoulder. "Hey! Can we get a table?" She was yelling and she could still barely even hear herself.

D laughed. "Yeah, for about fifteen hundred bucks! But don't worry. Just find a cute guy with a table. That's the only reason any of these guys are here. To meet girls like you."

Scarlett made a face. "Can we at least get a drink?" she said to Jane, who was moving her shoulders to the music.

"What?" Jane yelled.

"Bar!" Scarlett yelled. She pointed across the main room.

D shouted something that sounded like, "Come on, ladies. First round's on me," so they followed him.

When they reached the small wooden bar, D set a credit card down. "Jack and Diet and whatever they want," he said to the bartender. "Keep it open, please." The bartender began pouring a long golden stream of whiskey into a glass and glanced up at the girls.

"Tequila shot, please," Scarlett said.

"And a vodka soda," Jane added.

The bartender didn't say a word about IDs. *Yes!* When

he had poured their drinks, Scarlett raised her shot glass in the air. "Cheers."

"Cheers," Jane echoed, raising her glass too. She looked a little overwhelmed. "This place is, um, pretty amazing." She glanced at D, who seemed distracted.

"Listen, girls. I'm gonna do a lap. I'll catch up with you in a little. Have fun."

"'Kay, but we owe you a drink," Jane said.

"No worries, it's a write-off. Later." He disappeared into the crowd.

"I'm totally underdressed," Jane moaned before taking a sip of her vodka soda.

Scarlett glanced at Jane's light blue silk dress and gold wedge shoes. "What do you mean you're underdressed? You look great."

"Hardly," Jane grumbled. "Everyone here looks like a model!"

"Everyone here looks like a slut," Scarlett reassured her, even though it wasn't exactly true. "Besides, Janie, remember the cardinal rule: The only way to belong is to act like you belong. Or to not give a shit whether you belong or not, which works for me."

She downed her tequila neatly and set the shot glass on the bar with a *thunk*. "Another one, please," she said to the bartender.

Right at that moment, someone bumped into Scarlett, hard. She whirled around, ready to glare at the person . . .

. . . and was astonished to find herself eye-to-eye with Anna Payne.

The magnificent blond actress looked totally trashed. Her eyes were bloodshot and unfocused, and she was teetering a little on her five-inch heels.

"Uh, hey," Scarlett said. For once, she was at a loss for words.

"Ohmigosh!" Jane burst out. "You're Anna Payne, right? I love you!" She started digging through her purse. "I'm so sorry, but do you think I could take a picture with you? My little sisters would die; they think you're—"

Anna narrowed her drunk eyes at Jane, then scoffed as she staggered away.

Jane blanched. Scarlett was shocked by the actress's rudeness. What the hell?

"Okay, so we're officially no longer Anna Payne fans," Scarlett said quickly. "She's a drunk, hateful, no-talent bitch with the IQ of an amoeba."

"Yeah, but, I didn't see her waiting in any lines outside," Jane replied. She reached for her vodka soda and downed it in one gulp.

"I have to use the ladies' room," she told Scarlett. They weaved their way through the crowd, surprised to find no line outside the bathroom. Jane stepped inside— then stopped in her tracks, causing Scarlett to sort of walk into her. Two girls leaned on the counter, making out. The short, squat attendant just stood there, blithely holding a pile of paper hand towels for distribution, and seemed totally unaffected by the girl-on-girl action taking place against the counter next to her. Jane tried to hide her shock. Scarlett tried to hide her amusement at Jane's shock.

"Are we having fun yet?" Scarlett said. Then she walked toward a stall, just as three girls came out of it, giggling.

7

NO ONE MOVES HERE
TO BE A NOBODY

Trevor Lord sat at the corner booth—the best one in the room, next to the one Anna Payne had just disappeared from—barely touching his glass of eighteen-year-old Talisker Scotch. He was too busy watching tonight's parade of poseurs. Still, he felt hopeful. Maybe this was the night. Maybe he would get lucky.

"How about that one?" said the navy blue suit to his right.

"Next to the Justin wannabe with the unfortunate bleached tips?" said the gray suit to his left. "She's pretty hot."

"She's kind of *too* hot for my taste; she's trying too hard," said the only woman at the table. She tended to go for all-American, farm-raised, and milk-fed on these occasions.

Trevor gazed at the subject in question: size zero, glossy platinum (mostly purchased) hair down to her ass, black dress glued onto her Pilates-toned body. Why was it that when girls moved to Hollywood, they all eventually morphed into the same stereotype? Not that he wasn't fond of that stereotype. It had its uses. But she was a little *too* obvious. Besides, he already had a size 0 with platinum hair and a Pilates-toned body—a better one.

He turned to his companions and raised his eyebrows a barely perceptible millimeter. It was enough. They knew when he wasn't interested.

"What about her friend?" said Navy Blue Suit hastily.

The woman shrugged. "Too affected."

Gray Suit pointed. "What about the one dancing near the DJ booth? Red hair, big boobs?"

"Too plain," the woman dismissed. "Boobs notwithstanding, that is."

The three of them continued analyzing more girls on their weight, hair color, and cup size. But Trevor was starting to tune them out. He picked up his Scotch finally and took a long, thirsty sip. It slid down his throat like a river of pure heat.

While the three of them were comparing blondes versus redheads versus brunettes, and the DJ was playing "Jungle Love" by the Steve Miller Band, he spotted two girls trying to squeeze in at the bar. Petite, pretty blonde—not the run-of-the-mill Hollywood blonde, but softer, sweeter. She was *exactly* what he had been looking for. And she came with a tall, strikingly beautiful brunette friend who had a slightly exotic but not *too* exotic edge. The two of them managed to get the bartender's attention and were drinking and pretending to have a good time, but his razor-sharp instincts told him that they were nervous—awkward, even—knowing they didn't fit in, unaware that it may have been a good thing.

They were perfect.

He rose from the table. "I'll be right back," he said in the general direction of the table. He didn't wait for their response as he strode toward the bar, nodding and smiling at various people but not stopping to chat. This was not the time. He sidled up next to the brunette and caught the eye of the bartender, who knew without waiting to be told to hustle and pour him a Talisker with a splash of water, neat.

The two girls were talking, their heads bent close. Trevor leaned over and said, "Hi. Are you enjoying yourselves?"

The brunette glanced over her shoulder and fixed him with an icy stare. God, her eyes were amazing: intense green, like emeralds. Before she could say anything, the blonde grinned at him and said, "Yeah. It's our first time here."

Trevor nodded. The blonde was exactly as he had guessed her to be: fresh, innocent, vulnerable. *Perfect.*

"Do you two live in L.A.?" he asked them.

"We do!" the blonde said, as if it were the best piece of news ever. "We just moved here from Santa Barbara, actually."

"I've been there a few times," he said.

"It's beautiful there, huh?" the blonde gushed.

The brunette still hadn't said a word. Trevor took a sip of his Scotch, studied the two girls, and said, "So have the two of you ever thought about getting into the entertainment industry? Or maybe you're in the business already—"

The brunette cut in with "We're not really interested in guys who are technically old enough to father us."

"You think I'm that old, huh?" Trevor chuckled. "Listen, I'm not trying to hit on you. I promise. I'm a producer. I'm looking for girls to cast in a new TV show I'm putting together."

"The Real World: Hollywood?" the brunette said drily.

He smiled patiently. "I'm casting for a new documentary-style show. We're going to be following around a group of girls in L.A. Seeing what their days and nights are like. It's going to be really fun stuff. Kind of a reality version of *Sex and the City*, but totally PG, of course. Would you girls have any interest?"

The blonde leaned forward and regarded him curiously. Her eyes were big, blue, expressive. The cameras were going to love them, he thought. "You're a TV producer? Seriously?" she said.

"Yes," he replied. "You girls are exactly what I'm looking for. Why don't you come in for an interview, and we can talk some more about it?"

"What, do we look like we're totally clueless?" the brunette demanded. "We're really not interested in your low-budget project, or whatever you're doing."

He'd never met a girl who hadn't immediately softened at the words *producer, casting,* and *interview.* "Listen carefully to me," he said after a moment. "Thousands of girls like you come to L.A. for an opportunity like this, and it never happens. Except it's happening right now, to you. You can front all the confidence you want, but you don't fool me. You waited in line to stand at a bar in a place where you don't belong. I am offering you the chance to fit in at a hundred places like this—places where people would kill to be. Isn't that why you moved to this city? To take a chance? No one moves here to be a nobody."

Now the brunette was staring at him, a little stunned. So was the blonde. Good, good. It was working. The blonde he hadn't been too worried about. She was an open book. It was the brunette he had to win over.

He reached into his pocket, pulled out a slim silver case, and placed a business card on the bar. "In case you get tired of waiting in lines for tequila shots," he said, locking eyes with the brunette.

And then he turned and made his exit.

8

IT'S CALLED POSITIVE VISUALIZATION

At 6:05 on Tuesday night, Jane pulled out of the parking lot, away from Fiona Chen events. She had survived another day . . . barely.

She had accidentally hung up on three more people (she couldn't quite get the handle of the Call Waiting and Hold and Forward buttons), ordered the wrong kind of sandwich for Fiona, and almost spilled iced tea on a $100,000 wedding dress. (A hundred grand? For a dress that would only be worn once?) The bride—a famous Danish lingerie model named Petra—had been so upset that her therapist, acupuncturist, *and* psychic all had to be called in for emergency sessions.

Jane made a right onto Sunset and adjusted her shades. She drove past a row of trendy-looking sidewalk cafés, where pretty people were drinking pretty cocktails, laughing, and having fun. She wished she was one of those people right now.

She reminded herself that it would get better—it *had* to. She'd figure out the phones, she'd figure out Fiona. . . . By next week she'd think it was hilarious that she kept calling Fiona's favorite color specialist Max instead of Mav (she'd assumed Mav was a typo on the call sheet). Well, if Fiona didn't fire her before next week.

Up ahead, the early-evening sky was thick with smog; it was murky and gray, and it reflected Jane's mood perfectly. For the first time since moving to L.A., Jane felt troubled, uncertain. She had put off college and left the comforts of her home and family back in Santa Barbara to work for Fiona Chen. If Fiona fired her, what would she do?

Jane drove a few more blocks, wondering if she was going in the right direction. Wasn't the apartment this way? Or was it the other way? She reminded herself yet again to ask her parents for a GPS for Christmas (although that would leave a lot of months to still get lost). She slowed down at a stop sign and reached into her bag for her cell phone, to call Scarlett for directions. Despite living in L.A. for just over a week, Scarlett could direct a city tour.

As Jane waited for Scarlett to pick up, a guy crossed in front of her. He looked familiar. Jane took off her shades so she could see him better. It couldn't be . . .

"Braden?" Jane said loudly.

"Janie, are you lost again?" Scarlett's voice demanded. Jane forgot that she had her phone pressed to her ear.

"Call you back, Scar," she said quickly as she dropped the phone into her lap, thinking about luck or fate or whatever had brought her to this random intersection.

The guy kept going. Jane stuck her head out the window. "Braden!" she yelled at him.

He stopped in the middle of the street and turned around. It was definitely Braden. He looked at her for a second before he recognized her. "Hey! Jane!" he called out. He looked pleasantly surprised to see her.

"What are you doing?" Jane shouted.

"Just had my audition!" Braden shouted back. "I think I totally sucked!"

The car behind Jane honked. "You hungry?" she blurted out, before she'd had a chance to think.

Braden smiled and nodded. "Go left! I'll meet you around the corner!"

Jane smiled back. But even as she was smiling, her mind was spinning and racing. *Jane, what are you doing? He has a girlfriend. Don't be that kind of girl!*

"So I had to read this scene where my character mind-melds with an alien species that's part cyborg, part poodle. I thought I'd play it funny, you know? Because really, there's something pretty funny about a human mind-melding with a poodle from outer space," Braden said.

"Definitely," Jane said, nodding. She noticed that Braden's eyes looked more green than hazel today. Or was it the lighting?

After she had parked her car and given Braden a super-casual hug (she hadn't noticed the other night that he smelled really yummy, like the beach), he had taken her across the street to Cabo Cantina, which he said was one of his favorite hangouts in L.A. It was a really loud, colorful place with brightly painted chipped walls. (It was basically Fiona Chen's version of hell.) It reminded Jane of actual restaurants she'd gone to in Cabo during spring break. It also struck her as the exact opposite of the Hollywood glamour scene. To her surprise, she liked it. Or was it because she was there with Braden?

"But I guess funny wasn't what they were looking for, because the director just stared at me like I was completely out of my mind," Braden went on. "I don't think I'll be getting a callback."

"No, no. You have to think that you *will* get a callback," Jane told him, suddenly animated. "It's called positive visualization. It's like in that book *The Secret*. Scar and I do it all the time. Actually, I do it, and Scar just pretends to do it while silently mocking me." She grinned.

Braden grinned too. "It's cool how close you guys are. How long have you known each other?"

"We've been friends forever. We grew up together," Jane replied. "We're total opposites, which is why we're so close, I guess. I know that probably doesn't make any sense," she added apologetically.

"No, no, it does!" Braden said. "I grew up with my best friend, too. Jesse. It's that same thing. He and I are totally different. He's really into the whole Hollywood scene and that's never been my thing. We went to school together, at Crossroads."

"Where's that?"

"Santa Monica. When we were growing up he practically lived at my house. He loved it there because my family's so . . . I don't know, loud. Really close. Normal, most of the time. His parents weren't around that much."

"I know what you mean. Scar says she likes hanging out at my house because my parents aren't freaks, like hers."

"What are your not-freak parents like?"

"My parents are great," Jane said affectionately. "They've always been supportive of me and my two sisters. They've been married for almost twenty-five years, and they still love each other, which is amazing. We still catch them making out and stuff." She blushed. "I'm sorry . . . TMI."

Braden smiled. "Not at all. That's sweet. That's what I want someday. You know, to be married forever to someone I'm madly in love with."

"Yeah. It's just so rare these days," Jane said softly, wondering how the conversation had turned to marriage.

She took a long sip of her frozen margarita, keeping her eyes focused on the glass so she wouldn't do something dumb, like lean over and start making out with Braden right then and there. He was such a great guy. She hadn't met anyone she felt a connection with since . . . well, since Caleb, and in a way not even him, because although he was insanely hot and awesome, she had always sensed a distance with him. True, he was the first (and so far, only) guy who told her that he loved her. And true, they had lost their virginity to each other—something she had held out on doing for exactly six months, one week, and three days from when they first met. But despite their emotional and physical connection—their *passion*—Jane felt deep down that there was something ultimately aloof and untouchable about Caleb. The fact that, when it came time for him to decide on a college, he had chosen Yale over Stanford kind of proved her theory. With Stanford, they could have continued seeing each other, every weekend. But with Yale . . . Jane had hoped they could stay together and visit each other during vacations and holidays, and he had agreed initially. She was just always so happy to see him when he came home. It wasn't perfect, but they loved each other, and Jane was willing to deal with the distance. Sadly, Caleb wasn't. During his last visit he had told her that it would be better if they didn't "tie each other down like that," as though being in love was some sort of noose or trap. Or had he found someone else at Yale? Jane had always wondered.

"Jane? You still there?" Braden's voice broke into her thoughts.

Jane glanced up from her drink. Braden's hazel-green eyes were staring into hers.

"Still here," Jane said quickly. "I, um, just remembered

that I forgot to eat breakfast. And lunch. It was kind of a hectic day."

"What? You're kidding. Hey, Sarah!" Braden raised his voice and signaled to the waitress. "Can you bring us some chips and salsa? And a couple of menus?"

"I'm fine," Jane insisted, although her stomach *did* feel funny, and the tequila was making her head kind of spinny.

"No, you're not fine, crazy. You have to eat something now, before you wither away into one of those celery-sticks-and-bottled-water girls, which you're totally not," Braden said firmly. "And I mean that as a compliment. What do you feel like having?"

"Hmm. I dunno. What's good? I'll try anything!" Jane said. *God, that sounded slutty,* she thought.

She remembered that her hair was a total mess, and she must have looked so tired. She reached up and began trying to smooth down the loose strands that had escaped her hair clip. She licked her lips and glanced around, wondering where the ladies' room might be.

Braden watched her in amusement. "You look fine," he said, as if knowing exactly what was going through her mind.

"Thanks," Jane said, blushing again. Why did Braden make her feel like this? What was she? Ten?

"So. What kept you so busy today? You start your new job?"

"Day two," she said, and then regaled him with tales

from her first days at her first real job.

Braden smiled sympathetically. "Listen," he said when she had finished. "Don't stress. It's early days. I'm sure you'll be awesome at this job. And if for some reason it doesn't work out, then it wasn't meant to be, and you'll just have to be awesome at something else."

"Well, I don't know about that . . . but thanks," Jane said.

Braden reached across the table and grabbed her hands. "No, no. You have to *think* that you're going to have a really happy, successful career doing whatever. It's called positive visualization." He grinned.

Jane laughed and pulled her hands away. She didn't want him to feel how hot they were from her being nervous. "You're mocking me right after I tell you I had a bad day. Braden, you're not a very nice person."

"I'm most definitely not mocking you," Braden reassured her.

A moment passed, and Jane realized that she was still smiling and staring at him. She looked down at her phone and pretended to check a message. It was funny. She felt so anxious around him and he just seemed so comfortable with himself, like nothing fazed him. The waitress brought a red woven basket of chips and two dog-eared menus. Braden thanked her and handed one to Jane. She was about to tell him about meeting Trevor Lord the night before when someone's phone beeped. It beeped again.

"Jane? I think that's you," Braden said.

"What? Oh!"

Jane glanced at the screen. It was a text from Scarlett.

HELLO? DID U 4GET ABOUT ME? It said.

"It's Scar," Jane told Braden. She typed: **NO. IM @ SOME RESTRAUNT W/ BRADEN.**

WHAT!!?? Scarlett's reply read.

"How is she?" Braden asked her.

Probably freaking out and wondering what the hell I'm doing with you, Jane thought. "She's fine."

WILLOW THERE? Scarlett asked.

Oh, right. Willow. Jane had forgotten about her for a few minutes. On the other hand, Braden hadn't brought up her name. Not once. What did that mean? That Willow wasn't his girlfriend after all?

NO, she typed.

B CAREFUL, WOMAN, Scarlett responded a few seconds later.

"What's she saying?" he asked, leaning forward and playfully pretending to sneak a peek at her phone. Jane glanced up and smiled uncertainly at Braden, pulling her phone closer to her. She knew Scarlett was right. She wished she could ask him about Willow—girlfriend or not? He wouldn't have taken her to one of his favorite places if he had a girlfriend, right? He'd have said, "Nice running into you," and kept walking. Then again, maybe she was being presumptuous and he really had no interest in her at all, aside from being "just friends." Or maybe he was just hungry. She had no idea.

"Not much." And then, because what did she have to lose really, she added, "Did I tell you she's got this weird theory about actors? She says actors are professional liars." Maybe she'd subtly get him to fess up about Willow.

"Well, it's a good thing I'm an awful actor then," Braden joked. Then his expression turned somber. "Seriously, though. I really am an awful liar. In fact, I can't stand liars. That's why I can't stand Hollywood. I wouldn't even be here if it wasn't for . . ." He paused.

Jane leaned forward, waiting for him to finish. Her phone beeped with another text from Scarlett, but she ignored it. "What? If it wasn't for what?" Willow?

Braden shook his head and drank some beer. "Ya know, my acting and stuff. Come on, let's order. I'm hungry."

Jane took another sip of her margarita and studied him. She could tell that wasn't his original response. Guess he wasn't lying about being a bad actor.

9

THIS MUST BE THE
ENGINEERING QUAD

Scarlett held out the U.S.C. campus map. Where the hell was she, anyway? Day three and she still couldn't find anything. She looked around. Rows of trees. A fountain. A building called Olin Hall. A lot of geeky-looking guys with pocket protectors. Some of them—actually, *most* of them—were staring at her with undisguised lust, as though the closest they'd ever come to a girl like her was on the Internet, alone in their rooms, late at night.

Ah, this must be the engineering quad. How did she end up here?

Scarlett saw from the map that this area was called Archimedes Plaza—named after the ancient Greek mathematician. She remembered from some book that Archimedes had invented elaborate war machines, like the "heat ray," which supposedly reflected sunlight off a bunch of mirrors and burned enemy ships. That was kind of awesome, in Scarlett's opinion.

In another life, she could have imagined herself as a brilliant, bad-ass mathematician like Archimedes. But in this life . . .

Scarlett glanced down at her schedule, peeking out from behind the map. She knew that her parents really, really wanted her to be pre-med. Her mother, who thought she was such a clever shrink, liked to do that "reverse psychology" crap and would say things like, "Scarlett, sweetheart, it's probably best if you do some-thing *other* than medicine, so you can have your own identity," which loosely translated as: "Your father and I both went into medicine, so you should, too" (if you could call charging $400 an hour for telling patients not to be so hard on themselves, or vacuuming fat out of people's stomachs because they'd been brainwashed into thinking they weren't thin enough, "medicine"). Scar-lett knew that they were secretly waiting and hoping for her to sign up for courses like neurobiology and general physiology. Well, no, thank you.

She was perfectly happy with her English and philos-ophy classes. It had been hard to pick just a few from the catalog. Modern Philosophy and the Meaning of Life. Introduction to Contemporary East Asian Film and Cul-ture. Women Writers in Europe and America. Sex Simi-larities and Differences: A Multidisciplinary Approach. (That would be an easy class—most men are assholes, and most women are assholes, too, except with makeup?) She had to take some freshmen intro classes though, so while she couldn't have all these courses now, she was determined to sign up for them at some point over the next four years. Or however long she lasted at U.S.C.

Not that she would flunk out or anything. On the contrary, she wondered if she had done the right thing, coming here. Maybe she should have aimed higher, like an Ivy? Transferring was always on option. But then she and Jane wouldn't be able to live together. Scarlett knew that she wasn't an easy person to be close to. Jane was the only one who'd put up with her bullshit over the years and stuck around—no, not just stuck around, but been the most loyal friend imaginable. She didn't trust anyone else like she trusted Jane.

Just then, a voice interrupted her.

"Hi, there! Are you new here?"

Scarlett glanced up. A girl flashing two rows of perfect white teeth stood in front of her. She was tall and thin, with bleached blond hair and a pair of large, spray-tanned breasts practically popping out of her maroon U.S.C. tank. (Daddy issues, Scarlett concluded. Girls like her didn't get enough love from their daddies growing up, so they end up desperate for male attention. Girls like her would've fallen all over someone like Trevor Lord. Oops, was she starting to sound like Mom the shrink?) "Guilty as charged," Scarlett said.

"Hey, I'm Cammy! Welcome to U.S.C.!"

"Hi, Cammy! I'm Scarlett! Thanks for the welcome!" Scarlett's super-fake smile faded quickly, and she turned to go. Cammy would get the hint.

"Wait! I was just wondering, Charlotte—are you planning to rush?"

Scarlett frowned. "Scarlett. Umm, should I? I don't think Introduction to Contemporary East Asian Film and Culture is going to fill up before I get there."

Cammy giggled. "Ha-ha, good one! Next week is rush week! You should totally think about joining Pi Delta! Not to bid promise or anything."

Pi Delta? Scarlett thought. *A sorority? Seriously?*

"Pi Delt is awesome!" Cammy went on. "Rush week rocks, too! There's Unity Day, and there's Spirit Day, and there's Pride Day! We totally don't dirty rush but all the hottest girls join ours and you're really pretty."

Scarlett was well versed in sororities. She had seen *Animal House* about twenty-nine times on cable. She had also heard the "hazing" horror stories, in which new sorority sisters—"pledges"—were allegedly subjected to humiliating and sometimes dangerous rituals.

Cammy was going on and on about something called the "Greek Gala."

"I don't think sororities are my thing, Cammy," Scarlett interrupted her. "Didn't I read about you guys in the papers? Don't you make pledges stand in a cold room buck-naked, while you circle their cellulite with Magic Markers?"

Cammy gasped. Her mouth dropped open. "That is *so* not true!" she exclaimed. "Those are just horrible lies spread by jealous people who want to destroy us and everything we stand for!"

"If you say so. Thanks for inviting me, though! See you around campus!"

Scarlett suppressed a laugh as she hoisted her backpack on her shoulders and took off in the opposite direction. "Bitch!" she heard Cammy muttering after her. Whatever.

Scarlett turned left and headed toward what she thought might be the center of campus. As she walked, she passed racks of art posters for sale (Picasso's *The Lovers*, Van Gogh's *Starry Night*, and all the rest of the usual museum clichés to warm up those depressing little dorm rooms); a bronze statue of a Trojan warrior, nicknamed "Tommy Trojan," that reminded her of the mascot for the condom ads (maybe she *would* fit in here); maroon and gold U.S.C. banners; handpainted signs inviting her to join the Dancing Club, the SoCalVoCals, the Turkish Students' Association, or the Student Senate. She also passed people who were presumably her new classmates. A frightening number of them looked just like Cammy. What was the appeal, anyway? Why did they all want to be the same cookie-cutter, dyed-blond, plump-lipped, big-boobed, spray-tanned Barbie doll? Wasn't variety supposed to be the spice of life? To be fair, not everyone looked like that. Still, the Cammy clones were definitely not hard to spot.

Scarlett wondered once again if she had made the right choice in coming to U.S.C. Would she really fit in here?

On the other hand, would she really fit in anywhere?

10

TO BE UNCOMFORTABLE

Jane glanced around the waiting room and wondered how much longer it would be. It was so quiet, she could hear the ticking of the clock on the otherwise bare, white wall as it hit 6:45. She wondered what kinds of things they would ask her. And how long would the interview take? Also, if they were trying to make a savvy show about L.A., why would they be interested in someone like her? She knew nothing about L.A.

She was a little troubled by the fact that the waiting room was so—*ordinary*. Shouldn't a TV producer's waiting room be chic? With lots of glass and chrome and expensive art? Like Fiona Chen's office but louder. She leaned over to Scarlett, who was sitting next to her on one of the uncomfortable beige chairs. "His assistant said six thirty, right?" she whispered.

"Relax. When did you start caring about punctuality?

You're like half an hour late for everything," Scarlett reminded her.

"I'm really nervous. I'm a little scared to go in there," Jane admitted.

"Hey. *You're* the one who talked *me* into coming here. You were the one who was all excited about meeting with that guy," Scarlett said.

That guy. Jane reached into her pocket and fingered the business card he had given them at Les Deux. "Trevor Lord, producer, PopTV," it read. She and Scarlett had Googled his name right when they got home that night. He hadn't been lying. He was *the* Trevor Lord, TV producer, the creator of hit reality shows *The Beach* and *American Adventure.* He was kind of a big deal. Jane had read about how some of his recent shows had flopped. Was this new show going to be his comeback?

Scarlett had insisted that Jane do a Google Image search to make sure the person they'd met wasn't just *pretending* to be Trevor Lord using fake business cards from Staples. He wasn't. Trevor Lord—*the* Trevor Lord—had really and truly come up to them and asked them if they were interested in being considered for his new show. It was surreal. Things like that just didn't happen. Jane had never really loved being the center of attention, and with Scarlett as her best friend, she never had to be. But she had engaged in more than a couple daydreams at work—as she took notes for Fiona, while she brainstormed Sweet Sixteen party ideas with the infamous Marley twins—imagining what it would be like to be on TV. They hadn't agreed to call his office until Wednesday night—they did it together, when Jane got home from work—and were surprised when the girl seemed so eager to bring them in. She'd asked if they could come the next day. The thought had entered her mind that maybe she was only there because they wanted Scarlett on the show. She and Scar had, over their years of friendship, slowly become a two-for-one deal. If you wanted one of them, you usually got the other as well.

Jane had spent her entire lunch break on the phone with Braden on Wednesday while she went back and forth about whether or not to go for the interview. She was worried about even bringing it up with him, because he was so anti-Hollywood, but in the end, he had given her lots of good advice that had helped her decide to make the call to Trevor (like pointing out that being on the show could help her learn about good clubs in L.A., which would come in handy for her life as a party planner). Honestly, she didn't care what Scar thought of Braden (i.e., "guy-with-girlfriend on the prowl"). Attached or not attached, he was turning out to be an awesome friend.

Jane's parents had reacted with excitement plus a healthy dose of concern. "You're in L.A. for less than a month and you're going to be a TV star!" her mother had practically screamed over the phone. "Wait till I tell your sisters and your grandparents and Aunt Susan—"

"Mom, calm down. I'm not gonna be a TV star!"

"You're going to be a TV star!"

Jane laughed. "Okay, Mom, whatever you say." She had told her parents the whole story, except she'd said they were at a restaurant not a club.

"Honey, this is great, but what's the catch?" her father had piped in.

"Catch? What do you mean, catch?"

"Do you have to sign anything? Because if you do I want to run it by my lawyer first."

"Dad, it's just an *interview*." Of course, she had promised she wouldn't sign anything without consulting him because that was the only way she could get him off the phone. But as she sat in the waiting room she was happy to know her dad was looking out for her.

A door opened, and a girl dressed in jeans and a FREE TIBET tee appeared. "Jane?"

Jane glanced up at her.

"They'll see you first."

She rose to her feet and gave Scarlett a quick, nervous squeeze on the arm. "Wish me luck."

"You'll be fine, Janie," Scarlett assured her friend. She turned to the girl. "Who's 'they'? I thought we were just going to talk to Trevor."

"Sorry, they don't really tell me anything," the girl apologized.

Jane waved to Scarlett, then followed the girl down a hallway. "Have you been working here long?" she asked, trying to distract herself from her own thoughts with polite conversation.

"Like three weeks," the girl said.

"So is this, like, the main PopTV office?"

"No, this is one of the production spaces they rent." The girl stopped in front of another door and indicated for Jane to go in. "Right in here."

"Thanks!"

Jane entered, barely noticing the door close behind her, and found herself in an almost claustrophobically small room. It had the same dingy white walls and faded blue carpet as the waiting room. The only furniture was a single gray folding chair lined up neatly against one of the walls.

About five feet in front of the chair were a large camera on a tripod and a tall, industrial-looking light. Jane frowned at the equipment. What was it doing here? She turned to ask the girl, but she was already gone.

Then the door opened again, and a heavyset guy bustled in carrying a small black pack of some sort. The pack had an On/Off switch and a green light on top and a long black wire that ended at a tiny round ball extended from the bottom of it.

"Okay if I put this on you?" the guy asked Jane.

"What is it?"

The guy looked amused. "Microphone."

"Oh . . . I guess so. Sure."

"Great. Have a seat."

Jane sat down in the folding chair, which felt cold and hard against her bare legs. The guy handed her the wire and a piece of tape. "Run this wire down your shirt for me, okay?" he instructed. "And tape the mike to yourself, like right about here." He pointed to his chest, just about where her two bra cups would meet.

"Uh . . . okay."

The tiny round mike felt weird against her chest. Was it going to pick up the sound of her heart beating a million miles a minute? She was already nervous. The camera and impossibly small space weren't helping. *Relax,* she told herself.

The guy put on a headset and picked up a pack of equipment. He asked her to count to ten and began twisting knobs and flipping switches. Then the door opened again, and two men and a woman entered. One of the guys didn't even look at her as he went over to the camera and started pushing various buttons. The other two smiled pleasantly at Jane and took their positions on either side of the camera guy. They were both carrying notebooks and pens.

"Hi, Jane," the woman said. She looked like she was in her mid-thirties. Her thin brown hair hung just below her shoulders. She was wearing a blue striped button-down shirt over faded jeans and wore silver framed glasses over her tired eyes. "I'm Dana, I'm one of the producers of the pilot. And this is Wendell. He'll be helping out with casting."

Wendell had short, messy blond hair and wide brown

eyes and was probably at least a few years younger than Dana. He wore a navy T-shirt and cords. He didn't look like a Wendell.

Jane raised one hand and smiled awkwardly. "Hey. It's nice to meet you."

"We're just going to ask you a few questions, if that's okay with you," Dana went on. The camera guy flicked a switch, and Jane squinted as a bright white glare flooded the room. "Is that light bothering your eyes?"

"No, it's fine," Jane said quickly, afraid to complain about anything or ask any questions. The light felt hot on her skin.

"Great," Dana said. "So. You just moved to L.A. a couple of weeks ago, right? Do you work or go to school here?"

"I have an internship with Fiona Chen," Jane replied. "She's an event planner. She specializes in celebrity stuff, like charity events and showers and weddings. And birthday parties." Oh God, why was she still talking? Of course these people knew what an event planner did!

"Loooove her work," Wendell said, nodding.

"Have you made any new friends in L.A.?" Dana asked.

Braden came to mind immediately. And D, even though she had no idea what his last name was.

"I've met a couple of people," Jane hedged. "And my roommate, Scarlett, is my best friend from when we were, like, five. I'm really excited to meet more people. Everyone here seems so interesting."

Dana and Wendell scribbled in their notebooks. Jane shifted in her chair, trying to find a comfortable position. Her foot began to twitch. *Wow . . . Sounding a little desperate, Jane? And "interesting"? You couldn't come up with something more interesting than "interesting"? Way to show off that extensive vocabulary!*

The camera light was intense and bright, and it made it difficult to see Dana's and Wendell's faces. Jane struggled a little to read their expressions. She wished she knew what they were writing—and what they were thinking. She reached up and twisted a strand of hair around her index finger and continued to twist the same strand as Dana and Wendell fired more questions at her: Where did she grow up? What was her family like? Where did she go to high school? Did she plan on going to college? What were her career goals? Did she have a boyfriend?

Jane answered all the questions the best she could. *(Santa Barbara. My family's awesome. Santa Barbara High. I want to work for a couple of years, get some real-life experience, then go to college. Nope, no boyfriend.)* The questions went on and on like that. Jane felt as though they were trying to get her life story—the SparkNotes version, anyway—and couldn't imagine why. Her life had been pretty uneventful. That was why she'd moved to L.A., to make something happen.

At one point, there was a brief pause as Dana and Wendell wrote in their notebooks. (What were they writing?) The light was hot, and Jane could feel herself starting to sweat.

"Have you been going out in L.A. since you moved here?" Dana asked her.

"A few times. I'm still trying to figure out fun places to go. Apparently you guys have commitment issues with your clubs here," Jane said.

They both laughed at her joke. It sounded polite.

"You've noticed, huh?" Dana piped up.

"Drink of choice?" Wendell asked cutely, as if he were quizzing her out of the back of *Cosmopolitan*.

"For when you're legal, of course," Dana added, giving Wendell a cryptic look.

"Of course," Jane replied. Considering she'd met Trevor at a bar, she figured Dana's remark was a joke or something she had to say. "I'm partial to vodka . . . anything."

"My kind of girl." Wendell winked at her.

Jane smiled. She liked him. He was a little chattier than Dana. She felt more comfortable talking to him. Like she was having a conversation, rather than being interviewed. "So have you met any hot guys since you've been here?" Wendell leaned in toward her a little.

"Not really . . . I met one guy, but I think he has a girlfriend. Maybe." Ugh, saying that out loud made Jane realize how lame it was that she hadn't gotten up the nerve to ask Braden what the deal was with Willow. "I just broke up with my boyfriend a few months ago and I haven't really been dating."

"Awww, I'm sorry." Wendell made a little pout, then perked up. "But, you know, nothing cures heartbreak like a new cute boy," he said in an almost singsongy voice.

"Yeah . . . that or the vodka anything." Jane shrugged.

They laughed again—and this time it didn't feel just polite.

"Okay, so we're gonna read off a list of words," Dana said, all business again. "You say the first thing that comes to your mind. It's just for fun so don't think about it. Say whatever pops into your head."

"Okay." Jane straightened up a little.

"One-night stands," Dana said, staring.

"Umm . . . trashy," Jane replied, scrunching her nose a little.

"Shoes."

"Love."

Wendell nodded in agreement.

"Los Angeles."

"Big."

"Friendship."

"Long-lasting."

"Love."

"Rare."

Dana finished writing something in her notebook, then looked up at Jane. "And lastly . . . why did you move to L.A.? Besides your job, why L.A.?"

Jane thought for a minute. "To be uncomfortable."

Dana and Wendell looked at her, a little confused.

"My whole life I've always been safe, boring . . . comfortable," Jane explained. "I've had the same friends my whole life. I have a great family. I grew up in a beautiful place. I was really lucky, but I came to L.A. to get out of my comfort zone and do something different."

Dana and Wendell looked at each other, and Dana nodded almost imperceptibly.

"Okay, then, we're all done," Dana said. "We'll be in touch, okay?"

"It's over?" Jane said, surprised.

"It's over," Wendell told her. "You're free to go. You did great!"

"I did?" Jane felt like she'd only just gotten into the swing of things. Could she really have been great?

She got up, said her thank-yous and good-byes (she went to shake Wendell's hand, because it seemed like the right thing to do, and instead shared an awkward half-handshake, half-hug with him; Dana was fine with a brief but firm handshake), and headed back in the direction of the waiting room. In the hallway, she passed Scarlett and the girl with the Free Tibet tee. *How did it go?* Scarlett mouthed to her. *I don't know,* Jane mouthed back. She wished she had time to give Scarlett a quick lowdown before she walked into her interview. Although, knowing Scarlett, she would do just fine. Aside from her occasional bad attitude, Scarlett was extremely well-spoken and quick-witted.

While Jane sat in the plain room with the uncomfortable beige chairs, waiting for Scarlett, a thought occurred to her: If being filmed by one camera and examined by two people made her nervous, how would she ever be able to get used to filming a reality show? If two people noting and judging her words bothered her, then how would she handle being scrutinized by so many? She wondered just how many people watched PopTV.

"Hey, how'd it go?"

Jane pressed the phone closer to her ear as she curled up on the couch. It was late Thursday night. Scarlett had gone to the library after the interview to work on a paper for her English class.

The sound of Braden's voice made her feel immediately at ease. She had been on edge since the PopTV interview earlier that evening. Talking to Braden was like taking a long, hot bubble bath or eating a pint of chocolate ice cream, but better.

"I don't know. They said I did great. But I'm not sure they really liked me."

"Did *you* like *them*?"

Jane thought about Dana and Wendell. "They were okay. The guy—Wendell—was pretty nice."

"How did Scarlett's interview go? Did she say?"

"She said it was a piece of cake. I think she liked being a smart-ass on camera." Jane chuckled.

"So what happens next?"

"They said they'll be in touch. What does that mean?"

"That means they'll call you if they want you to come

in for a callback. That's like a second interview. And if not . . . well, their loss." Braden added, "The most important thing is, do *you* want to be on this show?"

"I'm not sure," Jane admitted. "I think Scar's actually kind of into the idea now that she knows it's totally legit. Plus, she already looks like a TV star. But why are they even interested in me? My life isn't exactly exciting."

"Maybe they don't want 'exciting.' Maybe they want you, exactly as you are."

"Um, thanks?"

Braden laughed. "You know what I mean!"

It was kind of weird, discussing all this with Braden. She and Scarlett had been in L.A. for less than two weeks, and they were being seriously considered for a TV show. Braden had been in L.A. for way longer, and he was still looking for steady work. But if he was envious, he kept it to himself. In fact, he sounded totally supportive. Which was one of the things that made him so amazing.

She didn't want to ruin a perfectly good conversation, but she *had* to ask him about Willow. He was no longer just a cute guy she'd met at a bar. He was becoming her *friend*. Friends know this kind of stuff about each other. "So. What's with you and Willow?"

There was a pause. "Willow," Braden said. "Hmm, how do I answer that? It's kinda complicated."

"Complicated?" Jane picked at some lint on her favorite embroidered pillow.

"Yeah, well . . . we've been hanging out for, like, three

years, since we were eighteen. It's an on-again, off-again thing."

On-again, off-again? Really? Jane wondered if that was how Willow saw things. Either way, he and Willow had definitely appeared on-again at Big Wangs.

"Oh. Well, Scar thought she was your girlfriend," Jane blurted out, then immediately felt dumb. Why was she bringing Scar into this? *Way to be totally juvenile, Jane.*

"Why would Scarlett think that?"

Because you and Willow were practically making out at Big Wangs? she wanted to point out. "She's not wrong," Jane said instead.

"But she's also not right." Braden laughed, a little uncomfortably, Jane thought.

They talked for only a little while longer before Jane realized that it was after midnight, so they said their good-byes. She had work in the morning—staff meetings were always on Fridays, and always promptly at 8 a.m.

But once she had slipped into bed, she had a hard time getting to sleep. Her mind churned with thoughts of the interview, rewinding to different moments. Why had she said *this*? *Why* hadn't she said *that* instead? And soon her thoughts drifted to Braden—she was glad that asking about Willow hadn't soured the conversation, but had to admit she was disappointed by his answer.

It was around 2 a.m., when she finally felt her eyelids growing heavy, that she realized that she actually *wanted* to be on Trevor Lord's new show. She had meant it when she told Dana and Wendell that she had moved to L.A. to be uncomfortable. What better way to push the boundaries of her small, safe, perfectly pleasant life than to put it on TV, for thousands—or millions?—of people to see?

11

WHAT JUST HAPPENED?

Scarlett and Jane got the phone call on a Saturday, while they were shopping at Target for "cute things to decorate the apartment" (according to Jane) and "crap we don't need so we can pretend that we don't live in a total shit hole" (according to Scarlett).

They had been talking about Braden, and Scarlett hadn't been telling Jane what she wanted to hear. Scarlett watched as Jane held up a bath mat in each hand. She wasn't positive, but they seemed to be the exact same shade of blue.

"Which one do you like better? I think the teal one may go better with our bathroom," Jane said.

"You're seriously holding two of the exact same mat."

"No." Jane dropped them both on the floor and took a step back. "The one on the left has a little more green in it. I just don't know which I like better."

"There is literally no difference between the two,"

Scarlett said, amused both at the way Jane had changed the subject and how seriously she was examining the mats. "I asked Braden to meet us tonight for a drink," Jane had said when they had first walked into the store.

Jane had looked like she was about to say something else but Scarlett interrupted. "Seriously? You're gonna bring sand to the beach? We'll be at a place full of guys. Why would you invite one? And one with a girlfriend?"

Scarlett could tell when Jane was in denial about a guy, which happened more often than not. In high school, before Caleb, Jane had fallen for more than a few boys with "complications" . . . aka boys with ex-girlfriends who refused to stay ex-girlfriends (like Rob, who kept getting wasted at parties and hooking up with his ex, Brittany, or Danny, who insisted on being BFFs with his ex, Rachel, who openly hated Jane and trash-talked her to Danny at every opportunity) or guys who were otherwise not prime boyfriend material. It was kind of a recurring theme for Jane. Although who was Scarlett to talk, since she wasn't exactly an expert on relationships?

"He said he couldn't anyway. He said he was busy all weekend with something he can't get out of," Jane said, adding a pout.

"Yeah . . . a relationship," Scarlett reminded her.

"I told you. She's not really his girlfriend. They have this on–again, off–again thing. It's complicated."

"How complicated could it be? She's into him. He's into exploring his options."

"Maybe." Jane had shrugged and wandered toward the Home aisles.

Poor Janie, Scarlett thought. *She needs another boy to distract her from this one—fast.*

Now in the bath aisle, Jane was studying each mat, ignoring Scarlett. Scarlett was about to say something else when she heard the muffled sound of a cell phone. She knew it wasn't hers, because she had left it in the car.

"Janie? I think that's yours," Scarlett noted.

"Huh? Oh!" Jane fished through her massive bag looking for it, spilling a couple items on the floor in the process: a tube of peach lip gloss, a balled-up receipt, and a tampon. "Crap!"

She bent down to retrieve them as she found her cell and shoved it against her ear. "Hello?" she said, sounding a little flustered.

Nearby, a little boy watched with interest as the tampon rolled down the aisle toward him. "Oh, jeez," Scarlett muttered. She walked toward him and snatched up the tampon before he did. "Stick to Legos, kiddo," she told him. The boy laughed and ran off.

"Yes, this is she," Scarlett heard Jane say to the person on the other end.

Stuffing the tampon into her back pocket, Scarlett glanced at the shopping cart, which Jane had somehow managed to completely fill with unnecessary items: silk pillows, lamps, frames, area rugs, vases, baskets, candles, and . . . did she seriously get a noise machine? It was going to take a little more than crashing waves and seagulls to drown out the big rigs flying by their windows all night long. Still, Jane did have good intentions. She was trying hard to make their home cute. Scarlett felt a little bad about giving her such a hard time for trying to turn their dump into less of a dump.

"Oh, hey! Trevor! How are you?"

Scarlett's head snapped up.

Jane grinned at Scarlett and pointed to the phone. *It's him!* she mouthed.

Scarlett was a little surprised. It had been nearly two weeks since they had gone in for the interviews. After so many days of not hearing from anyone, they had assumed Trevor had cast some other girls. Which had been a disappointment, since Scarlett had actually gotten into the idea of being on TV. The interview had been a blast. She had liked watching the shocked expressions on Dana's and Wendell's and the cameraman's faces as she described her philosophy about one-night stands and so forth.

And Jane had confessed to Scarlett that she, too, wanted to be on the show. Something about getting out of her "comfort zone." When it looked like they weren't going to get a callback, Jane had mourned the lost opportunity by playing hookie from work one afternoon and finishing off an entire pint of Cherry Garcia ice cream in front of the TV.

"Yeah, she's with me right now," Jane was saying. "Oh, she left her phone in the car." She gestured furiously for

Scarlett to come stand next to her, then pulled the phone away from her ear so they could both listen in. Scarlett leaned her head against Jane's.

Trevor continued, "So I'm sorry it's taken two weeks for me to get back to you guys, but I've been putting together a crew. It's been hell. Anyway, I watched both of your interviews and they looked great. Meet me for lunch and let's talk about the show."

What????

Scarlett grabbed Jane's hand and squeezed, hard. Jane squeezed back.

"What the hell does that mean? Are we in?" Scarlett whispered.

"I don't know," Jane mouthed back, her blue eyes wide.

"Jane? You still there?" Trevor said after a moment.

"Yeah!"

"How about the Ivy, tomorrow at one. My assistant will make a reservation."

"Sure," Jane said.

"Great! See you tomorrow."

"'Kay. Bye."

Jane snapped her phone shut and stared at Scarlett. "What just happened?" she asked, sounding puzzled. "Does that mean he wants us to do the show?"

"Why would he meet with us if he didn't?" Scarlett pointed out, although even as she said it she doubted herself because, really? He'd chosen *them*? Out of how many other girls? It just seemed so . . . unbelievable. But also, exciting!

"Oh my God," Jane whispered.

Scarlett couldn't decipher if Jane was feeling total disbelief or total fear. The two emotions on her face were harder to differentiate than the damned bath mats.

Jane just stared at Scarlett in the middle of the bathroom accessories aisle at Target. "Are we gonna be on TV?"

Scarlett stared right back at her. "Shit. I think so!" Then she told Jane to get both mats.

"We're living on the edge now," Jane joked.

"Yep. Watch out, world. Our bath mats are coming to entertain you!"

All the tension of the Braden conversation slipped away as they wheeled their cart down the aisle, trading quips about their impending TV stardom.

12

HOW INTIMATE AND UP CLOSE?

As Jane and Scarlett walked up to the pretty brick building with a white picket fence, Jane noticed several photographers holding cameras and camcorders. She headed for the restaurant's front entrance, past the ivy-covered trees and the thick, fragrant curtain of climbing roses.

The hostess led them to the beautiful patio and one of the umbrella-adorned tables, where Trevor was typing on his BlackBerry. He looked up from the screen and smiled at them, then rose from his seat to kiss each girl on the cheek. He wore black slacks, a black long-sleeved button-down shirt, and a silver Rolex watch. His curly, silvery black hair brushed his collar, and his intense brown eyes scrutinized both girls with a look Jane couldn't quite read. She detected the slightest trace of some subtle, expensive-smelling aftershave. She had found him very good-looking at Les Deux, and her opinion hadn't changed. She normally didn't find older men attractive (was he in his late thirties or early forties?), but he had a certain self-confidence that was appealing.

"Sit. Please. How are you guys?" He seemed like he was in a good mood.

"Great!" Jane replied. Scarlett nodded.

Jane sat down, tucked her bag under her seat, and surveyed the patio. She had seen pictures of celebrities eating at the Ivy in magazines, so it felt weird to be there. It was a nice day—a balmy Sunday—and the restaurant looked busy. It was smaller than she thought it would be. (She recalled her Jared Walsh sighting that day on Melrose and thought maybe everything in L.A. was smaller in person.) She recognized a blond man sitting two tables away. *Is that the guy from the cell phone commercial?*

"Have you guys eaten here yet?" Trevor asked as he opened his menu. "People won't shut up about the fucking vegetable salad."

"Seriously?" Scarlett grinned.

"Seriously. So." Trevor leaned forward and clasped his hands together. It occurred to Jane that he had a way of making a person feel like she was the only one in the room. "*L.A. Candy.* What do you think?"

"*L.A. Candy?*" Jane repeated.

"*L.A. Candy.* As the name of the show."

"It sounds like an adult video . . . or a bad board game," Scarlett joked.

"Or a number-one show?" Trevor smiled smugly.

"High expectations?" Jane teased him.

"No, very realistic. There's such a demand for programming for girls in your demographic right now. Network execs are really focusing on that group, and this show is exactly what they are looking for. *They're* willing to bet a lot of money on this show being number one."

Jane sat back. A number-one show? Since getting Trevor's call yesterday, she had imagined . . . what? That the show might or might not go forward, might or might not get canceled after one season, might or might not be a distant memory this time next year. She definitely hadn't imagined that it might be a top-rated show. The idea gave her goose bumps. She glanced over at Scarlett, who looked kind of stunned too.

"It's going to be the two of you, and two other girls," Trevor continued. "You'll meet them soon. The cameras will be following the four of you around at your jobs, at school, at home, at clubs. However you normally spend your days and nights. It will be very intimate and close-up."

Ohmigod, this is really happening! Jane thought.

"*How* intimate and close-up?" Scarlett asked. "Like are there going to be shots of me shaving my legs?"

"*Scarlett!*" Jane laughed. "I don't think he's interested in *that*."

Trevor smiled. "No worries. As I told you both, this will be a reality version of *Sex and the City,* but a little more PG. The cameras will definitely leave you alone during your personal grooming moments." He added, "As lovely as you are, Scarlett, I don't think anyone wants to watch you shave your legs."

After the waitress came by to get their drink orders, Trevor went on. "You're probably wondering about the practical stuff. As for your contracts, our lawyers are drawing them up as we speak. Dana will be in touch with you about the first day of shooting. If it works for you, we'd like to start the week after next. Most likely that Monday. In general, the shooting schedule is planned at the beginning of each week. Dana will keep you posted on that, check in with you about what you'll be doing and where you'll be that week, and so forth. Whenever there're locations involved, like a restaurant or club or school or office or apartment building—really, any place at all—my staff will have to get clearance to shoot. And speaking of apartment buildings . . . where do you girls live?"

Scarlett told him the address. Trevor pulled out a BlackBerry from his pocket and entered the information. "Right. I'll have someone contact the owner of your building," he said.

"They want to start the week after next?" Jane managed to ask.

"Yes. Maybe a night shoot at one of the clubs."

Jane looked a little concerned. "Because I work weekdays, and—"

"Yes! With Fiona. Her offices are beautiful. We just scouted them yesterday."

"Wait, you went there?"

"Yeah. I actually had a meeting scheduled with her

after this, but she just canceled. Some kind of floral emergency, I think."

"You talked to her?" Jane said, shocked. She couldn't believe they had called Fiona. She was so embarrassed. Shouldn't they have asked her before doing that?

"She seemed pretty excited to be working with us," Trevor breezed on. "She thinks that she'll be able to get some of her bigger clients to let us film their events."

"Really?" Jane felt a little relieved. Although she was a bit surprised, too. Fiona didn't seem like the type of person who would allow her space to be overrun by a camera crew.

"We also spoke to your school," Trevor said, turning to Scarlett. "We were able to get access to one of your classes."

Scarlett frowned. "You're gonna film me in class? Why would anyone want to watch that? That's more boring than watching me shave."

Ah, Scar, always finding a way to both charm and get the last word, Jane thought, though she could tell her friend was genuinely annoyed.

"Well, that's the thing about these shows. There's no story line or scripts, so we never know when things are going to happen. For all we know, you could meet your next boyfriend in class," Trevor explained.

Jane laughed. "True. But Scarlett's more likely to hook up with the professor than another student."

Trevor raised an eyebrow.

"She's kidding." Scarlett glared at Jane.

"Sorry," Jane apologized. But she wasn't totally kidding. In high school, Scarlett had had big crushes on their history teacher, Mr. Smith; their art teacher, Mr. Martinez; and their English teacher, Mr. Foster. It wasn't because they were older, though; it was because they were smarter than most guys Scarlett's own age.

"What do you want us to wear?" Jane asked Trevor. "And what about our hair and makeup and stuff?"

"You're on your own for that. You should dress however you would normally dress. And I wouldn't stress about makeup. Bill, our director of photography, is a genius. Everywhere you guys film will be lit perfectly and you will look beautiful. You'll see."

A commotion on the other side of the white picket fence caught their attention. A man in his mid-thirties stepped out of a silver Bentley. The group of photographers that had been gathered out front now circled him, yelling over one another and snapping their cameras furiously. The man smiled as he made his way through them. Jane watched people all around the restaurant discreetly glance up at him. His face looked familiar, but she couldn't place who he was.

"Amazing what *Dancing with the Stars* will do for your career," Trevor said drily. "I give it two weeks before he's back in rehab." He gazed thoughtfully at Jane and Scarlett.

"Rehab?" Jane repeated. She read about stars going in and out of rehab in the magazines all the time. But she had never actually seen someone who'd been in rehab in person. The guy *did* look a little weathered.

"I hope you realize that your lives are about to change," Trevor said.

His words and serious tone gave Jane more goose bumps.

"With *L.A. Candy,* you will become famous. Every girl in America will want to be you. Every guy in America will want to date you. And someday"—he nodded his head in the direction of the man from *Dancing with the Stars* who had just taken his seat two tables away from them—"you'll be back here, trying to have lunch while customers ask you for your autograph and photographers try to take your picture."

Jane laughed a little at the idea and tried to catch Scarlett's eye, but she was staring at her water glass. They were about to take off on a big adventure, but Jane wondered if either of them was ready for it.

It didn't occur to Jane until later that night, as she lay awake trying to ignore her fear and excitement so she could finally fall asleep, that not once during their unspeakably glitzy, glamorous, life-altering lunch at the Ivy had Trevor actually *asked* them if they wanted to be on *L.A. Candy.* He had just assumed they would.

He had been right.

13

TWO BEDROOMS,
A POOL, AND A VIEW

"Oh, Jesus," Trevor muttered. "This place is depressing."

Staring intently at his laptop screen, he clicked through a series of pictures. He had sent one of his PAs—production assistants—down to scout Jane and Scarlett's apartment. Peeling stucco walls in desperate need of a paint job. Spitting distance from the 101. A couple of cracked windows. A cheerless sign that read:

SUNNY PALMS APTS FOR RENT

STUDIO • 1BR • 2BR

Within seconds of buzzing for his assistant, Kimi, she came into his office, speaking to someone on her headset. "That was Tom. He's in New York trying to close the deal," she said, clicking off. "He needs you to call him before the end of business. Don't forget they're three hours ahead, so you'd better call soon. What do you need?"

"We need to find them a new place to live," Trevor said, sounding annoyed as he rubbed his head.

Kimi nodded. She didn't even ask him who "them" was. That was one of the things he liked about her, versus the seven other assistants he'd been through in the last two years. "No problem. Starting when?"

Trevor went through his mental calendar. "Starting Saturday."

"Saturday, as in the day after tomorrow?"

"As in the day after tomorrow."

She nodded again and then was gone.

Trevor scrolled through his address book and made the next call on his list.

"Hello?" It was Scarlett who answered.

"Scarlett. It's Trevor. How are you?"

"Broke!"

"Oh?"

"Yeah, Jane and I spent the day shopping. Apparently my whole wardrobe is 'soooo last season.' She's like a madwoman. I believe her exact words were, and I quote, 'What are credit cards for? We've gotta look good for TV!'"

Trevor chuckled. "Smart girl. She's right."

"So what's up?"

"I spoke to the owner of your building, and he wouldn't give us the clearance to shoot on his premises," Trevor said. The lie came easily, in part because he didn't believe in arbitrary labels like *facts* and *lies*. "Something about disrupting the other tenants' privacy. Anyway, I'm arranging for the two of you to move to a new apartment, starting this—"

"Wait! What?"

"—starting this weekend," Trevor went on, ignoring her interruption. "The network will take care of the details, like the security deposit, monthly rent, and movers and so forth. Do you want to run all this by Jane, or should I call her separately?"

"Wait. You want us to move? We just moved in here. Like a month ago! And I have a history test tomorrow and two papers due next week and—"

"We need to be able to film you guys at home, Scarlett."

"Seriously . . . Jane hasn't even unpacked yet. She's kinda slow with stuff like that. She was making a fort out of her boxes yesterday. And we signed a lease here."

"Don't worry about the lease. And we'll find you guys an amazing apartment. We'll get you one with a pool and a view. My assistant will email you the details this afternoon, including photos."

"You're fucking with me! We get a pool and we don't even have to pay rent?"

After hanging up, he buzzed Kimi on the intercom. "By the way, make sure the new place has a pool."

"No problem."

Lacing his fingers behind his head, Trevor sat back and stared out the window, at the all-too-familiar row of billboards and palm trees and overpriced cafés. He spent way too much time in his office. But really, that was fine with him, especially now that he had *L.A. Candy.* It was going to be off the charts. He could feel it. He had the girl next door; a gorgeous brainiac; a spoiled, rich heiress; and the loveable ditz, for comic relief. It was a perfect formula. This is what he was good at—people. Knowing what makes them tick and presenting that for America's entertainment. That's why he had been the top reality producer in Hollywood at one time, before the last couple of mistakes. And that's why he would be the top reality producer in Hollywood again, with *L.A. Candy.*

14

IT ISN'T AN ACTING JOB.
IT'S REALITY.

Pop!

Scarlett watched, amused, as Jane uncorked the bottle of champagne. A stream of white, frothy bubbles came shooting out of the top. Squealing, Jane angled it away from her, spilling some on the new cream carpet.

"Yes, Jane, I thought the carpet looked too clean, too!" she said. "We've been here an hour and you're already making a mess."

Jane handed her the bottle. "What do you care?"

Scarlett tilted the bottle back and took a swig. The champagne tickled her mouth. She glanced around their new apartment. The movers had left only an hour ago. The place was much larger than their last one and it looked practically empty. It wasn't like their last move. With the last apartment, they had moved themselves and it had taken forever. *These* movers had packed up their stuff and trucked everything over. Trevor had arranged it all. *And* sent over a bottle of champagne with a nice note about new beginnings, on beautiful blue stationery.

Scarlett was starting to change her mind about him. Maybe he wasn't a totally full-of-shit TV producer who made a lot of empty promises. Maybe he was the best thing that had happened to her and Jane since they had moved to L.A. They might not become famous like he'd promised, but Scarlett figured that their days of waiting in lines at clubs were numbered. And paying for their own drinks. Airtime was like currency in this town.

As for the apartment . . . it was amazing. They might not be here in a couple of months, but in the meantime . . . Scarlett stretched out across the cream carpet and stared up at the impossibly tall ceilings. The bare walls were freshly painted white. On one side of the room was a small fireplace that was controlled by a switch on the wall. In a corner, Penny swished around merrily in her new, larger fishbowl that Jane had bought for her at the pet store. Jane had remarked that it was only fair that Penny get an upgrade as well.

"I can't believe we live here." Jane looked around the apartment. "It's so much less depressing than the other one."

"Hey! You said it was 'charming.'"

"I was just trying to keep a positive attitude while we lived there." Jane reached for the champagne and took a sip. "But now that we're here . . . well, it *was* charming. A charming piece of crap."

Scarlett laughed. "Yeah. It was pretty bad."

Jane's cell began buzzing and vibrating next to her. She picked it up and checked the screen.

Her face lit up. "It's Braden!"

"Oh, really? You mean, the same Braden who texts you like a hundred times a day? Or a different Braden?" Scarlett teased her.

Jane had started typing. "Huh? What did you say?"

Scarlett shook her head. She wasn't sure what, exactly, was going on between Jane and Braden. She knew they were friends. She knew he had told Jane that he and Willow were on-again, off-again. But in her experience, "on-again, off-again" usually meant that the guy was not available for a relationship—or at least not a *real* relationship, beyond an occasional hookup that never went anywhere because the on-again, off-again girl was always waiting in the wings. She and Jane had been living in L.A. for more than a month now, and Jane hadn't been on a date yet. Scarlett wondered if she was holding out for Braden, which would be a huge mistake, with Willow in the picture. She had told Jane as much—not that it had done any good.

"You told Braden the news about *the show,* right? What did he say?" Scarlett asked Jane.

"He's really happy for us," Jane replied. "I get the feeling he's not that into reality TV, though."

"Sour grapes," Scarlett said. "He's just jealous because

you got an acting job before he did."

"It isn't an acting job, Scarlett. It's reality," Jane reminded her.

"Whatever."

While Jane exchanged text messages with Braden, Scarlett glanced at the piles of boxes in the living room. Trevor had asked them not to move anything for a few days. The TV crew was coming over at some point to film the girls unpacking their things.

She spotted a basket near the top of an open box and dug it out. It contained bottles of nail polish, nail polish remover, cotton balls, emery boards, nail clippers, and a cuticle kit. She set it down on the chrome coffee table and chose a purple polish.

"Can you hand me the pale pink?" Jane said, barely glancing up from her phone.

"Sure."

As she began painting her nails, Scarlett's thoughts wandered to the events of the last month. So much had happened so fast. First, the move to L.A., then starting school, then *L.A. Candy* . . . and now this new apartment. It almost seemed too good to be true. Sure, school wasn't perfect. Her classes seemed pretty interesting, so far. On the other hand, she was sometimes haunted by that familiar old feeling that she was smarter than everyone else in her class, that she was . . . *different*. And as for *L.A. Candy*—well, Trevor *had* hooked them up with this gorgeous place. And it *was* going to be a crazy experience being on TV. But there was also a big, huge question mark hovering over everything. As happy as she was with Trevor now, today, she didn't totally trust him. You weren't supposed to trust Hollywood producers, right? You were supposed to let lawyers, agents, managers, and people like that advise you about them. The problem was, Scarlett didn't have anyone to ask for advice about this whole business. Forget about lawyers, agents, and managers. She didn't even have a kind, wise dad or a business-savvy mom to ask about stuff. When she had called her parents to tell them about *L.A. Candy,* their response had been to ask her if the show was going to interfere with her studies and affect her grades. Her father had added something about the harmful effects of reality TV on teen self-image and society in general. What bullshit.

"You want more champagne?" Jane said, holding the bottle gingerly between two freshly manicured fingers.

"Why not?" Scarlett said, reaching for the bottle. She didn't feel like thinking about *L.A. Candy* anymore.

15

BUY THE GIRL A DRINK FIRST

It was late on Monday night when Scarlett and Jane hopped out of a cab down the street from Les Deux. They had opted to get out on the corner, rather than run up the meter while waiting in the line of cars that extended down the block.

Jane was wearing a charcoal shift dress. The back dipped into a low V accented with a large black chiffon bow. A layer of delicate black lace peeked out from the bottom of her dress. Her long blond hair was pulled back tightly into a straight ironed ponytail. Her makeup was simple: coral blush on her cheeks and a gunmetal shadow brushed under her blue eyes.

Scarlett wore dark skinny jeans and a thin black T-shirt with a deep V. She had several gold necklaces layered over her tanned chest. Jane had even persuaded Scarlett to wear a little more makeup than usual. Even if it *had* required practically pinning her down, Jane had managed to apply mascara, bronzer, and lip gloss to her face. Scarlett had also reluctantly allowed Jane to tidy up her smudged black eyeliner into sleek lines. She looked lovely, like a slightly more polished version of her usual self.

The street was extra busy tonight. Closer to the parking lot, Jane noticed what appeared to be doors to another club. She hadn't noticed it the last time they were there. A large crowd of people spilled out of the messy line and into the street. She and Scarlett made their way past the mass of clubgoers and walked through the parking lot of Les Deux.

As Trevor had promised, Dana had called over the weekend to arrange for tonight's shoot—their very first. She had told the girls to find the tech van in the lot next to the club. She would meet them there so they could be miked and given further instructions.

Scarlett peered around the lot. "Did she say where they would be?" she asked Jane, frowning. "Can you call her?"

Jane pulled out her phone and dialed the producer's number.

"Jane!" Dana sounded anxious when she picked up. "Are you and Scarlett here yet?"

"Um, yeah. We're in the parking lot. Where are you guys?" Jane asked, looking around her.

"We're in the very back. Look for two white vans."

While walking farther into the lot, Jane spotted two minivans parked side by side at the far end. They were a little more soccer mom than she had expected.

"There!" Jane pointed as she started heading toward them.

Scarlett's eyes followed. "Oh my God! They're rocking minivans! They're like you at sixteen." She laughed.

When Jane got her driver's license, she had been so excited to pick out her first car. Unfortunately, due to her less-than-stellar GPA, her parents had refused to buy her a new car. Instead, she was forced to drive the family minivan for the first six months. She had hated that car so much.

As they got closer to the vans, they saw a bunch of crew members, dressed in various versions of all-black outfits. There had to be almost a dozen people from PopTV to film her and Scarlett. A few of them were unloading large pieces of camera equipment out of the back of one of the vans. Jane wondered how the camera guys would maneuver those huge cameras in the crowded club. She was about to ask Scarlett when the passenger door of the second van swung open.

"Great, you found us. You ready to get started?" Dana said, climbing out of the van and adjusting her earpiece. Her eyes looked even more tired than they had at Jane's initial interview three weeks ago, with her and Wendell. Had she been pulling all-nighters? Jane fought the impulse to offer the woman some concealer.

"Yes. So are we getting miked out here?" Jane asked her.

"Right over here," Dana said, motioning toward the

closer of the two vans. The back was open and a younger-looking guy was sitting on the bumper. He had a large pack of sound equipment strapped to the front of him by a padded harness. He unhooked the equipment and set it in the back of the van. Jane watched him as he reached in and pulled out two small microphones. They were smaller than the ones she and Scarlett had worn during their interviews. They were only a half an inch thick and silver. He unwound the thin black cord from around the first silver pack.

"Scarlett?" He looked at both of them.

"Present." Scarlett stepped toward him.

He eyed her outfit for a moment. "You're wearing a bra, right?"

She looked only a little taken aback. "Um, yeah."

"Okay." He took out a piece of double-sided tape and began peeling the paper off one side. "Well, I'm gonna have you tape this microphone to the inside of the front of your bra and run the wire around your side, then I'll clip the mike pack on the back of your bra."

He pressed the tape down, securing it against the tiny mike, and handed it to her. Then he pushed both his thumbs against the tiny mike pack, holding down two buttons at once. After a couple seconds, a small green light glowed on the top.

"You can go in the van if you want." He glanced back up at Scarlett. She had her shirt pulled up over her bra as she tried to get the tape to stick to the inside of her lacy black cup. "Oh . . . Or you could do it out here."

A couple of guys passed them. One in a trucker hat yelled out at Scarlett.

Jane laughed, amused at her friend's total disregard for acceptable parking lot etiquette. "Don't be shy or anything, Scar," she joked.

Scarlett turned to the sound guy, holding up the round metal piece at the end of the wire. He clipped it into the pack, wrapped the extra wire around the silver pack, and hooked it to the back of her bra. Scarlett pulled her shirt back down and turned her back to Jane.

"Hunchback?" she asked as she attempted to look over her own shoulder.

"Actually . . ." Jane examined the back of Scarlett's shirt. "You can barely see it."

"Okay, then, you must be Jane," the sound guy said. She noticed a white piece of what looked like surgical tape on the bottom of the second pack. Her name had been written across it with a black Sharpie.

"Yes, but, um . . ." Jane turned around, revealing her exposed back. "No bra. I'm sorry, I didn't know."

"It's cool." He shrugged. "What are you wearing under the dress?"

"Underwear."

"What kind?"

"Shit, buy the girl a drink first." Scarlett laughed.

"What do you mean? Like what brand of underwear?" Jane asked, slightly flustered.

"No." The guy laughed. "I need to know if it can support

the pack. I can always use a leg strap, but they're just a little uncomfortable and tend to fall off."

"Well." Jane looked a little embarrassed. "They're actually bathing suit bottoms. It was laundry day."

"That should be fine. I'm just gonna have you tape the mike onto your skin." He touched the center of her chest with his index finger, indicating the placement. "You wanna hop in the van to put it on?"

"Yes, please." Jane opened the door to the van and stepped in, closing it behind her. She moved a stack of notebooks and folders to the side and sat down. She looked around as she reached down the front of her dress and stuck the mike to her skin in the spot he had indicated. The van smelled like smoke and cheap vanilla-scented air freshener. The carpeted floors were stained. She noticed the key was still in the ignition and had a round white keychain hanging from it that said "Enterprise." On the seat behind her was a red ice chest and a clear plastic storage bin containing bags of chips, crackers, and different kinds of snack bars. It looked like it had been stocked at the corner gas station.

She opened the door and reached for the mike pack. The sound guy attached it to the wire and wound the slack around the pack as he had done before. She closed the door again to lift up her dress and hook the mike pack onto her bikini bottoms. The metal pack was cold against her skin. She pulled her dress down and got out of the car. Scarlett and Dana were waiting for her.

"Okay, so they're almost done setting up the cameras," Dana said. "We're gonna have you walk back out to the front of the club. Don't get in line. Go right up to the door. Paul, the doorman, knows to let you in. The cameras will be shooting the entrance, so act natural, okay? Anyway, once you're in, just wait for us. We have to re-po cameras inside. It will just take a minute."

"Then what?" Scarlett asked her.

"Then just have fun. Act natural," Dana advised. "The cameras will be shooting the interior club scene the whole time, too, but they'll be very unobtrusive. And we've already gotten releases from everyone who's seated in your area."

"We have an area?" Jane said, surprised, at the same time that Scarlett said, "They made everyone sign releases?"

"Yeah," Dana answered them both. "We have PAs go into the bar ahead of you and ask anyone who might be in a shot to sign a release form saying it's okay for their images to appear on TV," she explained. "Otherwise they have to blur their faces and it doesn't look—"

Dana stopped short. She looked distracted for a moment. She reached down and unhooked the black walkie-talkie that was attached to her jeans. "Yes, all miked up."

For a second, Jane wondered what the hell Dana was talking about, but then she remembered that the earpiece was there for a reason.

She smiled wearily at them. "Okay. I think we're ready to . . . wait, hang on." She pulled a cell phone out of her back pocket. "Oh, it's Trevor.

"Yes?" Dana said into the phone as she glanced at her watch again. "Don't worry, we're right on schedule. The girls are here and miked and . . . What? *Oh.* Yes, I'll take care of it."

Dana hung up and began rummaging through a beige canvas bag with a PopTV logo on it. She dug out a manila envelope and pulled out two sheets of paper. "I almost forgot. I have releases for you girls," she said apologetically. "I guess they haven't finished your contracts yet so we're just going to have you sign day releases for tonight."

Scarlett took the paper from Dana and started scanning it.

"It's a standard form. Like I said before, everyone who's supposed to has already signed one." Dana reached into her bag and pulled out two pens. "Here you go. Just sign and date on the bottom of the page."

Jane turned to Scarlett, feeling a little unsure. She was hoping Scarlett would say something, tell her what to do. Should they insist on delaying the shoot until they had the actual *L.A. Candy* contract? She had promised her dad she'd send it to him as soon as she got it so he could show it to his lawyer.

Scarlett only sighed and took one of Dana's pens. "Whatever," she said.

I guess that's that, Jane thought.

Jane sank back into the plush velvet booth as she squeezed a lime into her vodka soda. The DJ was playing one of her favorite songs, Madonna's "Material Girl."

This is so totally different from the last time we were here, she wanted to say to Scarlett. But she was aware—very aware, actually—of the fact that they were being filmed. Not that it would be obvious to anyone who didn't have to sign a release—the cameras were tucked away in the corners of the room, as Dana had promised.

She knew that she and Scarlett were supposed to "act natural," which meant that they weren't supposed to talk about the fact that Paul the doorman (the same one who had made them wait for forty-five minutes before D had gotten there) had let them in immediately, as though he had been expecting them (he had), with a smile as though he knew them (he didn't). Or the fact that the stylishly dressed hostess had led them—all friendly as though they were regulars or celebrities, or both—to what seemed like the best table in the club, with a perfect view of the room and just the right level of throbbing beat emanating from the DJ's booth. Or the fact that the waitress had offered them "bottle service," bringing over a bottle of Grey Goose vodka, ice, and all the fixings, so they could mix whatever drinks they wanted (for as many rounds as they wanted) on their own. All without asking them for ID. It was . . . *unreal* was the word that popped into Jane's head. Which was kind of funny—and a little ironic—since this was supposed to be a *reality* show.

Jane peered around the packed room, wondering if the crowd knew that they were being filmed by a PopTV crew.

120

And what about the people at the neighboring tables who had presumably signed releases—were they self-conscious, like she was? Were they worried the cameras were going to catch them doing something embarrassing?

"Sooo." Scarlett poured her second shot of Patrón and tipped it back smoothly. She glanced around the room, looking a little uncomfortable, then shifted in her seat. Jane was surprised to find that her friend was as unsure as she was about how to act in this situation. Scarlett *always* knew what to do. "How was work today?" she asked before biting into a lime wedge.

"Oh, the same," Jane replied. "I'm finally getting used to the phones, though. I don't hang up on people anymore. Maybe Fiona won't fire me, after all. Not this week, anyway." She laughed nervously.

She continued to people watch, when she noticed her phone had started buzzing. She pulled it out of her bag and glanced at the screen.

It was a text message from Dana. SORRY BUT CAN YOU REPEAT WHAT YOU JUST SAID? she had written. SOMEONE GOT IN THE FRAME.

Scarlett was staring at her curiously. "Braden? Or not Braden?"

Jane shook her head. She tried to remember her exact words about her job. "I'm getting used to the phones," she said after a moment, trying not to sound completely weird and unnatural. "I don't hang up on people anymore. Maybe she won't fire me. Not this week, anyway."

Scarlett frowned, confused. "*What?* You just said that. Janie, you okay?"

"Hey, we're doing a Sweet Sixteen party for the Marley twins next weekend," Jane blathered on, which seemed easier than explaining. "It's going to be amazing."

"Hey, can we borrow a couple of limes? We're totally out."

Jane turned around to see a girl in the next booth smiling at her and Scarlett. She was pretty—Southern California pretty—with long, platinum blond hair and a deep tan. She was with another girl with shoulder-length, light brown hair. They both looked to be around Jane and Scarlett's age. It seemed no one got carded in L.A.

Jane handed the blond girl a small crystal glass full of sliced limes. "Sure. Here you go!"

"Thanks!" the girl said. "We've been trying to get our waitress's attention for, like, forever. She's totally disappeared."

"She probably fell into a black hole," Scarlett said drily.

The brown-haired girl scrunched up her face and peered anxiously around the room. "A black hole?" she said. "Is that, like, dangerous?"

"It's not only *not* dangerous, it's scientifically impossible," Scarlett assured her.

The girl looked blank. "Oh."

The blonde extended her hand. Jane noticed that she had long, slender fingers and perfectly French-manicured nails. She seemed very put-together, although she was wearing more makeup and hair products than clothing. Her gorgeous black minidress had a plunging neckline. Jane could smell her heavy perfume from where she was sitting.

"I'm Madison," the blond girl said. "And this is Gaby."

"Hey," Gaby said, waving.

"I'm Jane and this is Scarlett."

Scarlett nodded to the girls.

"What do you guys think of this place?" Jane asked.

Madison grinned. "It's awesome. I practically live here. Atmosphere is great, and the DJ is prime hookup material—don't you think?"

"Madison, you can't say things like that!" Gaby gasped. She took a sip of her cosmo and accidentally spilled some on her pale pink silk blouse. "Oops! Oh shit, am I going to get electrocuted?" she cried out, swatting at her chest.

Jane and Scarlett looked at each other as Gaby unbuttoned her blouse and studied her boobs with a worried expression. Jane watched in confusion. What was she doing?

Then Jane saw the flash of familiar black wire and realized Gaby was wearing the same kind of microphone as they were. Was Madison miked too? Jane saw that Scarlett had also noticed.

They looked at each other, puzzled. *Did they mike everyone in the room? Or just Madison and Gaby? Were they more important than the others in the room?* Knowing that she was—that they *all* were—still on camera, Jane refrained from voicing her questions out loud.

Madison's voice cut into her thoughts. "Jane, I love the color of your nails. Where did you get them done?"

Jane glanced at her hand. "I did them myself."

"Seriously?" Madison gasped. "They look so good. I can't paint my own nails." She held out her French acrylic nails.

"Yeah, Jane is independent like that. She totally bathes and feeds herself too," Scarlett said.

Madison arched her eyebrows and gave Scarlett a look. Jane knew that look well . . . that "WTF is your problem?" look. Scarlett got it often.

But instead of saying anything, Madison just took a deep breath and squeezed a lime into her drink. "Gaby and I were talking about doing a beauty day this Saturday," she said brightly. "You should come. Both of you. We'll get facials, get our hair done, maybe nails. It'll be a total glam day."

"No, thank—" Scarlett began.

Jane stepped on Scarlett's foot with her silver wedge. "Sounds fun!" she said quickly. "I could use a girls' day."

Scarlett kicked Jane's shin under the table. Jane suppressed a cry of pain and kept smiling.

She glared at Scarlett. *These must be the other girls Trevor had mentioned. Why else would they be miked? So we'd better get to know them,* Jane thought, rubbing her shin, then reaching for her vodka soda and wondering what-the-hell kind of "reality" she'd just signed herself up for.

124

★ ★ ★

The next evening, Jane and Scarlett received their *L.A. Candy* contracts at home, by messenger. The two of them went through the thick documents at the kitchen table, over beers.

"Does this make sense to you?" Jane said, skimming the pages. Everything was in tiny print, and in really convoluted English.

Scarlett skimmed through the pages, too. "Uh . . . not really. Hey, do you know how much they're paying us to be on this show? Trevor didn't say anything about that. *Holy shit!*" Her eyes grew huge.

Jane's head whipped up. "Holy shit *what*? What's wrong?"

"Nothing's wrong! It says, 'two thousand dollars episodic fee.' They're paying us two thousand dollars *per episode*!"

For a moment, Jane felt as though she couldn't breathe. "Seriously?" she finally managed.

"Seriously. It says so right here, on page twelve."

Jane flipped quickly to page twelve. There it was, right there at the top of the page. She didn't understand the rest of the legal jargon, but she understood *that*. "Holy shit!" she agreed.

"Dana said they're filming ten episodes this first season, which means—"

"Twenty . . . thousand . . . dollars," Scarlett said slowly.

Jane said nothing. She stared at Scarlett as she took a long sip of her beer. Then they sat back in their chairs, not speaking for a while. Jane tried to absorb this *new* reality. Twenty grand—just for being filmed doing stuff she would have done anyway, like going to work and hanging out with her friends. She couldn't believe it. She had never made that much money in her entire life, not from all her part-time jobs put together. And of course, Fiona was paying her minimum wage, basically. Maybe now she wouldn't need to dip into her savings as much, or she could tell her parents they didn't need to help her out anymore.

Was this really happening?

Then she remembered what she'd promised her father. "Dad told me to send the contract to him, so he can have his lawyer take a look," she said to Scarlett in a serious voice. "We shouldn't sign until then."

"Absolutely," Scarlett said. "Let's send these to your dad first thing tomorrow."

"Perfect."

"So what do you think? You wanna go out and spend our first paychecks before we get them?" Scarlett grinned.

16

WHO'S AFRAID OF THE BIG, BAD ENGLISH PROFESSOR?

"Hello, everyone," Dana called out from the front of the classroom. It was Scarlett's Wednesday-morning seminar on twentieth-century American playwrights. Scarlett had just seen Dana the night before yesterday at Les Deux. She was not particularly happy to see her now, with the *L.A. Candy* crew invading her class.

"My name is Dana," she went on. "I'm one of the producers of a show we're filming for PopTV. You may have noticed the cameras when you came in. We are here to film Scarlett." She motioned toward Scarlett.

Scarlett sunk low in her seat. This was so embarrassing. She could feel the other students staring at her.

"We won't be interrupting your class at all, and we're going to try and stay out of your way as much as possible," Dana continued. "That being said, Alli will pass around some releases. If you don't wish to be on camera, please move to the back right corner of the classroom."

The girl sitting next to Scarlett quickly rose from her seat and gathered her things. "This is bullshit," she grumbled as she shoved past Scarlett.

You're telling me, Scarlett thought. *The first semester has barely begun and I'm already a social pariah.*

Scarlett watched a couple more students around her relocate to the back corner of the classroom, each one giving her a disapproving glare as they passed her seat. She totally understood their frustration. She was just as annoyed by the cameras' presence as they were. Scarlett buried her face in her laptop while Alli, the girl Dana had pointed out, made her way around the classroom, collecting signatures and snapping digital pictures of the students who were willing to be on camera. When she was done, Dana thanked the students and left the classroom.

Professor Cahill moved to the spot Dana had just vacated. "So. Can anyone tell me what Edward Albee was saying in *Who's Afraid of Virginia Woolf?*" he began.

Professor Cahill was uncharacteristically dressed up today. Decked out in a beige linen suit and bow tie, he bore an odd resemblance to the popcorn guy, Orville Redenbacher. It was better than his usual attire, which was a pair of baggy Dockers and a button-down white shirt with the inevitable coffee stain blooming across his enormous stomach. Apparently he couldn't drink coffee without spilling it on the exact same spot every day.

Professor Cahill also seemed to be sweating a lot more than usual. He was slightly more animated in his lecture today, like he was starring in an American play of his own. *Who's Afraid of the Big, Bad English Professor?*

Three camera guys had set up in the classroom, one in the back filming the professor, and one in each of the front two corners of the room. The two in front seemed mostly to keep their lenses focused on Scarlett, occasionally panning over to get shots of Professor Cahill and the other students, all of whom were trying their hardest to appear unaffected by their presence.

Scarlett's phone started vibrating. She pulled it out of her jeans pocket and looked at the screen.

It was a text message from Dana. **CAN YOU PLEASE TILT DOWN YOUR COMP SCREEN. IT'S BLOCKING YOUR FACE**, she had written.

Scarlett lowered the screen of her laptop, her annoyance growing. It hadn't really occurred to her before that being on this show was going to be such a pain in the ass. And this was only day two! She hoped it would get better, not worse. Or that she'd get used to it.

No one had answered Professor Cahill's original question. The classroom was totally silent.

"Anyone? *Who's Afraid of Virginia Woolf?*" The professor scanned the students with narrowed eyes.

Scarlett sighed and raised her hand. Professor Cahill turned to her, beaming. "Yes, Ms.—" He glanced down at the seating chart, as if to find her name. *Ummm . . . yeah, I'm the girl with the crew of fifteen that took over your class-room with stage lighting and cameras. No biggie, you probably just forgot.* "Ms. Harp."

"Yeah, well, *Who's Afraid of Virginia Woolf?* is about one unhappily married couple getting tanked and abu-sive in front of another unhappily married couple," Scarlett said loudly. "So Albee was saying that marriage basically sucks, and that when it comes right down to it, it's impossible for people to be kind or even civil to one another."

"Yes, yes, that's right, isn't it?" Professor Cahill said, nodding. He ran his hand through his nonexistent hair, in the process of smearing his bald head with blue chalk marks. A few students tittered. "With Ms. Harp's insight-ful comment in mind, let us turn our attention to the scene on page . . ."

Scarlett was barely listening. She closed the page of notes she had been taking. She had read the play twice. She got it. She checked her emails and noticed that she had a new message from Madison, the blond chick from Les Deux the other night. Dana must have given Madi-son her email. *Note to self, change email immediately*, she thought.

TO: JANE ROBERTS, SCARLETT HARP, GABY GARCIA
FROM: MADISON PARKER
SUBJECT: GIRLS' DAY!

Hey Bitches!! So this Saturday I'm planning a girls' day for us. We're all meeting at Kate Somerville (go online to pick the treatment you want), then lunch and blowouts at Warren Tricomi. So fun! Be prepared for a whole day of beauty treatments. Also bring a cute outfit so we can go out after. (Gotta go out and show off our gorgeous new selves, right?) Don't bother with an RSVP because I'm not taking no for an answer!!
XOXO,
Madison

Jane had already responded: CAN'T WAIT!

Gaby had responded, too: SO IN! HEY, DOES KATE SUMMERVILLE LET U BRING DOGS?

Awesome. I guess this means I have to go, too, Scarlett thought. She wondered if Trevor or Dana—or both—had been blind copied on the message.

After Les Deux, Dana had confirmed that Madison and Gaby were the other two girls on *L.A. Candy. Thanks for the heads-up,* Scarlett had thought. *You could have told us before we walked into the club.*

So who, exactly, were Madison Parker and Gaby Garcia? According to Dana, Trevor had "discovered" them at a posh gym in Hollywood. Madison was a socialite from out East. Gaby worked for some publicist. Scarlett wondered what Trevor's plan was for the four of them. Were they supposed to become insta-friends? Was this what he meant when he said they should "act natural"? Because hanging out in a spa with girls like Madison and Gaby was most definitely *not* natural. She and Jane had just met them two days ago. Not to mention Scarlett wasn't huge on spas—or girls like Madison and Gaby.

When class finally ended at 10 a.m., Scarlett scooped up her books and laptop and made a beeline for the door. Fortunately, Dana had not scheduled her to be stalked by the cameras after this. If she remembered correctly, they were filming Jane at work next. Scarlett thought it was hilarious that this show that Trevor had guaranteed them was going to be the Next Big Thing basically had one camera crew—she guessed "reality" happened only in scheduled intervals?

"Charlotte?"

Scarlett paused in the doorway and looked down the crowded hall. It was Cammy, the blonde she had met the first week of classes. She was hugging her books against her huge, fake chest and waving frantically at Scarlett. Scarlett pretended not to see her and turned the other way. But as she headed in the other direction, she saw that one of the cameras that had been inside the classroom had been repositioned in the hall. Damn. It was blocking her exit strategy.

"Charlotte!" Cammy cried out again.

Scarlett reluctantly turned back around. "Hi, Cammy." She forced a smile.

"How has school been going for you?" Cammy asked cheerfully.

"Um, you know." Scarlett remembered their last

encounter ending on a not particularly friendly note. Was Cammy so blond that she'd forgotten?

Then she noticed Cammy staring past her, over her shoulder. Cammy tucked her hair behind her ears and stepped a few inches to the left. It didn't take a genius to figure out Cammy was positioning herself to be in line with the camera.

Scarlett rolled her eyes. "Well, I'm gonna be late for my next class." She made her way through a cloud of Cammy's desperation and toward the next camera guy she saw. She pulled her shirt up, revealing her perfectly toned tummy, and ripped the mike off her chest. She then slid the mike pack out of her back pocket and held it out to the camera operator.

"Can you give this to whoever's doing sound? I'm late," Scarlett said as she shoved the pack and tangled wire into his hand.

"Sure." He pulled his eye away from the viewfinder and smiled at her. He was cute. He had a folded bandana wrapped around his forehead, holding back a full head of light brown waves. She hadn't noticed him before. She actually hadn't paid attention to any of the camera guys. They were always stationed behind their equipment by the time she entered a room. She glanced back over her shoulder at the camera that had been blocking her original path. Another guy in his mid-twenties was standing next to it, talking into a walkie-talkie.

He was wearing a faded black T-shirt that showed his chiseled arms. *Hmmm, eye candy . . .* , she thought as she turned and headed toward her next class. *Maybe this won't be so bad after all.*

17

YOU'RE PROBABLY WONDERING
WHY I CALLED YOU IN HERE TODAY

Jane peered at her watch as she rushed out of the elevator, into the world of soft lighting and trickling waterfalls. She had an excuse for being late this time, though. She'd spent most of the morning running errands for Fiona. Plus, the *L.A. Candy* crew was following her around for the rest of the day. They had intercepted her in the parking lot, miked her, and filmed her getting out of her car and walking to the lobby of the building. Five times. Now they were setting up in the front waiting area of Fiona Chen Events, filming her "arriving for work."

She knew the crew had been with Scarlett this morning, at school. She wondered if they were filming Madison and Gaby sometime today too. Maybe they had their own camera crew? Dana hadn't mentioned that. Dana had said something about Madison being from a rich East Coast family that owned a bunch of hotels. And Gaby worked at an L.A. PR firm called Ruby Slipper. Apparently Gaby had been born and raised in L.A., where her mother and stepfather still lived; her father and stepmother lived somewhere in the Southwest. In any case, Jane liked these girls. They seemed fun. She was looking forward to their spa day on Saturday. In fact, she wished the spa day was *today*. She was feeling a little stressed, and could use a relaxing facial.

"Hi, Naomi!" Jane said, waving to the receptionist. She tried to speak at the usual, acceptable low decibel, but she knew that would only guarantee her a text message from Dana to tell her to say it again, a little louder.

Naomi adjusted her silver headset and peered out at Jane from behind a huge bouquet of white tulips. She glanced self-consciously at the two camera guys zooming in on her. "Hi, Jane. Fiona wants to see you in her office right away," she whispered.

Jane felt her blood freeze. Those words were never good. Fiona never called Jane into her office unless she was in trouble. It was always something like, "Jane, the last time I checked, ivory and eggshell weren't the same color," or "Jane, is this message from Jeffrey with a *J* or Geoffrey with a *G*?" What had she done this time? Either way, she preferred that her humiliating lectures take place in private—just her and Fiona behind closed doors. *Guess not today.* She frowned at the cameras, which were supposed to be capturing "an average workday." *Well, now, the* L.A. Candy *viewers are going to see my average butt getting yelled at,* Jane thought.

She sighed and hoisted her bag higher on her shoulders. "Thanks, Naomi," she said, then started down the hall toward Fiona's office.

"Wait! Jane!" A man wearing an earpiece and holding a small monitor rushed up to her. "Hey, I'm Matt. I'm directing today's shoot."

Jane tried to hide her confusion. What did he mean, directing? She thought they were just following her around. What needed to be directed?

"Hey. Sorry, Naomi said Fiona wants to talk to me."

"Yeah, we know. We just need a few minutes to set up cameras," Matt explained, moving to the side as several crew members passed them, carrying cameras and other equipment.

"Her office looks beautiful but it's all white. Makes it hard to shoot. They spent two hours lighting it this morning," Matt went on.

"What's wrong with white?" Jane asked.

"It just doesn't look great on camera. Color looks way better."

Jane looked down at the summery white lace dress she was wearing. *Crap,* she thought.

Jane and Matt proceeded to Fiona's office and stopped right outside. Jane waited while Matt stood next to her, fussing with buttons on the small monitor in his hand. The screen alternated between shots of Fiona and an empty chair. Jane watched as Fiona sat there, patiently waiting for Jane's entrance. She looked lovely on the screen.

"Okay, you can go in now," Matt instructed Jane as he stepped away from the door.

Jane knocked lightly before going inside. Fiona looked up from her computer screen. "Good morning, Jane! Please come in and sit down." She sounded more pleasant than usual. *She must enjoy humiliating people,* Jane thought.

As she stepped into Fiona's office, Jane looked around her. Two metal stands flanked Fiona's desk, securing large lights. The intensity of the lights was muted by wide sheets of what looked like tracing paper, wrapped around the fixtures and held in place by wooden clothespins. The same kind of paper had been taped over one of the tall windows. The result was an overall softening of the lighting in the room.

Jane sat down in one of the chairs, set her bag on the floor, and crossed her legs. Her foot began twitching.

Fiona clasped her hands and leaned forward. "So. Jane. You're probably wondering why I called you in here today."

Jane nodded, her eyes wide.

"I realize you've been here at Fiona Chen Events for only a short time," Fiona said. "But during that short time, you've—"

—managed to screw up just about everything I've asked you to do, Jane finished silently.

"—handled the pressure very well. I think it's time for you to move up to the next step. To that end, I would like to offer you a promotion. How would you like to be my full-time assistant?"

Jane's jaw dropped. Was she serious? Fiona was offering her . . . a promotion? To be her assistant? Why would she do that? Fiona's assistant would never confuse eggshell and ivory.

"Of course, it will be strictly on a trial basis," Fiona went on. "Let's say three months. During those three months, you will work harder than you have ever worked before. At the same time, you will have opportunities that you have never had before. And if you succeed, your future as an event planner in this town will be virtually guaranteed."

Fiona leaned back in her seat and stared at Jane, waiting for her answer. All of a sudden, Jane noticed that Fiona was wearing makeup. When had the boss lady started wearing makeup?

"Well, Jane?" Fiona prompted her.

The camera zoomed in on Jane. She took a deep breath. Was she ready for this? A real job was better than an internship because it meant she would get paid a little bit more. It also meant that she would get more responsibilities, more respect . . . more *everything*.

"Yes!" Jane said, nodding. "I'd love to. Thank you so much!"

Fiona smiled. It was not her usual chilly, arctic, I-am-the-boss-lady-and-you-are-my-slave smile but a cordial, friendly smile. It didn't look entirely natural on her. "Fabulous! Let me show you where you'll be sitting. Then we can have Human Resources draw up your paperwork."

Jane couldn't believe what had just happened. In a daze of excitement and confusion, she thanked Fiona once more. She was just about to stand when Matt opened the door and popped his head in. "That was great! We just need a wide shot real quick. Give us a quick min to set up," he said.

A couple of the crew members rushed into the room. One peeled the thin paper off the far window and another began pulling back the lights. Jane watched as they bustled around her. She noticed Fiona eyeing their sneakers on her immaculate carpets. Her expression made Jane cringe a little. She was surprised Fiona hadn't made them take off their shoes.

"Okay," Matt said, putting a hand on Jane's shoulder. "So count to ten after I leave the room, then thank her again and walk out the door."

"Okay." Jane nodded as he turned and left the room. She took a breath and looked back up at Fiona, trying not to feel totally overwhelmed by everything that was going on. *One, two, three . . .* , she counted mentally.

Then Fiona did the most surprising thing yet. She leaned in toward Jane and whispered, "You're doing just fine, dear." And then she smiled softly, kindly.

Jane barely had time to react before Fiona's smile vanished, as though the moment had never happened. Fiona straightened up in her chair and resumed her usual cool, businesslike expression.

"Jane? You still counting? We're ready for you!" Jane heard Matt say from behind the closed door.

★ ★ ★

Jane opened the bottom drawer of her new desk and tucked her bag inside. She opened the two others, too—each drawer had a different vintage crystal knob—and started planning what would go where. The top drawer would be for pencils, pens, and stationery. The middle drawer would be for energy bars, breath mints, makeup, tampons, and other personal stuff.

She still couldn't believe it. She had walked into Fiona's office expecting to get reprimanded. Instead, she had gotten promoted. And now, she had a desk of her own, in an office across the hall from Fiona's. It was simple, bare-bones. In fact, Jane was pretty sure it had been a storage room the week before, albeit a large storage room. She leaned her face on her hand as she stared into the Mac on her desk. The screensaver was a black-and-white picture of a Buddha statue. In the monitor, she saw the reflection of one of the camera operators changing angles behind her. She felt bad for him. He was edged up into the corner and had no space to move.

"Roomy back there?" Jane teased.

The guy shrugged and laughed a little.

"Excuse me."

Jane spun around. Standing in the doorway was a guy with short, cropped blond hair and blue eyes. He was carrying a big, sleek leather portfolio.

"Hi," Jane said, a little startled.

"Hey, there," the guy said. "I'm looking for Fiona Chen,

but I think I got lost. I have an appointment to show her my portfolio."

"Across the hall," Jane said, pointing. "She actually has someone in there . . . you may want to wait a minute."

"I'm sorry. The girl at the front told me to come straight back."

"Oh, no worries. She just pulled someone in there for a sec. Some mix-up with peonies. He'll be out in a minute . . . a little less of a man."

The guy laughed. "I'm Paolo."

"I'm Jane. Are you a model?" Jane asked, pointing at the portfolio in his hand.

Paolo laughed again. "No, no. I'm a photographer."

"Oh!"

Paolo smiled at her. He had the cutest smile. "Hey, this may be a little forward, but . . . could I call you some-time? Maybe we could go out for coffee or something? I just moved here from San Francisco, and I don't know too many people in town."

Jane was taken aback by his forwardness. They had met all of sixty seconds ago. Still, he *did* kinda look like a young Brad Pitt. Besides, when was the last time she'd been on a date? Braden didn't count. She had met him for drinks again at Cabo Cantina, over the weekend, to celebrate her being on the show and moving into a new apartment. It had been her idea. So that wasn't a date. It never was with him. "Sure," she said.

"Great!"

Jane blinked. Oh, yeah. The cameras were still rolling. Paolo was being filmed. But he didn't seem to be fazed by it.

Did that mean he had walked into her office knowing there would be cameras? Had Dana talked to him already and gotten him to sign the release papers? Had she *told* him to ask her out? Or did he just happen to be there for a meeting, like he said?

Just then, Fiona's door opened and Damien, an intern, shuffled out and shamefully dropped his head.

"I'll grab your number on the way out," Paolo said before he disappeared into Fiona's office.

"Okay."

Despite just meeting him, Jane couldn't help but be excited. She looked past the camera in the hallway and spotted Dana. Jane grinned and mouthed, "He's so cute!" Dana nodded in agreement and gave her a thumbs-up. Jane noticed a release form in Dana's hand. Did that mean Paolo had been released? Did that mean it *had* been a setup? Jane smiled to herself as she realized she didn't care. She was already thinking about what to wear on what might turn out to be her very first on-camera date . . . her first date, period, since Caleb. Okay, so Paolo wasn't Braden. So what? It was nice to have a guy interested in her. It had been a long time. *Too* long.

18

GIRLS' DAY

Scarlett stood outside Kate Somerville. The spa was located on a small, shaded street that broke off of Melrose, amid plush trees, rows of boutiques, and one-man valets. She glanced at her phone. It was a few minutes past ten. Except for the camera crew, she was the first to arrive. Apparently no one believed in punctuality anymore.

She would have driven over with Jane, but her friend had to run an errand for Fiona Chen first. Early on a Saturday morning, no less. Four days into Jane's big-deal promotion from intern to assistant, and she was already busier than ever. Jane had worked until almost midnight on Wednesday and Thursday, and she had canceled a Friday-night movie date, just the two of them. Instead she'd had to babysit a young up-and-coming actress at an event Fiona was throwing for a children's foundation. (In Hollywood, putting on Manolos and stopping by for a glass of champagne apparently said, "I care.") In any case, it seemed like she and Jane hadn't had much together time since they'd started filming *L.A. Candy.* Scarlett was convinced that the show was somehow responsible for Jane's promotion and new, crazy-busy hours. It sounded dumb and probably selfish, but she missed their regular old boring lives, before PopTV.

Speaking of Jane . . . she came rushing up, her long blond hair flying all over the place. "Hey, I'm sorry. I've been trying to find parking for, like, twenty minutes." She sounded out of breath. "Where is everybody?"

"No one's here yet." Scarlett shrugged.

"Oh, well, let's go in. I'm sure they'll be here in a few minutes."

The front door opened onto the bottom of a winding staircase. They climbed the black carpeted stairs, admiring the long crystal chandelier above. When they reached the top of the stairs, they found themselves in a spacious room, where two women at a large white receptionist's desk checked them in. A couple of cameras were already set up inside. One of the guys proceeded to mike the two girls.

Scarlett had to admit that the place was beautiful, all vintage ivory wallpaper and polished oak floors. In the center of the room, a circular glass table displayed a single white orchid and an artfully fanned spread of *Vanity Fair, Harper's Bazaar,* and *Vogue* magazines. Tall silver vases, with bunches of pink hydrangeas spilling out of them, stood on each side of a square fireplace covered with small opal tiles and filled with shiny black stones. The remaining walls were mirrored, with shelves of boxed products in teal, lavender, and periwinkle packaging. Other than some soft music, it was silent.

Beautiful or not, Scarlett didn't want to be there. She wasn't a spa type of girl. And she didn't feel like wasting a few hours—actually, the whole day and night—hanging out with Madison and Gaby, whom she hardly knew and didn't particularly want to get to know. She was seriously tempted to persuade Jane to bail and spend the day at the beach instead. But she knew Jane would probably stare at her in horror and point to the cameras and shake her head, like, "Are you insane, Scar? They're already here!" Jane was hyper-obedient when it came to doing whatever the producers or directors or other crew members told her to do. Scar was just the opposite. It fit with their respective personalities. Still, it made her kind of sad and nostalgic for the days when it was just her and Jane. Before Trevor, Dana, Wendell, Madison, Gaby, and the rest of them had ruined everything.

But you wanted to be on this stupid show, Scarlett reminded herself.

Jane dropped onto one of the plush couches, seemingly oblivious to Scarlett's mixed feelings about being there. Sighing, Scarlett followed suit. She saw one of the cameras zooming in on her, so she reached for a *Vanity Fair* and began flipping pages. That was the sort of thing one did in the reception area of a spa, right? A moment later, she heard the front door open and chatter drifting up the stair-well. She turned to the doorway to see Madison and Gaby coming around the corner.

"Hey, ladies!" Madison's voice erupted into the quiet room. Gaby trailed in behind her, waving. Because of Gaby's RSVP email to Madison, Scarlett had expected her to be carrying a teacup poodle or something. But she was dogless today.

As a soundman miked them, Madison smiled at one of the receptionists, who greeted her by name. "Let Ana know I'm here," Madison instructed her, then quickly turned back to the girls. Scarlett had the same impression of her that she'd had on Monday night at Les Deux. She looked so . . . fake. Like there wasn't a single real thing about her. Why had Trevor cast her for this show, anyway? And as for Gaby . . . well, the woman needed cue cards just to help her process her next thought.

"Hey, guys!" Jane cried out. She sounded excited to see them. Scarlett didn't say anything.

Scarlett felt Jane elbow her ever so subtly. "Be polite!" Jane pleaded in her ear.

God! When had Jane turned into Miss Manners? Scarlett gave Madison and Gaby a quick wave, barely glancing up from her magazine.

"Sooo." Gaby sunk onto the couch next to Jane. "What are you getting done?"

"I played it safe. Facial." Jane shrugged.

"Oh, they're really good here!" Gaby exclaimed.

"What about you?" Jane asked.

"I'm just getting a Lipocell treatment," Gaby replied.

Jane cocked her head. "What's that?"

"It's where they—"

"She's getting the cellulite removed from her ass," Madison interrupted, chuckling.

Scarlett looked up just in time to see Gaby's smile fade a little.

"Oh, well, sign me up for that one!" Jane joked.

Scarlett leaned back into the comfy couch. Yup. Gaby was definitely a flake. And Madison was definitely a fake. A fake with a mean streak to boot. Seriously, why would she pick on Gaby? It was like kicking a dumb puppy that was trying to follow you home.

"So . . . Madison? What do you do, anyway?" Scarlett asked her. She was curious about what kind of job a "socialite" like Madison might have. If she even had a job. Or did she go to school? She could totally see her fitting in perfectly with Cammy and her Pi Delta friends at U.S.C.

Madison grinned. "Lots of stuff. I'm kind of between jobs right now. I tried PR, but it wasn't really me. I tried retail, too. And I worked as an intern at a literary agent's office. But it was so boring."

"How old are you?" Scarlett said, not caring that she sounded bitchy. "Seems like you've been around the job block."

"I'm only twenty," Madison said, either unaware of Scarlett's bitchiness or choosing to ignore it. "I might try college next. Aren't you at U.C.L.A.? How do you like it?"

"U.S.C. Jury's still out."

"What jury?" Gaby piped up.

"So what are you getting done, Scarlett?" Madison said, changing the subject.

Scarlett turned her attention back to her article: "Inside the Private World of Anna Payne." Oh, yeah, *that* bitch. Still, it was more interesting than talking to *this* bitch. "Laser hair removal," she replied, pretending to yawn.

There was a silence. Scarlett glanced up just in time to see Madison's and Gaby's faces simultaneously twisting into the same horrified expression. Gaby let out a little "Ouch!"

"What? I was reading about it online. It's supposed to be a 'noninvasive' and 'comfortable' procedure. Besides, I hate waxing," Scarlett explained, feeling defensive, then frustrated for feeling defensive.

The two girls exchanged knowing glances.

"What are you getting lasered, sweetie?" Madison asked, concern in her voice.

"Bikini."

Madison stared at her for a moment, and then reached into the quilted Chanel clutch next to her. She pulled out a prescription bottle and spilled one long white pill into her palm. She handed it to Scarlett.

"What is it?" Scarlett asked her.

"Just take it. You'll thank me later."

"Yes, definitely!" Gaby agreed.

Scarlett peered suspiciously at Madison. She wasn't too high on Scarlett's trust list. But Madison's reaction to the laser was the first real emotion Scarlett had seen register on her face. Scarlett opened her mouth, tossed in the pill, and swallowed.

"So! What are we doing after our beauty treatments?" Jane asked Madison. Scarlett made a face. Why did her best friend have to sound so positive?

"Oh, I made fun plans for us." Madison smiled mysteriously.

Great, Scarlett thought bitterly. *Wonder which will be more painful, the laser or a night out with these two.*

"Who wants more champagne?" Madison sang out. "Don't be shy, ladies!"

Scarlett glanced up from her spot on Madison's luxurious leather couch, which felt like butter against her skin. She was lying down with her head on some guy's lap. Through the haze of champagne, martinis, and tequila shots, she was vaguely aware of Madison standing on top of her Italian marble coffee table, waving a gold champagne bottle in the air.

Scarlett tried to sit up, willing her drunken brain fog to dissipate. Nearby, she saw that Jane was perched on a boy's lap, giggling, while he played with her hair. Across the room, Gaby was dancing with three guys to an AC/DC song. She was wearing an oversized man's white button-down shirt open over her black sequined dress. Just behind her, two cameramen from *L.A. Candy* were there, filming everything. Scarlett wasn't positive, but she thought they were the same cameramen that had been with them all day, starting at the spa.

What time is it? Scarlett wondered groggily, sitting up a little more. She remembered Madison saying something about the penthouse apartment belonging to her parents. What had Dana said about them? That they were fifth-generation Parkers from somewhere on the East Coast who owned fancy cribs like this all over the world, or something like that? Not that Scarlett was impressed. Like its occupant, the place looked fake, unnatural—as though the decor had been copied straight out of an interior design magazine.

The girls had been out all night and Madison had insisted they all go back to her place, including the handful of guys they had collected throughout the night.

"Where do you live?" the guy cradling Scarlett's head asked her.

"What?" Scarlett murmured.

"Where . . . do . . . you . . . live?" the guy repeated, kissing her forehead.

"She lives with me!" Jane spoke up. She stumbled a little over her words. "Scar and I are roommates!"

"Let's move the party there," said Jane's guy, stroking her hair.

"Why? Don't leave! We're having fun!" Madison cut in. "Besides, I have spare bedrooms."

Scarlett staggered to her feet. She was drunk, but she wasn't *so* drunk that she wanted to get even more wasted and hook up with some random guy for the *L.A. Candy* cameras to see. She wouldn't let that happen to Jane, either. "Come on," she groaned as she shoved away from the guy trying to kiss her. Where were her shoes? "Janie. Come on. We should go."

"Oh, don't go!" Madison cried out. She twirled on the coffee table, balancing a drink in one hand and the champagne bottle in the other.

"Madison, this music sucks. Don't you have any eighties?" Gaby demanded.

"This *is* eighties, moron. Gaby's officially cut off!" Madison laughed hysterically.

Blurry. Everything was blurry. Scarlett spotted her shoes under the coffee table and clasped Jane's hand. Scarlett's guy and Jane's guy trailed behind them, one still holding a bottle of vodka. There were good-byes and thank-yous between the girls as Scarlett dragged Jane out the door and toward the elevator. Scarlett pressed the Down button and steadied Jane as the doors opened. She stepped into the elevator and watched as the two guys began to follow them. One of the cameramen brought up the rear, filming.

"You boys going home?" Scarlett stopped them before they walked in.

"No, your friend said we could come back with you," one said, pointing at Jane, who was resting her head on

Scarlett's shoulder.

"Oh. Okay, then. Good night." Scarlett smiled at them as the door closed in their faces.

"What the . . ."

She could hear one of them yell as the elevator began to drop. Good-bye, losers. Good-bye, camera. She placed her hand on top of Jane's head and brushed away the hair that had fallen into her face. "Come on, Janie. Let's go home."

"Hmmm? Why're we going home, Scar? We were having fun." Jane's voice sounded slurred.

"Yeah, but now it's time for bed."

"Yes, Mom."

When they got outside, Scarlett sucked in a lungful of the cool autumn air, fortifying herself. It wasn't easy to make an escape, but she was glad to get away from it all. She began looking up and down the noisy, neon-lit street for a cab. She and Jane would have to come back for their cars tomorrow. Neither of them was in any shape to drive. In fact, Jane wasn't in any shape to *stand*.

"Can we go home now?" Jane murmured, slumping against Scarlett.

Scarlett draped an arm over her friend's shoulders and held on tight.

"Yes, Jane, we're going home now."

19

WHEN IS THIS EPISODE GOING TO BE ON TV?

Jane pushed her pasta with truffles around with a fork. She didn't have much of an appetite. Yesterday's marathon girls' day out—which had turned into a girls' night out, which had turned into a girls' and guys' night out—had left her feeling a little drained. But she knew she should at least make an effort. She was at Bella with Paolo, the hot photographer she had met at work.

And a TV crew.

That meant three camera guys, one director of photography, two producers, five production assistants, one soundman, one lighting person, one guy helping out with electrical issues, and a writer who was noting everything they said on camera. *Intimate.*

It turned out that Paolo had indeed signed a release and also agreed to have their first date filmed. So the cameras were rolling on the two of them sharing a candlelit dinner.

She was pretty sure she looked like a mess after the night she'd had.

Paolo didn't seem to notice. Which was a relief. But how could he not notice? He was smiling at her expectantly. "So? Do you like it?" He pointed to the pasta dish he'd recommended to her.

Jane took a bite. It tasted like . . . *vodka* . . . like everything else she had tried to eat that day. "Love it," she lied, forcing a smile.

"Great! If you're still hungry after this, we should order dessert."

"Mmmm." Jane's stomach turned. Why had she let Madison talk her into all those martinis? And champagne? She felt awful. Her head throbbed, and she had had the shakes all day. She had contemplated canceling the date, but Dana had told her that they had already paid for their filming permit and that it was too late to reschedule.

Paolo was apparently a big foodie. He was going on about the dishes he had grown up eating (his father was Italian, and his mother was French), and about how he had almost gone to cooking school but had decided to become a photographer instead.

Jane listened, or attempted to listen, trying to remember why she had agreed to go out with him. He was definitely cute. And he seemed nice enough. But they had zero in common. Although how could she have guessed that after only a few minutes of talking to him? She noticed he liked to talk about himself. Normally it would have bothered her, but it was kind of a blessing tonight. She was hardly capable of witty date banter right now. She was more focused on trying to make the room stop spinning.

It was sad, really, because no matter how great this guy might be, he didn't stand a chance. And not just because she felt awful. If she was being honest with herself, she had to admit there had been no real spark when they met, and even now, the conversation was polite. He was cute, sure, and getting asked out by a cute guy is always nice, but talking to him felt so forced. It wasn't Paolo's fault, though. The truth was, Jane would have preferred to spend any night on a non-date with Braden than a real date with a cute guy she didn't really care about.

Jane's cell buzzed. Now that she knew texted directions were a part of her "reality," she'd put her phone on the table for easy access. She glanced at the screen; yep, it was from Dana. It said: **YOU LOOK MISERABLE. POOR GUY. COULD YOU ACT A LITTLE MORE DATEY?**

Jane did feel bad for him. He had to know that she wasn't having a good time. She leaned forward and touched Paolo's arm; that was a "datey" gesture, right? But Paolo barely seemed to notice. He was too busy talking about whether paella was better with seafood or meat. Jane tried to look interested. *I want to die,* she thought.

She struggled through the rest of dinner and felt a wave of relief when she saw the check heading their way. Thank God, the end was near. Once they got up from the table she was so happy she could have cried. All she wanted to do was get into bed. Alone.

When she saw Dana standing outside the restaurant as they exited, her heart sank. Obviously, a quick escape wasn't an option.

"The camera crew will meet you back at your apartment for a nice good-bye shot," Dana said. *Good-bye? Outside my apartment? Couldn't we just double-park in front of the building and say our awkward good-byes in the car? This night is never going to end,* Jane thought. But at least she would get a break from the cameras during the drive home.

The valet pulled up with Paolo's BMW and Jane slid in. "So where are the cameras?" Paolo asked her after shutting his door. He looked around. "Are they following us?"

"Yeah, they're meeting us back at my apartment," Jane said. "They aren't filming the drive."

"Oh," Paolo said. Even through her haze Jane could hear the disappointment in his voice. "So! When is this episode going to be on TV?"

Jane frowned. How was she supposed to know? "I'm . . . not sure."

"My friend knows one of the guys that was on *The Beach*," Paolo went on eagerly. "He said he gets paid to go to clubs and travels everywhere. So cool. Do you have an agent?"

Jane was quiet for a minute. "Paolo. Be honest. Did they ask you to ask me out?" She didn't look at him.

"No. Of course not," Paolo reassured her.

Good, Jane thought. She felt a little better. At least he

had asked her out on his own.

"I had an appointment with Fiona. I didn't even know what you guys were filming until I got there," Paolo went on. "I saw the sign out front and—"

"What sign?" Jane demanded, turning toward him.

"The sign outside the Fiona Chen offices. It said PopTV was filming."

"Oh." Jane felt anger rising inside. "So you just saw the sign and followed the cameras and thought you'd try to get on TV by talking to me and . . ." She paused. "Stop."

"What?"

"Stop the car!" Jane yelled.

Paolo turned right off Hollywood and pulled over to the side of the road. "What the hell is your problem? I just took you out for a nice dinner and—"

Jane quickly opened her door, leaned her head out, and began to throw up. Her mouth tasted like vodka. She spit then wiped her face with her sleeve. She sat back up in her seat and closed the door.

Dead silence. Paolo looked horrified.

Well, Jane thought. *At least I know he won't try to kiss me good night.*

The following night, Jane walked into Lola's and headed into the back room. Even though it was a Monday night, the place was packed, but she didn't mind. Braden was at the bar, waiting for her. She couldn't imagine anywhere she'd rather be than here with Braden without the cameras.

She hadn't seen him since last weekend at Cabo Cantina.

"Hey!" she said, giving him a quick kiss on the cheek.

"Hey!" Braden said, kissing her back. "It's good to see you."

"You too!"

She sat down beside him, smiling. She took a moment to admire his appearance without making it obvious that's what she was doing. He was wearing tailored dark jeans and a navy-and-white-striped sweater. He had more stubble than usual. Tonight more than ever he struck her as the kind of guy who had no idea how hot he was—which, in Jane's opinion, made him even more attractive. But friends weren't supposed to think of each other as *hot*, she reminded herself.

Braden handed her a menu. "They have a full bar here, but they're known for their martinis. They have every kind you can think of."

"Eww . . . a garlic mashed potato martini?" Jane said, glancing at the menu. "I think I will play it safe with apple."

Braden motioned to the bartender and ordered her drink. "So how's life as a big TV star?" he asked play-fully.

"Ha-ha," Jane said. "Actually, it's not at all what I expected."

"What do you mean?"

"I mean . . . well . . . I thought it was going to be easy. Fun. Like Scar and I would have to show up at a club a couple times a week and be filmed or whatever.

And maybe they'd film me at a work event once in a while. But it's way more intense than that, and it's only been a week. The cameras are always following me around, you know? They film me answering phones at the office. They film me at home. They film me when I go out, even if it's just to the Starbucks around the corner. It's kinda weird."

Braden glanced over her shoulder. "Uh-oh. Are they here now?" he joked.

Jane grinned. "Nope. I made my escape."

"Good! Next time, we'll have to wear disguises."

"Yeah . . . they'll be looking for me."

As the bartender set their drinks in front of them, Jane thought about how Braden seemed like the only person in her life who *didn't* want to be around when the cameras were—besides her parents, that is. Her sisters had already begged to come visit her, her cousin suddenly wanted to hang out—even Fiona had jockeyed for airtime.

Jane clinked her glass against Braden's. "Cheers."

"So when do I get to see you on TV?"

"Soon! I think in a month? Trevor, he's the main producer, said they're going to film us for a few more weeks, then edit a bunch of stuff. Then the series premiere is going to air. They're going to keep filming us for a few months after that though, until the season's over. So there's this overlap."

"Sounds like it's happening pretty fast."

"It is! There's going to be a series premiere party, too. I'll text you when they tell me where it is. Scar and I are pretty excited about it. Well, *I'm* excited about it. Scar's acting like she couldn't care less. Anyway, you *have* to come." Before he could say no, Jane rushed on. "So what's going on with you? Have you been on any more auditions?"

"I have one coming up next week. It's another sci-fi pilot."

"No shortage of those, I guess. What's this one about?"

As Braden talked, Jane found herself leaning closer to him. She loved listening to him. She loved being with him, period. Why hadn't it been like this with Paolo? Or with any other guy she'd met since Caleb?

"—so if it works out, I can be a big, fancy TV star like you," Braden was saying.

"Funny."

Braden reached over and pulled a thread off her tank top. His fingertips brushed against her bare shoulder, sending a chill down her spine.

"You get that's what's going to happen to you, don't you?" he said, suddenly serious. "Clubs, tabloids, fans— the whole messed-up Hollywood scene?"

"Hardly," Jane said. "The show is probably going to get canceled after the first episode. Seriously, you should see the stuff they film. Nobody is going to want to watch a bunch of random girls getting yelled at by their bosses or gossiping with their friends while doing laundry. It's kind of boring, if you ask me."

"You? Boring? Never."

Jane stared at him. *So what's with you and Willow?* she wanted to say. *Are you guys on or off right now? Oh, she's moving out of the country? That's awful!* But she couldn't bring herself to even mention Willow's name. It was so nice, just being here with Braden. Talking about his sort-of girlfriend would definitely be a buzzkill.

And then Jane realized something else—something almost as depressing as the subject of Willow.

When the *L.A. Candy* episodes finally hit the air, Braden would see Jane on a date with Paolo and flirting with those guys at Madison's apartment. Not that anything had come of either of those nights. Quite the opposite, in fact. Still, she felt a wave of guilt. Even though she and Braden were just friends. She wondered if it would even bother him . . . and kind of hoped it would.

Yeah, like my date with Paolo is going to make any guy jealous, Jane thought drily.

"Penny for your thoughts," Braden said.

"What?"

"It's an expression. My mom says it a lot. It means—"

Jane laughed. "Oh! I know the expression. I was just confused because I have a goldfish named Penny."

"You do? I thought you were a dog person."

"I am. But my mom's allergic, so I never had one growing up. That's why I have Penny. She's kind of my pretend puppy."

"Oh, that's kinda sad, actually." Braden fake-pouted. "So . . . what were you thinking before? You had this look on your face."

"Sorry, Braden." She fished an apple slice out of her drink and took a bite. "It's gonna cost you a little more than a penny to hear my thoughts."

The next morning, Jane woke up to the shrill tone of her cell phone ringing. She glanced groggily at her clock. It was 7:00 a.m. Wait, 7:00 a.m.? She wondered if it was a wrong number. Or maybe it was her father making sure she and Scar had signed the *L.A. Candy* contracts. He'd called over the weekend to tell her that his lawyer had said they were standard contracts and okay to sign. Or maybe it was Fiona, getting an early start to the day. She often phoned Jane at odd hours, giving her crazy instructions like "Hurry over to Olivier's design studio and pick up the white silk dress for Leda Phillips; she needs it in exactly twenty-three minutes." Or "Drive up to Malibu and take your camera. I need some shots of a space called Wave for a possible Buddhist wedding ceremony at dawn . . . Oh, and make sure the sun is just starting to rise, because our client is very particular about lighting."

Fiona. Work. Tuesday—it was Tuesday. Crap, she had a meeting in an hour!

Jane managed to pick up her cell just before the call went to voice mail. "Hello?"

"Hey, Jane, this is Trevor. Were you sleeping?"

Jane rubbed her eyes. Trevor? Why was Trevor calling her? She hadn't really heard from him since they'd started filming. It was hard to believe that was less than two weeks ago. It felt like so much longer than that.

"Hey, Trevor. Nope, I'm up."

"Good. Listen, I just wanted to let you know what a great job you're doing. I've watched the edits and they're looking amazing. I'm so excited for you guys to see."

"Thanks," Jane said, rubbing her eyes again and feeling a little funny about being complimented on living her life.

Trevor went on, describing different scenes to her. He sounded genuinely excited. Jane rolled out of bed and stumbled into the kitchen. She was going to have to hurry if she was going to make the 8 a.m. meeting. Scar's door was closed; she was probably still sleeping. Lucky girl. Trevor was laughing because Dana had told him that Jane had thrown up on the way home from her date with Paolo. Trevor said they'd had to color-correct her face because she had looked so sick at Bella, but he didn't blame her because he couldn't stand listening to that guy either. Jane laughed. At least Trevor thought Paolo was as lame as she did.

He also mentioned Madison and Gaby and how much they liked hanging out with Jane and Scarlett. Jane hadn't seen them since their girls' day (and night) on Saturday. Madison had texted her and Scarlett, asking them if they wanted to have another girls' day soon— maybe lunch followed by mani-pedis? Jane had texted back with a definite "I'm in!" As far as she knew, Scarlett hadn't responded. She picked up that Scar wasn't too crazy about Madison or Gaby. Jane had meant to bring it up with her, but they'd barely spent any time together without the cameras around lately. She wished Scar would be more open to the girls, though. They were really fun and nice. And it seemed as though the four of them were expected to hang out once in a while for the cameras—at least when Jane wasn't at the office, and Scarlett wasn't at school, and Gaby wasn't at Ruby Slipper, and Madison wasn't . . . well, doing whatever Madison did with her days. What *did* she do with her days? Judging from her super-put-together appearance, she probably lived at the gym and spent the rest of her time at the spa and boutiques (with the *L.A. Candy* cameras in tow, no doubt).

Then, out of the blue, Trevor said, "Were you at Lola's last night?"

Jane frowned. "Um, yeah. Why?" How did he know that?

"Oh, one of my friends said he saw you. That place is great, right? I think I wanna film there."

"Yeah, it was cool."

"Who did you go with?"

"I met my friend Braden there," Jane said.

"Just a friend?" Trevor asked. And by the way he said it, Jane assumed it had been accompanied by a suggestive eyebrow raise.

"Yes, Trevor . . . just a friend," Jane assured him, hoping Trevor's interest in Braden would end there.

"Great. Well, Jane! Keep up the good work! Dana will be in touch with you very soon, maybe even today. We're sending you and Scarlett out to a few magazines to do some publicity for the show. We're also getting the four of you together to do a photo shoot for the promo poster. Series premiere's coming up; there's a lot to do."

"Okay."

They said their good-byes. Jane shut her phone and set it on the counter next to her. She opened the refrigerator and pulled out a bottle of water to throw into her purse. Fruit? Yogurt? Nope, no time. She still had to shower, get dressed, and get out of here. Fiona was a punctuality freak, and Jane didn't want to be subjected to one of her death-ray stares because she was rushing into the conference room even five minutes late.

As she headed back to her room, she wondered about Trevor's interest in Braden. He had *tried* to sound casual about it, but she couldn't help feeling totally weirded out that he had known where she was the night before. It was like she was being watched even when she wasn't being filmed. The thought gave her chills, but she quickly shook it off. *Stop being so paranoid,* she told herself. She had to get dressed and get to work or suffer the very real wrath of Fiona Chen.

20

DO THEY FOLLOW YOU INTO THE BATHROOM?

"So. It's Scarlett Harp and Jane . . . uh . . ."

"Roberts," Jane quietly filled in for what felt like the millionth time to Scarlett, but was probably only the third.

"Right. Jane Roberts. So how long have you girls been acting?"

Tiffani, the inexperienced assistant pretending to be a reporter, glanced up from her notepad and gave Scarlett and Jane a barely disguised look of total and utter boredom. It was the same look they had received from multiple reporters in the past few days. PopTV had them doing a round of publicity interviews with four different magazines this week. The bleached blond bimbo and her SAT-challenged sidekick were apparently doing the same, at four other magazines. First, Scarlett and Jane had interviewed with someone at *Star*. Then *Life & Style*. Followed by *In Touch*. At each of those magazines, Scarlett and Jane had been assigned the lowest of the low on the journalism totem pole—that is, newbie reporters who (A) had no idea how to conduct an interview, (B) got their names wrong, (C) got the show's name wrong, or (D) all of the above. Now they were sitting in Tiffani's cubicle at *Gossip,* yet another tabloid magazine. The kind that plastered the racks by grocery market registers. And in the first thirty seconds of the interview, Tiffani had managed to place herself in the "D" category.

Scarlett glared at Tiffani. Jane, noticing, squeezed Scarlett's arm with gentle but unmistakable firmness. It was her friend's way of saying, "Shut up and let me handle this."

"Actually, it's a reality show, so there's no acting," Jane explained pleasantly. "*L.A. Candy* is the name of the show. It's kind of like a reality version of *Sex and the City*, but it's younger and based here in L.A. The cameras follow Scarlett, me, and two other girls, Madison and Gaby, around L.A. while we work, go to school, go to clubs . . . stuff like that."

Scarlett sat back and folded her arms across her chest. Okay, so Jane was good at this. And by good, she meant Jane had the patience to smile and bullshit reporter after reporter with the same bullet points they had memorized from the press packet they had been given by Trevor's assistant. With Tiffani, and the three others before her, Jane had managed to be polite, deliver PopTV's cute little promotional speech, *and* not vomit in the process. Scarlett, not so good in the bullshit department, hadn't said much.

"Cool," Tiffani said, scribbling in her notepad. "So are the cameras with you, like, all the time, then? Do they follow you into the bathroom? Are they with you twenty-four/seven?"

"Do you see any—" Scarlett began.

"Ha-ha!" Jane cut her off, laughing lightly. "No, the cameras aren't with us *all* the time. They're just there for the important stuff."

"Gotcha. So . . . Jane?" Tiffani crossed her legs and turned toward Scarlett. "What can we expect in the series premiere of *Eye Candy*?"

"Listen, my journalism experience may be limited to writing for the high school newspaper," Scarlett snapped, "but I don't think knowing basic information like the interviewees' names and the title of our show is asking too much."

"*Scaaaarlettttt!!!*"

Scarlett whirled around, wondering whose girlish high-pitched voice was shouting her name in the hallowed halls of the *Gossip* magazine offices. She looked up and saw D. Was this guy everywhere they were?

"Scarlett! Oh, and Jane!" Diego shrieked, noticing Jane sitting next to Scarlett. "Oh! My! F'ing! *G!*" He stopped in front of Tiffani's cubicle and grabbed both girls in a manic hug. "Tell me! What are you lovelies doing in this sad little hellhole?"

"D!" Jane squealed happily. "Better question. What are *you* doing here?"

"I work here! I'm Veronica Bliss's assistant."

Veronica who? Scarlett wanted to ask, but the so-called reporter cut in.

"Diego, do you mind?" Tiffani said impatiently. "I'm right in the middle of an interview."

"Interview? What interview? What does this she-demon want with the two of you?" D asked, turning to Scarlett and Jane.

"What is your problem?" Tiffani demanded.

"Go fact-check something. Shoo!" D hissed, waving his hands at her.

"I'm interviewing them for the *Eye Candy* piece, you asshole," Tiffani snapped.

Scarlett's seething boiled over. "Seriously? Are you that dense? It's *L.A. Candy.*"

"*L.A. Candy?* You mean, the new PopTV show?" D interrupted. "Girls, you're on that show? Why didn't you say anything at Les Deux?"

"We met the producer that night, right after you disappeared," Jane explained.

"Well, color me clueless! This is unbelievable!" D crowed. "Listen, girls. What are you doing this Saturday? Wait! It doesn't matter! Cancel. We're going to celebrate! I want to fall in love with you before I have to hate you."

"Oh, fun!" Jane exclaimed.

"Sure," Scarlett agreed. D might be a tad on the dramatic

side, but she'd take hanging out with him over a night out with Madison and Gaby any day.

Tiffani's phone rang. She picked it up, listened, then hung up quickly. "Diego? Your master's looking for you," she said. "You'd better run!"

D turned pale. "Uh-oh. Listen, ladies. Here's my card. Text me later, 'kay? We'll figure out what, when, where, and what to wear!"

"Sounds good," Jane said, hugging D good-bye.

Scarlett watched as he hurried into an office with mirrored windows. She studied the card he'd handed her. It said: "Diego Neri, assistant to the editor in chief, *Gossip*." So . . . his "master," Veronica Bliss, must be the boss lady of this magazine. And judging from D's freaked-out expression when he took off just now, she must be intimidating. Scarlett was sure Jane could relate to that.

21

WE COULD USE SOME FRESH MEAT

Veronica Bliss sat admiring the framed, oversized *Gossip* magazine covers that adorned the wall across from her desk. The one of super-stud actor Gus O'Dell trading spit with his male costar while Gus's wife was pregnant with their first child . . . and the other of super-saint actress Leda Phillips standing next to her smashed Mercedes, just moments after the now-famous DUI.

She sighed as she looked over this week's mockup spread across her desk. Another week. No one was in rehab . . . no one new, at least. No one was being lazy about hiding their affairs. No one had become desperate enough to leak their own nude photos onto the Internet. Nothing new. She was bored. Every "it girl" had either cleaned up her act or simply gone off the deep end and now failed to surprise.

Veronica gazed out the glass wall of her office. It was mirrored on one side so she could see out, but no one could see in. She eyed the two girls sitting in Tiffani's cubicle and gabbing away with Diego. Who was that assistant of hers talking to? The first girl was tall, brunette, and strikingly beautiful. The second girl was shorter, pretty, with long, wavy blond hair. She didn't recognize either of them.

Veronica picked up her phone and buzzed Tiffani's extension. "Ask Diego to come to my office, please."

A moment later, Diego came rushing through her door. "Sorry, sorry! I heard you were looking for me. Did you need something?" Worry marred his smooth, cute, Asian-American face.

Veronica smiled tightly at him. "What's Tiffani working on today?"

Diego looked confused. "Tiffani? She's, uh, interviewing two of the girls from PopTV's new reality show."

Veronica arched her eyebrows. "Oh. And who are they? Do we know anything about them?" she asked casually. She knew about the show. Her spies at PopTV had told her all about it. If it was anything like the network was pitching it to be, those girls were about to become household names.

"Well . . . their names are Scarlett and Jane. Scarlett's the brunette. She's a student at U.S.C. Jane's the blonde. She interns for an event planner."

"Really? Which planner?"

"Uh . . . I'm not sure. I can find out for you."

"Please do. And ask Tiffani to email me the notes from her interview as soon as the girls are gone."

"Yes, of course."

"Good." Veronica looked back at the girls. She watched as Jane tried to untangle a strand of hair from her finger. "We could use some fresh meat. Things are getting a little boring around here."

Veronica knew the only thing America loved more than watching their stars rise was watching them fall. These girls were so unprepared for what was about to happen to them—instant fame—that the inevitable rise was practically guaranteed to be followed by a quick descent. And capturing those heartbreaking, tragic, nose-dive-from-the-pedestal moments was what Veronica—and *Gossip* magazine—did best.

22

MY NAME IS JANE

Jane pulled into a spot marked RESERVED. It was the only empty space she could find in the recording studio's parking lot. Even though it was the weekend, the place was packed.

She hopped out of her car and walked toward the long gray building. There were several brightly painted doors along its side marked with numbers above each. She looked down at her new BlackBerry and tried to pull up the email that Trevor's assistant had sent her. She was still figuring out how to use it. Trevor had given a BlackBerry to every girl on the show a couple of days ago, so it would be easier for Dana to get hold of them and send them their schedules.

"Building One," Jane read aloud, finally finding the email.

She made her way toward the door with the large blue number one painted above it and headed inside. At the end of a long hallway, she found the door marked SOUNDBOX STUDIOS and went in, her Miu Miu heels sounding loud against the cement floors. She had never owned a pair of $400 shoes before. They had been her first splurge, part of her new wardrobe for the show.

"Can I help you?" A young girl with long black hair smiled at Jane from behind a cluttered desk.

"Hi. I'm supposed to be meeting Dana from PopTV." Jane looked around, hoping she was in the right place.

"Studio three," the girl said, pointing at the door to Jane's left. "I think she's already in there."

"Thanks."

Jane slipped inside and found herself in a dimly lit room. Dana was sitting on a red couch and talking to a tall bald man. In one corner of the room was a big-screen TV, which was currently turned off. Across from that, there was a control board lit up with hundreds of buttons, switches, and dials next to a large glass window through which Jane could see another, smaller room encased with black padding. In the center of the smaller room was a wooden bar stool and a round mike hanging from a black stand.

"Hey, Jane," Dana said as Jane came in.

Dana looked even more stressed and exhausted than usual—if that was possible. The woman seriously needed to check into a spa, for like a month. She wore a blue sweatshirt over jeans, and she had on no makeup. Trevor had mentioned that all the producers had been editing until

2 or 3 a.m. every morning, trying to get the show ready for the premiere, which was now just two weeks away. Two weeks! Jane could hardly believe it. She reminded herself to go shopping for something cute to wear to the party, which was going to be at a club called Area. She also reminded herself to invite her family and friends—particularly Braden.

"Hi. Sorry I'm late. I couldn't find the building," Jane apologized.

"Jane, this is Tim. He's gonna be running the session."

Jane shook the bald guy's hand. He had big, friendly brown eyes and a toothy smile.

"Here." Dana handed Jane a sheet of paper. Jane scanned it quickly.

```
JANE'S V.O.S.
My name is Jane. I just moved to L.A. with
my best friend, Scarlett. I intern for one
of the best event planners in the busi-
ness. So far it's been (pause) a learning
experience.
    Scarlett just started as a freshman at
U.S.C. The only thing hotter than her SAT
scores is her.
    Gabrielle works at a PR firm called Ruby
Slipper. She's finding out fast that she
isn't in Kansas anymore.
```

That's Madison. She's always between jobs.
She's tried almost every career there is,
but there's one thing she's always been good
at (pause) spending money.

We all moved to L.A. this summer. Some of
us to work . . . and some of us to play. So
let the games begin.

Jane laughed a little as she read through each line. "'The only thing hotter than her SAT scores is her'? Seriously, who wrote this?"

Dana didn't look amused. "Me."

Awkward, thought Jane as she quickly tried to backtrack. She saw Tim trying not to smile at her comment.

"No, it's funny. I like it." Jane smiled, attempting to hide her embarrassment.

"We're running a little behind. Why don't you hop in there?" Dana said, motioning to the smaller room on the other side of the large glass window. She was all business again, so maybe Jane's comment didn't faze her. Or maybe she'd get her revenge in the editing room. "Take the script with you, okay?"

"'Kay."

Jane followed Tim back out the door and into the smaller room. She climbed onto the stool as Tim started plugging and unplugging different wires from the wall. He stood up and handed her a set of headphones. Then he left the room, closing the door tightly behind him. Jane could hear herself breathing through the headphones.

"Can you hear us?" Tim's voice echoed loudly.

"Yeah," Jane replied and then jumped at the amplified sound of her own voice. It was weird.

"Okay, then." Tim made a few adjustments to the control board. "Let's start with the first line." He pointed at her, signaling for her to begin.

Jane looked down at the script and began to read. "My name is Jane. I just moved to L.A. with my best friend, Scarlett. I intern—"

"Jane?" Dana's voice interrupted her.

Jane looked up from the script. She could see Dana through the window. "Yeah?"

"Can you read it a little more . . ." Dana tilted her head to the side like she was searching for a word. "It's sounding a little flat. Try reading it like you're telling a story."

"Okay," Jane said, confused. In fact, she didn't really understand what she was reading, much less why she needed to read it like she was "telling a story." What was this for? All Trevor's assistant had said in her email was that Jane should show up at this studio and that she didn't need to dress up since there wouldn't be any cameras. When she'd asked Scar what she thought it was about, she found out Scar hadn't been invited. Jane had been surprised, since they had done the four magazine interviews *together* last week, and she, Scarlett, Madison, and Gaby were scheduled to do a photo shoot *together* tomorrow, for the promo poster. Why was Jane being asked to do this—whatever this was—without Scar or the other girls? "I'm sorry, Dana. I don't really get what you're asking me to do. You want me to read these lines like they are a story?"

"Like you're narrating. This goes at the very beginning of the first episode. You're basically introducing all the girls. Didn't Trevor explain this to you?"

"No, his assistant just told me to show up here and ask for you."

Dana exhaled loudly, sounding frustrated. "Okay, Trevor was supposed to explain. At the beginning of every episode we need a quick recap of the previous week. Instead of having an actor come in to do the voiceovers, Trevor wanted to have one of you girls do it."

"Wait, I'm doing this for *every* episode?" Jane asked.

"Yeah. Apparently you're the most relatable. They tested the pilot with several groups."

"Groups?"

"Focus groups. We showed a rough cut of the pilot to a bunch of people in our demographic to get their feedback. According to them, you're relatable."

"Scarlett's relatable."

"To *you*, Jane. Not to middle America."

"Really?" Jane sounded puzzled. "What about Madison?"

"Jane. No one thought *that* blonde is relatable."

Jane laughed. It was true. There weren't many people like Madison. "Well, Gaby's not blond."

"Gaby's wonderful. She's sweet and very pretty. But we

all know Gaby isn't exactly the brightest crayon in the box."

Jane tried to process what Dana was telling her. Did this mean the story was being told from *her* point of view? Or was she just narrating what had happened to everyone? And why hadn't Trevor talked to her about this before she came in here today?

"So do you understand, Jane?" Dana asked her.

"I think so," Jane said, adjusting her headphones as she began to read again. "My name is Jane. . . ."

23

CENTER STAGE

Madison surveyed the enormous room inside Stage 5 of the PopTV studios. Half of the space was entirely white, and the corners were rounded so that the walls flowed seamlessly into the floors. The far end was filled with couches, makeup stations, and racks of clothing on one side, a table topped with boxes of hot Starbucks coffee, assorted food—and a lot of people—on the other. She sipped her coffee, making sure not to mar her perfectly applied makeup. Nothing was going to ruin this day for her. She was even wearing a terry cloth robe over her outfit, in case of accidental spills. Not that Madison was prone to accidents. She never made mistakes and never left anything to chance.

Today was the photo shoot for the *L.A. Candy* ad. The place was a beehive of activity as people set up, their voices echoing weirdly in the massive space mixing with the eighties music blaring from somebody's iPod.

Madison spotted Dana dodging a clothing rack as she

headed in the direction of the hair and makeup area. Dropping her half-full coffee cup into a trash can, Madison followed Dana to see what was going on. Mostly she was curious to see how the other girls looked. Inside, Dana was talking to Jane and Scarlett, who seemed to have arrived just a few minutes ago. (Madison had arrived early of course.) The makeup girl was done up in jet-black eye shadow, a full set of false lashes, and hot pink lipstick—at the crack of dawn, no less—which made Madison feel doubly smug about having had her makeup done by her own person, in advance. Each station had its own rectangular mirror framed with bright, round lights, and each had a vast assortment of products (eye shadows, liners, lip glosses, blushes, and bronzers in every possible color).

"Hi, Madison!" Jane called out in a tired but friendly voice. "Your hair and makeup look great."

"Thanks!" Madison reached up and touched the halo of tight ringlets on her head. She noticed that Jane had dark circles under her eyes, her skin looked pale and blotchy, and her brows were unkempt. God, how could she leave her apartment looking like that? She was lucky no one knew who she was.

"Where's Gaby?" Jane asked.

"Running late," Madison replied.

"Late? How late? I've left her three messages," Dana snapped, glancing at her watch. With the *L.A. Candy* premiere just a couple of weeks away, she had been even more tense and cranky than usual.

"She'll be here," Madison said. "She texted me like five minutes ago. She overslept. Hi, Scarlett."

Scarlett nodded but didn't say hi back. She was dressed in an oversized navy sweatshirt with the hood pulled over her wet hair, jeans, and sunglasses. She was holding a plastic plate heaped with soggy scrambled eggs, bacon strips, and half an onion bagel. *Ew.* How could the girl eat so much before a photo shoot? Was she always such a pig?

"Whose insane idea was it to have a six a.m. call time?" Scarlett complained to no one in particular. She bit into the bagel, then made a face and dropped it onto her crowded plate.

"Mine. Scarlett, this is Lana. She'll be doing your makeup," Dana said, pointing to the woman in the hot pink lipstick. "Ann'll be here any minute. She'll be doing yours, Jane." She paused to listen to someone on her head-piece. "Uh-huh. Oh, jeez. Back in a sec, girls," she said, hurrying out of the room.

Scarlett glanced warily at Lana. "I don't like to wear a lot of makeup."

"Don't worry, honey, I'll make you look beautiful," Lana reassured her.

"Yeah, well. Think of the lightest possible makeup you can do. Then do it even lighter than that," Scarlett said testily. *Yeah, good plan,* Madison thought. *Offend the woman who's about to do your face.* Although, in this case, Scarlett was right to be cautious. On the other hand . . . if Lana made Scarlett look like a freak, then all the better for Madison. Jane and Gaby were cute but they weren't exactly turning heads. But Scarlett was stunning. Of the three girls, she was the only one who rivaled Madison in the looks department.

A petite blond woman walked over and smiled brightly at Jane. "Good morning!" Madison heard the woman introduce herself as Ann, her makeup artist. "Well, aren't you just beautiful? You're gonna make my job so easy!" she said cheerfully.

Apparently 6 a.m. call times didn't bother Ann. Neither did lying about someone's physical appearance.

"I don't know about that," Jane said, laughing.

Yeah, Madison didn't know about that either.

Jane sat down at one of the stations, then glanced at Madison in the mirror. "So when'd you get your hair and makeup done, Madison? Did you get here at four a.m. or what?" she joked.

"Oh, I used my own people," Madison said. "I don't trust just any stylists doing my hair and makeup. They never get it right."

Both Lana and Ann threw her dirty looks. Whatever.

"Well, I was so excited about this shoot that I barely slept last night," Jane said quickly to Ann. "So if you can make *me* look good, you're a genius!"

Madison watched as Ann began to apply a creamy moisturizer to Jane's face with a makeup brush. Jane pointed to some magazine clippings on the mirror that showed different models, all with long lashes and doll-like pops of color on their cheeks. Then she gestured to Madison, who had the same lashes and cheeks. "Are we all gonna look like that?" Jane asked Ann.

"Yes! You girls are going to look amazing!" Ann replied.

"It's a retro, fifties concept. Trevor told me about it last week. We're all gonna be holding big, round lollipops," Madison explained. "*L.A. Candy*, get it? He said this picture's gonna run in all the magazines. And they're making posters out of it, too."

"So cute!" Jane said.

Scarlett rolled her eyes.

"We're all wearing these, in different colors," Madison went on. She stripped off her white terry cloth robe to reveal a fifties-style swimsuit. It was hot pink and hugged her perfect curves. Light pink lace trim lined the top where her cleavage spilled out.

"Ohmigod! How cute is that?" Jane cried out.

Scarlett looked horrified. "What are you wearing?" she demanded.

Madison twirled around, showing off her tanned behind peeking out from the bottom of her suit. "Don't you love it? I'm obsessed! They had them made for all of us."

"You have got to be *kidding* me." Scarlett's expression shifted from horrified to pissed off. "I don't do bathing suits in pictures. And I don't do pink."

"Relax, princess of darkness. We're all wearing

different colors," Madison said, smirking. "Obviously, yours is black."

Scarlett jumped out of her chair and shoved past Madison. "Where's Dana? I gotta talk to her. I'm not wearin' that."

"Scarlett, I'm not done with you yet!" Lana called out after her, waving a brush. But Scarlett was gone.

Madison smiled to herself. Of the four girls, she was obviously the only one who knew how to behave at photo shoots, which was fine with her.

"This is bullshit!" Scarlett stood with her arms crossed over her chest, clenching a brightly colored lollipop in one hand. Her long black hair had been curled and pinned into an updo. Her face had been made up to look like the other girls'. "Seriously, why didn't you people run the 'bathing suit that rides up my ass' concept by me before I got here and had no other option?"

"I'm sorry, Scarlett," Dana said, sounding irritated. "I must have missed the part where you had wardrobe approval in your contract."

"You know what Catherine McKinnon would have to say about this crap?"

"Catherine who?" Dana glanced impatiently at her watch.

"She's a well-known feminist scholar, and she—"

"Well, *I'm* ready to get started," Madison cut in. She

patted her tight curls. "Where do you want me to stand? Here?" She pointed to center stage. She envisioned herself in the middle of the shot, with the other girls fanned around her in a semicircle.

It had taken twenty minutes to get Scarlett into her bathing suit, and she hadn't stopped complaining since. Jane had also made a comment about how revealing the suits were, although she hadn't made a big stink about it like her friend. She had just whined a little until Ann put some bronzer on her not-so-slender legs to placate her.

Gaby, who had finally arrived, was fiddling with the trim on her yellow suit, seemingly oblivious to all the commotion. Madison had to admit that the color looked nice against Gaby's golden skin. And Gaby, who usually dressed conservatively, actually had a decent body. Jane, on the other hand, could stand to hit the gym. She was nowhere near Madison's size 0. The truth was the girl looked almost dumpy in her pale blue suit with the small white bow in the center.

Gaby leaned over to Madison. "You wanna do something later? I hate Sundays; they're sooo boring," she whispered.

"Sure, sweetie."

"Like what?"

"I don't know. I'll think of something." Madison didn't understand why Scarlett had freaked out—she looked hot in her black bathing suit.

"So what are you wearing to the series premiere?"

"I'm not sure . . . Gaby, let me focus, okay?"

"Focus on what?"

"On the photo shoot."

Gaby frowned. "What's there to focus on? They're just gonna take our pictures, right?"

Madison waved her hand dismissively, not wanting to talk anymore. Of course she had to focus. She had to focus on making sure she was photographed in the most flattering possible light and angle, more than the other three, to ensure that she was the obvious star of *L.A. Candy*. The show didn't actually *have* a star. It was supposed to be about all four girls equally. But a certain dynamic in a promo poster or an ad could convey so much. So it was crucial that Madison did what she could to help shape that dynamic.

The photographer, Jeremy, was English. He appeared to be in his late forties, with salt-and-pepper hair and bushy eyebrows. Straight? Gay? It was so hard to tell with Brits. Just in case, she made a point of throwing a dazzling smile in his direction and pushing her shoulders back, which made her boobs look—well, apparent.

Jeremy smiled back at her. Then he pointed to Jane and said, "Jane? We're going to have you sit on that big candy heart there—with your back against Scarlett's. Yeah, uh-huh, darling, that's right."

"Where do you want me?" Madison called out pleasantly.

"Madison, Gaby . . . I want you to sit on the ends, on either side of Jane and Scarlett."

Madison complied, and a moment later, Jeremy began clicking away. This was not a pose *she* would have chosen.

But these were probably just test shots. There was still time for Madison to jockey for a better spot.

The doors to the studio opened, and Trevor strolled in. He waved as he walked toward Dana, who stood behind the photographer, watching. Madison hadn't seen him in a while, although she *had* called him a few times in the last couple of weeks to try to find out what was going on with the edits, the photo shoot, the series premiere, everything. He hadn't said much about the edits, although he had revealed that he was very, very happy with Madison's and the other girls' footage.

"Wow. You all look great!" Trevor said.

Dana pointed to the computer screen where the test images were being displayed. "What do you think, Trevor?"

Madison watched as Trevor and Dana studied the screen for a minute. Then Trevor called the photographer over, and the three of them stood there, talking quietly. Madison couldn't hear what they were saying, but they kept looking at the screen, then over at the girls.

A moment later, Jeremy resumed his position behind the camera. "Okay, we're going to move you around a little, girls."

Aha, Madison thought. Smart man. Trevor knows Madison should be in the center, not hanging out on the edge of the shot.

"Miss Jane," Jeremy continued, "instead of profile, we're going to have you face forward." He stepped back and looked at the group as Jane shifted her legs around to the front of the big candy heart. "Okay, can you slide a little more forward? And Miss Scarlett, let's have you sit on the back corner. Now, I need all you girls to get closer together."

Madison felt a frisson of alarm. "Um, Jeremy?" She forced herself to smile charmingly. "Can we do this differently? I feel like Jane's blocking me. I'm practically in the background."

"Madison, you look great just where you are," Trevor spoke up. "We just want you all close together for the group shot."

"But—"

"Now say 'cheese'!" Jeremy called out.

Madison tried to hide her frustration. This was not the way she had planned it.

She and the others settled into their new spots, and the photographer snapped a picture. Madison watched Trevor's face as he regarded the computer screen, waiting for the image to appear.

Trevor waited . . . then leaned forward . . . and smiled. "It looks perfect," he announced. "Thanks, Jeremy."

Madison was seething. Her eyes went to Jane, who was smiling and looking pleased with herself. That pudgy little nobody had just stolen Madison's moment. Who did she think she was?

24

WE'RE **NOT** TV STARS

Jane checked her makeup in her round, gold hand mirror one last time before walking up to Area. It was strange not seeing a long line outside of one of L.A.'s hottest clubs, but it had been closed off for the private PopTV viewing party.

"I'm a little nervous," she whispered to Scarlett as she reached for her hand.

"What do you have to be nervous about?" Scarlett said with a grin. "So millions of people all across America are about to get an intimate, inside, up-close-and-personal look at the very private life of Jane Roberts. Big deal."

"And the very private life of Scarlett Harp, too!" Jane reminded her. "Aren't you scared?"

"Nope. I don't have anything to hide."

"I don't have anything to hide either. It's just weird knowing that so many people will be watching."

"Or maybe no one will be watching," Scarlett said cheerfully.

Sometimes Jane felt like Scarlett *wanted* the show to fail. *L.A. Candy* had completely taken over their lives. For the last month, the cameras had been with them almost every day: at work, at home, at clubs, shopping, having lunch, and everywhere else. Every Sunday, Dana called to set up the shooting schedule for the upcoming week. Jane no longer thought of a typical week as being from Monday through Sunday, but from one scheduling phone call to the next. Dana and the show had become her calendar. And she no longer thought about an outfit as being complete without a mike under her clothes, taped to her skin.

Jane had no idea what the *L.A. Candy* producers had done with all the footage. The only thing that she had seen was the short trailer that had been running on PopTV all week—a quick montage of her, Scar, Madison, and Gaby around town. Several strangers had already recognized her from it. Tonight would be the first time the four of them would see an actual episode. None of the girls really knew what to expect. Deep down, Jane still had her reservations about the whole *L.A. Candy* concept. After all, how interesting could it be, watching the day-to-day, unairbrushed lives of four average, ordinary California girls? A trailer with clips and fast music was one thing. Would the producers really be able to pull off a whole series?

Jane's phone beeped. She checked it quickly. It was Fiona, saying that she was really sorry but she was going to miss the party. Jane hadn't seen much of Fiona lately, or at least that's how it felt. It was weird. The first few days after Jane got her promotion, Fiona had her running around like crazy. But after that, she'd barely had any responsibilities— at least none that took place off camera.

A six-foot-tall poster of the four girls had been placed by the door of Area. It was the image from the photo shoot two weeks ago, of the girls wearing those skimpy bathing suits and holding large, round lollipops. The poster had L.A. CANDY written in hot pink letters across the top and ". . . anything but sweet" in smaller writing along the bottom.

The same image had appeared in a bunch of magazines. When Jane first saw the full-page ad, she'd been pleasantly surprised. The image was less slutty than she'd thought it would be, and more tongue-in-cheek.

Still, it was bizarre seeing herself on a six-foot-tall poster. It was so . . . *huge*.

Jane and Scarlett stood there a moment, gazing at themselves.

"Kind of a weird moment, isn't it?" Scarlett remarked. "The real us staring down the pretend us."

"I guess that's one way of putting it."

Next to the poster was a small white backdrop covered in PopTV's logo with a lone photographer standing in front of it. When he saw Jane and Scarlett, he waved eagerly at them.

"Pose for me in front of the step and repeat," he called out.

"The step and . . . what?" Jane said, confused.

The photographer pointed to the white PopTV backdrop. "That."

"Uh, sure." She clutched Scarlett's hand tighter.

As the photographer lifted his camera and began clicking, the girls made their best attempts to appear natural. Neither had any idea how to pose. It was her—*their*—first red carpet experience. It was so strange. Jane had seen pictures of *real* celebrities in front of logo-covered banners with a swarm of photographers (well, more than one photographer, anyway) snapping away. And now . . . *she* was standing there having her photo taken. It felt like she was dreaming, except that she wasn't sure yet if it was a good dream, a bad dream, or something in between.

Inside, the club was packed. It looked like it would on any other night, except the twentysomething hipsters that usually filled all the white leather booths had been replaced by executives, advertisers, and family members.

"Wow," Scarlett said, glancing around. "It looks kinda like the Men's Wearhouse took over Area."

"Yeah."

Jane started working her way through the crowd, looking for familiar faces. Scarlett followed. Jane spotted Trevor, Dana, Wendell, and a bunch of the *L.A. Candy* staff and crew. She hadn't seen Wendell since the interview back in August; he caught her eye, gave her a huge smile, and waved. Madison and Gaby were talking to an older couple. The woman looked a lot like Gaby. They had to be her mom and stepdad. The place was mostly filled with people Jane didn't recognize. She knew D was coming late. As for Braden—she wasn't sure. She had texted him an invite (with a vaguely worded "Feel free to bring your friends!" which could've included Willow, but also not), and he had promised to "try to be there."

Jane spotted her parents and sisters, Lacie and Nora, standing near a table of food. They looked as excited and nervous as she felt inside. She was beyond happy that they were here. She'd seen them only once since moving to L.A., when she and Scar had driven to Santa Barbara for a quick overnight trip for Lacie's sixteenth birthday party.

"Hey, guys!" Jane called out. She grabbed Scarlett's hand and ran toward her family, teetering precariously on her four-inch stiletto heels.

"Jane! Oh my gosh." Her mother, Maryanne, clasped her in a warm hug. Her father, Mark, did the same. The two of them hugged Scarlett as well.

"We are so proud of you girls!" her father said, his eyes twinkling. "Wow, TV stars! This is really exciting."

"Dad," Jane said, blushing. "We're *not* TV stars."

She turned and smiled at her sisters. Lacie's curtain of long blond hair was clipped back and her hazel eyes were wide with awe. Nora, who was fourteen, had their father's curly brown hair (a strand of which was currently twisted around her index finger—like sister . . . like sister) and golden brown eyes. She smiled back at Jane, revealing her purple-tinted braces.

"So what celebrities are gonna be here tonight?" Lacie asked immediately. Lacie never minced words.

Jane laughed and shrugged. "I don't know."

"I heard Anna Payne might stop by," Scarlett joked, elbowing Jane.

"*Whaaaaat?*" Lacie and Nora practically screamed.

"Just kidding, just kidding!" Scarlett held up her hands.

Nora wrinkled her nose. "Not funny. So are you dating anyone famous yet?" she asked Jane.

Jane noticed her parents staring at her, as if waiting eagerly for her answer to Nora's question. "Uh, no," she said, embarrassed. "I'm not dating anyone *not* famous, either."

Her mother reached out and smoothed a nonexistent wrinkle in Jane's dress. "Are you doing okay, sweetheart? Do you need anything?"

"I'm fine, Mom," Jane said. Her mom—and her dad, too—always worried about her and fussed over her. Actually, she kind of missed that, now that she was on her own.

"Ohmigod! Isn't that Jesse Edwards?" Nora exclaimed.

"He's soooooo hot!" Lacie cried out.

Jane turned. Standing in front of the step-and-repeat where Jane and Scarlett had posed for some shots, his arm draped casually around some girl who looked a lot like one of the Victoria's Secret models, was a gorgeous guy dressed in a black suit and collared white shirt, no tie. He was tall and broad-shouldered, with a medium build and light brown, wavy hair.

"He looks so familiar," Jane said.

Nora gaped at her. "Jane, you're so ignorant! Jesse Edwards is in, like, *all* the magazines."

"Yeah, Jane," Scarlett scoffed exaggeratedly, causing Nora to playfully stick her tongue out at Scarlett.

"He's the son of Wyatt Edwards and Katarina Miller," Lacie clarified after a not-so-subtle eye roll.

Oh, yeah—*him*. Now Jane remembered. Jesse Edwards was the twenty-year-old celebuspawn of those two famous actors, who had met on the set of a movie and spent the last two decades splitting up and getting back together again. In the tabloids Jesse was always with some B-list starlet, in front of a trendy restaurant or club. He had had some small roles in a couple television series, but he was mostly known for his looks and the girls he dated. He was a notorious playboy.

Jane watched him as he escorted his date in the direction of the bar, waving and smiling at everyone he passed. What a player. Still, he was *hot*.

"Scarlett!"

Jane turned around. Mr. and Mrs. Harp—actually, Dr. and Dr. Harp—were walking toward them, champagne glasses in hand. Scarlett's dad, in his expensive-looking gray suit, fit right in with the crowd. Scarlett's mom's silver dress hugged her rail-thin frame.

"You came." Scarlett sounded less than thrilled. Jane knew that her BFF and her parents had never been close. In fact, after Lacie's birthday bash, Scarlett had elected to spend the night at the Robertses' house rather than her parents'.

"Your father never misses a party," Scarlett's mom said wryly. "How *are* you, Scarlett?"

"What exactly is *L.A. Candy* about, anyway? It's not like that awful reality show where kids compete for dates, is it?" Scarlett's dad spoke up.

"No, Dad. Actually, it's PopTV's first X-rated reality show," Scarlett replied. "They've installed a stripper pole in our living room." Her parents gaped at her. Jane's parents looked at each other uncomfortably. Lacie and Nora just giggled.

"She's kidding," Jane added quickly.

Someone's cold fingers touched her shoulder. She turned around; it was Madison. Gaby was there too, holding a martini in each hand. Madison was wearing a beaded gold minidress. Her bleached hair was in full, loose curls. Gaby's black corset dress went down to her knees, and her hair was styled in a smooth updo. Her makeup was flawless. Jane hadn't seen either of them since the photo shoot.

"Jane!" Madison trilled. "Scarlett! Are you two sooo stoked about tonight!?" She sounded louder than usual and a little drunk.

"Hey, guys," Jane said, hugging them both. "This is crazy, right?"

"It's the best!" Gaby agreed. "Hey, does anyone want a martini? I accidentally ordered two."

"I'll take one!" Madison said, giggling. Jane noticed her parents raising their eyebrows. Her parents were cool with her drinking wine with dinner occasionally, and there's no way they didn't know she'd tried more, but still, she was glad she and Scarlett hadn't had time to grab any drinks. Her mom and dad were most likely about to see her drinking at least once on the huge screen at the front of the room—might as well not rub it in their faces any more than PopTV was about to.

Jane and Scarlett introduced Madison and Gaby to their parents. "My mom and dad are over there, talking to Trevor," Gaby said, pointing. "Hey, Madison, when are your parents getting here?"

"They're not. They're in Beijing." Madison shrugged and took a sip of her martini, spilling a little. "They're closing some deal on a resort they're building over there. They wanted to take the jet and come back just for this party. But I told them we could celebrate the next time they're in town."

"Your parents are hotel developers?" Scarlett's mom asked Madison, with interest.

Madison leaned over and took a sip of one of Gaby's martinis. "Among other things."

The Harps started telling Jane's parents about some fancy

new hotel in London they'd stayed at recently. Lacie and Nora wandered away, in search of celebrities. Jane turned to Scarlett, Madison, and Gaby so they could gossip about the other people in the room when she noticed a familiar figure walking into the club. Her heart practically jumped out of her chest. It was Braden! After his noncommittal RSVP, she wasn't sure if he was going to make it. He was dressed in a black button-down shirt and dark jeans. He looked lost and uncertain, as though he had never stepped foot in a club before. Which, knowing him, was totally possible. The more Jane got to know him, the more she understood how *not* into the Hollywood scene he really was.

She was about to shout out his name when Trevor's voice came on over the speakers. He was standing in the front of the room by the massive plasma screen. People turned to face him.

"Could I please have everyone's attention?" Trevor called out. "Jane, Scarlett, Madison, Gaby, could I get you guys up here?" Jane threw her parents an excited, nervous smile and followed the other girls to the front.

"It's exactly one minute and twenty-two seconds until the big moment," Trevor went on, holding up his Rolex. "Before we get our first look at this very exciting new show, I just want to say what a wonderful time we've all had working on it. And it's just the beginning! These last few weeks have been tough, but we did it. So I hope you all enjoy *L.A. Candy* as much as we've enjoyed creating it."

The room went dark. "With that, I want to invite everyone to take a look at the very first episode of a show that I hope will be around for a long, long time. Ladies and gentlemen, *L.A. Candy*!" Trevor announced.

Everyone clapped and cheered. Trevor stepped back just as the screen came to life. Jane's face appeared, smiling at someone or something in the distance. "My name is Jane," she heard herself say over the speakers, in surround sound. She was mesmerized.

Then the opening credits began playing over the new Rihanna song and a montage of all four girls doing different things, the final image of Jane unpacking a box in the new apartment then collapsing on the couch with Scarlett and smiling.

Jane leaned against Scarlett. "Oh my God! It's us," she whispered.

"Yeah, yeah," Scarlett said. She was pretending to be bored, but Jane could tell that she was mesmerized, too.

The girls fell quiet as the opening credits faded out, followed by a shot of Jane walking into Fiona Chen Events. There was Naomi at her desk, telling Jane that Fiona wanted to see her. Then Fiona offering Jane the promotion. They showed Fiona telling Jane that she was trusting her not to screw it up. Then it cut to a shot of Jane with a worried expression. People around her laughed. After that was a scene of Jane setting up her new desk. Then Paolo stopping by and asking her out. Jane couldn't *believe* they were showing this clip. She couldn't stand Paolo. She had never heard from him after their unfortunate first date.

Next came Gaby at her job, at the PR firm called Ruby Slipper. She was at the front desk, answering phones and getting people's names mixed up in funny ways. That got big laughs. (Jane was glad her first day at Fiona Chen hadn't been filmed!) Then Madison working out at the gym with her personal trainer, Byron . . . who was hot! Jane felt a sudden urge to get in shape. Then Scarlett in one of her classes at U.S.C., taking notes. She raised her hand and gave some smart-ass answer. It cut to several of her classmates' faces and then back to the professor. All stunned. People around them laughed again.

By the time it got to all four girls together at a club, Jane could sort of watch herself without feeling uncomfortable. Except . . . *oh shit!* Jane knew what night that was. She squeezed Scarlett's arm. Were they going to show her wasted at Madison's? With her parents and little sisters not ten feet away? Eyes glued to the screen, she watched them all going back to Madison's apartment joined by a group of guys. There were shots of the girls dancing, laughing, drinking champagne. To Jane's surprise it looked rather harmless. Phew! Then it showed two boys announcing that they were going home with Jane and Scarlett. It cut to a closeup shot of them pounding fists and giving each other knowing glances. *Ew,* thought Jane. *Those guys are such tools!* Music began to play as Jane, Scarlett, and the two guys made their way toward the door. Then it cut to a bird's-eye view of downtown L.A. all lit up. The words

"Created and Produced by Trevor Lord" appeared across the screen, and then the credits began to roll.

With that, the room broke into wild applause. Scarlett moved closer to Jane. "What the fuck?" she whispered.

"I know! They totally made it look like we went home with those guys," Jane whispered back. "Didn't we leave them at the elevator?"

"Yes," Scarlett said. "I can't believe they did that."

Jane turned to Madison and Gaby. "What did you guys think of that?" she said in a low voice.

"That was *awesome*," Madison said, although it seemed a little forced. "So when did you do the recording at the beginning?"

"Oh, it was kind of a last-minute thing," Jane explained. She had only told Scarlett about the producers asking her to do the narration.

"Well, you did great. It all looked so good!" Gaby raised her martini glass in the air and twirled around, doing a little dance. "Madison, you want to get another one?"

"Sure, sweetie!"

As the two girls walked away, Jane and Scarlett exchanged a glance. Scarlett shrugged and mouthed, *WTF?* Jane shrugged back.

"Jane! Scarlett! *O-M-G!*"

D was rushing toward them, followed by an older guy Jane didn't recognize. He hugged Jane and Scarlett tightly. "It looked amazing! I'm totally TiVoing every episode!"

Then D turned to the guy beside him. "I want you two to meet my friend, Quentin Sparks."

"Pleasure," Quentin said, extending his hand.

"Quentin is a club promoter," D continued. "He does a night at Les Deux and one at Teddy's. He does all the best nights."

"I told D you girls are welcome at any of my clubs. We can comp you a table and a bottle. Just let me know," Quentin added.

"Cool," Scarlett said.

D and Scarlett made small talk, but Jane's eyes were scanning the room. There was someone she *had* to talk to. Jane noticed Braden sitting at the bar, alone. "Excuse me," she said to Scarlett, Quentin, and D. "I just spotted my friend. It was really nice meeting you!"

"Stay out of trouble, you!" D called after her.

"That's exactly where she's headed," Scarlett said under her breath.

"Speak for yourself!" Jane said, waving good-bye and hurrying to the bar.

Braden's eyes lit up when he saw her. "Hey!" he called out.

"Hey!" Jane threw her arms around his neck and hugged him tightly. He hugged her back. She hadn't seen him in ages—not since that night at Lola's. She'd been so busy with work and everything.

"I can't believe you're here!" she told him.

"Of course I'm here. I wouldn't have missed your big

night," Braden said, grinning. "Show's awesome. Well, you were awesome, anyway."

Jane blushed slightly. "Yeah, well, they kinda edited some things in a weird way. Like that final scene? That's not how it happened."

"Yeah, that's typical with reality shows, I think. Here." Braden handed her a box wrapped in pale blue tissue paper. "I brought you a present."

"A present? Seriously? Aww, you didn't have to get me anything!"

"It's no big deal. It's kinda lame."

Jane tried to hide her eagerness as she ripped open the box. Tucked away in a nest of white tissue paper was a stuffed puppy doll. It was white with floppy brown ears and brown spots.

"Awwww!" Jane said, holding it up. "Braden! You got me a puppy!"

"I figured he could keep you company until you got a real one," Braden explained.

"That's so sweet. I'm naming him B, after you."

"You are not!"

"Too late, I already named him." Jane smiled at him. Screw "friends." She liked him so much. "Seriously, Braden, I can't believe you did this. Thank you so much!"

Jane hugged him again. She knew any other guy would have brought her flowers or something generic, but not Braden. He was different from any guy she had ever met. Why did Willow have to be in the picture?

She knew she should ask Braden what was up with Willow these days.

But not tonight. Besides, he *had* come alone.

As Jane tightly hugged Braden, she felt someone's gaze on them. Over his shoulder she noticed that someone was watching them intently from across the room.

For a moment her eyes locked with Trevor's. She gave him a little wave, breaking from her hug. But Trevor showed no response. He should have been happy, right? His show was a huge success, at least if this crowd was any indication. So why did she feel like she was in trouble?

25

A CREATIVE SOLUTION

The clock said 3:05 a.m. Trevor couldn't sleep. It was always like this on the night of a series premiere. He wouldn't know for hours if *L.A. Candy* was a hit or a bust. But until then . . . his mind wouldn't stop churning.

He thought about the mood tonight at Area. There had been no mistaking it—it had been electric. Everyone loved the pilot. But ultimately, there was no way to tell from a small crowd of friends, family, cast and crew, and a handful of industry people if the show was going to have a future or not. So—he would have to wait.

He glanced at the clock again: 3:06 a.m., 3:07 a.m.

If the show *was* a hit, he was going to have a minor problem on his hands. Actually, it was not so much a problem as an interesting challenge. And he of all people relished challenges. He would wrap his brain around this one and figure out a creative solution, just as he always did.

Jane was very important to the success of *L.A. Candy*. Which meant that her love life was very important to it too.

26

HERE'S TO ALL **FOUR** OF US GETTING INSANELY RICH AND FAMOUS!

Scarlett glanced at her watch, then at the menu, then at her watch again. She tapped her foot restlessly.

Jane leaned over. "What's wrong, Scar? Do you have someplace else you have to be?"

"Where is everyone?"

"We're early. Trevor should be here any sec—and Madison and Gaby, too."

Scarlett leaned back in her chair and peered around at the other tables, trying not to feel totally annoyed. Trevor had summoned her and the other girls for a lunch meeting at Toast. What did he want with them, anyway? Hadn't they all seen enough of one another at the series premiere party last night? Besides, she was still in a foul mood over the episode. It had *not* reflected her "reality"—not at all. Jane had been put off by it too, but not for long. Braden had shown up at the party, and after that she'd been way too cheerful about everything—including the fact that Trevor and the rest of them had completely twisted everything. Like Jane's nonrelationship with Paolo and that stupid, drunken night at Madison's apartment.

Scarlett didn't look forward to—what? Nine more episodes of the same? She wondered if it was too late for Jane and her to get out of their *L.A. Candy* contracts.

"Hey, they're here!" Jane's voice interrupted her thoughts.

Scarlett saw that Jane was waving eagerly at Trevor, Madison, and Gaby, who were walking toward their table. Jane looked . . . excited. Happy. *Maybe she likes being a part of all this,* Scarlett thought. *Maybe she doesn't want to get out of her contract.*

Trevor was striding toward their table, his cell glued to his ear. Madison and Gaby trailed a few feet behind him. Both girls were wearing shades and looking unusually pale, as though they had been out partying until about five minutes ago. Which was a likely scenario, from the way they had been putting away martinis last night.

"Jane! Scarlett!" Trevor snapped his cell shut and kissed each girl on the cheek. "Traffic on the 101 . . . ," he said in response to Scarlett looking at her watch. "I ran into Madison and Gaby out front."

"You don't have to yell, Trevor," Gaby whined, rubbing her temples as the hostess pulled out her chair for her.

"Sweetie, do you want me to get you some Advil or something?" Madison offered.

Gaby nodded. "Yes, please. I feel like crap."

"Can you have our waitress bring us water right away? Flat?" Trevor asked the hostess. "I have news," he told the girls mysteriously.

Scarlett raised her eyebrows. "News?"

"You're giving us a raise?" Gaby piped up.

Trevor laughed. "Better than that."

A waitress came by a few moments later with glasses of water. Trevor waited until she had set a glass in front of each of them and walked away. "So. I wanted to tell you all personally that *L.A. Candy* is a hit! It was the number-one rated show for women eighteen to thirty-four last night— and, surprisingly, men eighteen to thirty-four as well."

"Oh. My. God!" Madison threw up her arms, her bracelets jangling noisily. "This is *amazing!*"

Gaby glared at the bracelets and rubbed her head.

"So, what does that mean?" Scarlett asked him. "For us."

"It means that things are going to be very different now," Trevor replied. "Twenty-four hours ago, almost no one knew who you were. Starting today, you won't be able to leave your apartment without being recognized. Case in point . . ." He nodded his head in the direction of two girls in their early twenties waiting for a hostess. Both were looking in their direction and whispering to each other.

Scarlett looked over at the girls and then back to Jane. Her friend hadn't said a word; she looked dazed. Her mind reeled as she tried to take in Trevor's news. *L.A. Candy* was a hit? For real?

Trevor turned to Jane as well. "Jane? You okay?" he said, sounding concerned.

Jane blinked. "Yeah. I'm fine. It's just . . . well . . . it's just that I didn't really expect this. I'm kind of blown away. No offense, but I thought no one was gonna watch this show." She laughed.

Trevor reached over and squeezed her arm. "Well, *everyone* watched last night. And it's just beginning. I guarantee you that over the next few days and weeks, it's gonna get a little crazy. You have no idea. This is a big deal. Your face is going to be everywhere. You'd better get ready because it's going to happen fast."

Scarlett glanced at Trevor, then at Jane, and back to Trevor again. She noticed he was directing his comments to Jane. Why wasn't he saying all this to her, Madison, and Gaby, too?

Madison seemed to notice this also, because she cleared her throat noisily and raised her glass. "Well, here's to all *four* of us getting insanely rich and famous!" she blurted out.

Scarlett turned to Trevor. "This is all really pretty exciting and all that," she said, sounding less than sincere, "but let me ask you this. On last night's episode? Why did your editors make it seem like Jane and I went home with those guys?" she demanded.

"Scarlett," Trevor said slowly. "It was just an ending shot. No one said you all went home together. Maybe they were just walking you out. Besides, I wasn't there, but you did all leave together. And we have Jane on camera inviting them all to your place. We aren't making up crazy stories here."

"But—" Scarlett began, but Trevor stopped her.

"Honestly, Scarlett, it's not a big deal. You're on a number-one show. It's exciting. Trust me on this. You just enjoy the ride and let *me* worry about how the show is edited, okay?"

Scarlett was about to argue with him some more. But Jane threw her a look—it was somewhere between a pleading "Can we talk about this later, in private?" look and a frustrated "Do you always have to be such a pain in the ass?" look. Not that Jane would ever call her a pain in the ass to her face. But Scarlett knew that she and Jane had their differences about the show, about being "friends" with Madison and Gaby, and about everything that had happened in the last month or so since the first shoot at Les Deux. Jane was, for the most part, into it—and even when she wasn't *totally* into it, she was at least open to the experience, ready to be a team player. Scarlett, on the other hand, was starting to have serious regrets about ever signing on.

Jane continued to stare at her with that *look*. Scarlett sighed, then turned to Trevor. "Whatever. But don't do that anymore, okay? Don't make it look like stuff happened that didn't happen."

Trevor smiled charmingly at her. "Of course not."

Yeah, right, Scarlett thought.

27

YOU'RE THE ONE WHO
GOES TO U.S.C., RIGHT?

Jane's cell buzzed on her desk, loudly intruding on the "serenity" of Fiona Chen's office atmosphere. She quickly grabbed it before any of her coworkers noticed. The last few days had been filled with calls and text messages from people she didn't even know still had her number. She rubbed her eyes and stared blankly at the screen, wondering who wanted to talk to her now. She decided just to let her voice mail pick it up.

Other than her family and a few close friends, Jane had not told many people that she was filming the show. She hadn't had very high expectations, so she didn't want to make a big deal out of it. But it seemed like a lot of people she knew watched PopTV, judging by all the surprised phone calls and texts she'd gotten since the show aired. Now she knew what people meant when they talked about their lives changing overnight.

"Jane? Could you come in here, please?"

It was Fiona, summoning her on the intercom. Jane dropped her cell into her bag, and headed into Fiona's office, notebook and pen in hand.

Fiona was sitting behind her desk, leafing through a book of fabric swatches. Behind her, one of the *L.A. Candy* camera guys angled his lens to get a clear shot of Jane entering the room. On the corner of Fiona's desk was a light box that was about two feet tall, casting a soft light over Fiona's face. The director had mentioned to her that Fiona was not pleased with the way she looked on screen. So now they had to light her face differently to make her look more "fresh." Translation: Fiona didn't like them cutting back and forth from her face to Jane's because she felt it made her look old. In addition, Fiona had hired a hair and makeup artist for the days they were scheduled to film at the office.

"Jane! Sit down." Fiona looked up from the swatches. "I wanted to talk to you about a very important new client."

"Sure!"

"Anna Payne has hired us to do a New Year's Eve party," Fiona explained.

Jane stopped. Anna Payne? She remembered how the actress had been so rude to her at Les Deux. But while she wasn't the politest person in the world, she *was* an A-list celebrity. Jane knew this job was a catch. Besides, Jane never got to work directly with Fiona's clients. Actually, she usually had little-to-zero interaction with any of them.

"She's coming in next Tuesday to talk to us," Fiona went on. "I want you in on the meeting. In fact, you will be involved in the planning of this party, from start to finish. It will be excellent experience for you."

So much for little-to-zero interaction, Jane thought. Fiona was asking her to meet with Anna Payne *and* help plan her New Year's Eve party.

"What do you think, Jane? Are you ready to move up to a higher plane of responsibility?"

Ever since the *L.A. Candy* cameras had begun filming at Fiona Chen Events, Fiona had started talking like this. She had developed a talent for making the simplest task seem like an impossible challenge, where anything could go wrong and Jane was not to let her down. *"Are you ready to move up to a higher plane of responsibility?" "Do you have the courage to take on this challenge?" "Life is a series of choices." "What choice will you make here, today?" "Don't let me down, Jane. I'm counting on you."* Jane was helping to select centerpieces and color schemes, not curing cancer.

"Absolutely," Jane said, nodding. She opened her notebook to a clean page. "Is there anything you want me to do to get ready for the meeting?"

"I'm getting to that. The budget is a quarter million, but she seemed flexible. We need to run some preliminary concepts by her when we meet. Why don't you come up with some ideas by, say, Friday, and we can discuss?"

"No problem."

Jane could barely breathe as she headed back to her tiny office. Fiona was actually going to let her help plan an entire New Year's Eve party, from start to finish. Jane was aware that the camera's presence had a large part in

Fiona allowing her to participate, but she didn't care. And it wasn't just any party, either. Jane was going to help with Anna Payne's party. Sure, Anna was a huge bitch, but Jane would just have to deal. Jane felt like she was finally getting an opportunity to do what she wanted.

She was already searching for venues on the Internet when her cell vibrated—again. Jane glanced around before she pulled it out of her bag. It said: MADISON PARKER.

Jane picked it up. "Hey!"

"Hey, Jane."

"I'm so glad it's you. My phone's been nonstop. My third-grade teacher emailed me this morning." Jane laughed. "Seriously, the woman is like sixty-something. What the hell is she doing watching PopTV? Has everyone been driving you crazy?"

There was a brief silence. "Yeah, it's so annoying," Madison said after a moment. "Listen. Are you shooting today?"

"Yeah, but they're just wrapping up. Why?"

"Yeah, me too. I was thinking. Wouldn't it be fun to sneak away from the cameras and grab a drink, just me and you?"

"Is Dana listening? You're gonna get in trouble, lady." Madison had never invited only Jane to go out. She wondered if something was up with her.

"No Dana. I'm in the locker room. I took that stupid mike pack off and stuck it in my gym bag. So, what do you say? Drink?"

Jane glanced at the time on her computer screen. "Sure. Just tell me when and where."

"Perfect!"

Jane admired the peach color of her Bellini before taking a sip. "What *is* this place, anyway?" she said, glancing around the dimly lit Bar Marmont. She took in the red lanterns lined with fringe hanging above them and a stuffed peacock in the corner of the room. Small fake butterflies covered the ceiling. Jane and Madison were seated at the bar.

"It's one of my favorite places in L.A.," Madison replied. She clinked her glass to Jane's. "So. Here's to stardom! What a bitch, right?"

"It's crazy! People have been coming up to me and asking me to take pictures. And, oh my God! Some woman stopped me on the street and asked me to sign her arm today. It's weird, right?"

Madison didn't reply.

"You okay?" Jane asked her.

Madison reached up and ran a hand through her hair. "Yeah. It's just that . . . well, I'm not sure I'm really into it."

"What do you mean?"

"I don't know. I make jokes about wanting to be famous, but I didn't come to Hollywood to be a celebrity. I came out here to try to find *me.* I know that sounds kind of lame," Madison apologized.

Jane shook her head. She wouldn't have been shocked to hear this from Scarlett, but Madison? "No, not at all."

"It's just that, I grew up in a very wealthy family, right? My parents have more houses than I can count. My childhood was all about benefit balls and society pages and making sure I picked up the right fork at Le Cirque. I wanted to get away from that for a while, move to a whole new coast, and figure out what I want to do with the rest of my life."

Jane nodded. "Well, that makes sense. I think that's why we all came here."

Madison took a sip of her drink. "I've been out here for about a year. I've had a few jobs, and now, I'm thinking about school. It's not like I'm not grateful for what my mom and dad gave—*give*—me. It's just that I don't want to turn into some spoiled brat who spends all her time shopping and partying. I want to *do* something, you know? I want to have something that I accomplished all on my own. Have my life mean something."

Jane stared at her, impressed. This was a totally different side of Madison. She was used to rich, party girl Madison, who lived in a stunning penthouse apartment, flashed her black AmEx at every opportunity, and never said no to a martini. She didn't know this other side of Madison even existed.

"I feel the same way," Jane said earnestly. "My family's not insanely rich like yours, but we were pretty well off. Not that they ever spoiled me or anything. They always insisted I work and stuff. Anyway, I feel like you can never really know who you are until you put yourself into a completely different environment. Like you're who you are because of *where* you grew up and *who* you grew up with. I wanted to get away from all that to see who I really was, on my own."

"And figure out who your real friends are?" Madison added. "Hollywood is full of users. It's so hard to know who to trust here. And as if friends weren't hard enough to find, guys are impossible. I'd give anything to meet a guy who just loves me for me."

Jane nodded. "Yeah, I'll take one of those too."

Madison's eyes sparkled. "Any candidates?"

Jane's thoughts flashed to Braden. She felt a blush creeping into her cheeks. "Well . . . there's a guy I really like," she admitted. "Except he already has a girlfriend, sort of. Well, not a girlfriend, exactly, but this on-again, off-again thing."

"Minor technicality," Madison joked. "What's his name?"

"Braden. He's really cute. And he's sooo sweet. He gave me a stuffed puppy at the series premiere party because he knew how much I love dogs."

"Wow. That's so lame!" Madison laughed. "But yes, very sweet."

"He is!"

Madison was the first person Jane had told about Braden, besides Scarlett. She didn't want to tell anyone because she felt stupid having feelings for a guy who had feelings for someone else. But the Bellini was making her feel so relaxed, and Madison was a good listener. It was nice, just sitting in this cozy, pretty bar and talking about guys, careers, Hollywood, life—everything. She couldn't do things like this with Scarlett. Scarlett would spend the majority of the evening mocking everyone around them and complaining about how sceney the bar was.

Still, enough about Braden. Jane switched subjects. "So. How long have you and Gaby been friends?"

Madison twirled the stem of her nearly empty champagne glass. Her nails were perfectly shaped and painted a dark violet hue. "I don't know. A couple of months?" She shrugged.

Jane was surprised to hear this. She'd had the impression that the two girls had known each other forever. "Oh, I thought you guys were best friends."

"Yeah, well, Gaby's sweet."

"What about Trevor? I can't remember—did he 'discover' you at a club too? Did he give you the cheesy speech about opportunities?"

Madison laughed. "Nah. I met him at the gym. Actually, his wife used to be my personal trainer. She—"

"His wife?" Jane asked, surprised. "Trevor's married?"

"Yeah. You didn't know?"

A voice interrupted their back and forth. "'Scuse me!"

Jane glanced up. Two college-aged girls approached them at the bar. They were grinning shyly at Jane and holding out a couple of cocktail napkins and a ballpoint pen.

"Um, you're Jane from *L.A. Candy,* right?" one of them said. "We don't mean to bother you, but could we get your autograph?"

"I love your show!" the second girl exclaimed.

"Thanks," Jane said hesitantly. Why were they asking her and not Madison, too? They probably just didn't recognize her. "This is Madison; she's on the show too," she said, nodding at Madison.

"Right!" The first girl stared at Madison. "Cool! You're the one who goes to U.S.C., right?"

"Can we get your autograph too?" the second girl piped up.

Madison blinked. She looked kind of pissed. "No. That's Scarlett."

"Oh." The girl looked a little embarrassed. "Sorry. I get you all confused. Can I get yours?"

As Madison signed her autograph for the girls, Jane's cell buzzed on the bar next to her. She glanced at the screen. It was a text from Braden.

HAVING A SMALL PARTY SAT NITE MY HOUSE 9 P.M. TILL WHENEVER. CAN U COME? BRING SCAR AND ANYONE ELSE U WANT.

"Thanks!" the two girls said to Jane and Madison, then took off.

"Who texted you?" Madison asked Jane, watching the girls as they walked back to their table. "It must be somebody good, 'cause your face just got all glowy."

"It's Braden. He's inviting us all to a party Saturday night."

"Us? What do you mean, us?"

"He said I could bring whoever. You have to come. I want you to meet him. I'll ask Scar and Gaby, too."

"Definitely," Madison said, finishing the last of her drink. "I wanna meet the sort-of girlfriend so we can figure out how to get rid of her."

"Madison! That's awful!" Jane tried to look shocked, but she couldn't help but laugh a little.

"The guy gave you a freakin' stuffed animal."

"So, it could have been an 'I'm glad we're friends' stuffed animal, not an 'I really like you' stuffed animal."

"No, Jane. Trust me, I know guys. I practically have a Ph.D. in them."

Jane raised her eyebrows. "Yeah? Well, if you're so well versed in guys, then where is your Prince Charming?"

Madison smiled mischievously. "I'm working on it."

28

OUT OF SYNC

Scarlett dropped her backpack on the floor and tossed her keys on the kitchen counter. God, what a morning. That jerk Professor Cahill had given her a B-plus on her paper on David Mamet's *Speed-the-Plow*. B-plus—how dare he? That paper was better than any of his pathetic, impossible-to-sit-through lectures. The only good part of her day was when Dana had inexplicably canceled the scheduled shoot. The cameras were supposed to film a couple of Scarlett's classes, plus follow her around campus to get some general walking-around-campus footage. But this morning, she had called to say they were postponing those scenes— new schedule TBD. Scarlett hated how last minute all the scheduling changes were, but was really happy not to have to film today.

Scarlett had enjoyed the break from the cameras. It was a pain in the ass, having to get there a half hour early and get miked only to attend classes full of students who either loathed her presence or wanted to become insta-friends with her and ask her questions about the show.

The thing was . . . as much as she hated the cameras, it seemed like that was the only time she got to see Jane. Between her school and Jane's work, most of their time together was while being filmed. Ever since the series premiere, and even before then, she had felt out of sync with her best friend. Jane was getting along well with Madison and Gaby, whom Trevor and Dana had basically forced on Scarlett and Jane. But Scarlett couldn't stand hanging out with them. Gaby was nice enough, but the girl had the I.Q. of a sandworm. Scarlett had made many failed attempts to carry on a normal conversation with her. And Madison struck her as a royal bitch posing as a—what? She couldn't even hold a job. Although, maybe that is difficult to do when your talents are limited to drinking, spending your parents' money, and subjecting your hair to an abnormal amount of bleaching. Scarlett hadn't quite figured Madison out. In any case, she didn't like her. She didn't trust her either.

Scarlett could tell that Jane got annoyed with her for being rude to Madison and Gaby or talking shit about them behind their backs. It didn't make sense. She and Jane always sided with each other against girls like them. What had changed?

The front door opened with a noisy jangle of keys, and Jane walked in. "Hey, Scar," she called out. Her blond hair tumbled carelessly out of her clip, and she looked really tired.

"Hey, Janie. Bad day at work?"

Jane set her bag on the kitchen counter. "It was okay. I had drinks with Madison after. And guess what? Fiona's finally gonna let me help with a party. But you'll never guess whose . . . Anna Payne!"

Scarlett stared at her. She wasn't sure which part of this statement to process first—drinks with Madison or the Anna Payne party.

She chose the more palatable option. "Anna Payne? That should be super-fun!" Scarlett said sarcastically.

"Yeah, well, I told Fiona that we really hit it off when I saw her at Les Deux, so . . . ," Jane joked.

"I thought I read that she just got married to somebody recently."

"Oh, yeah. To Noah Moody, right? I saw that in *Gossip* . . ."

Noah Moody. Scarlett tried to remember what she knew about the guy. He was an actor, hot, a little older, and had a history with drugs. Yeah, pretty much ideal husband material.

Jane went to the refrigerator, opened it, and grabbed a container of take-out sesame noodles. She got a fork out of the dishwasher and leaned against the counter. "Madison took me to this bar over on Sunset. We should go sometime; it was really cool," she said between bites. "Oh, and Madison said we should check out this movie theater called the Arclight. She said it's the best place to see movies in L.A. You can pick your seat ahead of time and—"

"I didn't know you were filming tonight," Scarlett interrupted her.

"I wasn't. I met her at Bar Marmont after work, just for fun."

Scarlett frowned as Jane continued on. Madison said . . . Madison said . . . It was getting a little nauseating. When had Jane and Madison become such good friends?

"I've gotta take a shower," Scarlett cut in, hooking her thumb in the direction of the bathroom.

Jane stared at her. "Oh! 'Kay. I'm gonna see what's on TV."

"'Kay."

Scarlett headed to the bathroom for the shower she really didn't need, except to escape from Jane's Madison-fest monologue.

Scarlett knew she should try to talk to Jane about how she was feeling—about their friendship, the show, their new "friends," *all of it*. But she couldn't. At least not now. The idea of it exhausted her. She headed to the shower and she felt as far from Janie as she'd ever felt.

29

SMALL PARTY, HUH?

"So who's gonna be at this party?" Madison asked. She smoothed a coat of lip gloss across her mouth, then loudly kissed the passenger's-side window of Gaby's BMW: *mwah!* The shimmery pink imprint looked ghostly against the neon-lit darkness outside.

"Braden said it's gonna be small," Jane replied from the backseat, where she was sitting next to Scarlett. She tapped her foot absentmindedly to the beat of Rihanna's "Disturbia" playing over Gaby's speakers.

"Small? Lame. I hope I didn't just waste a good outfit," Gaby complained.

"Not sure if I'd classify that as 'good,'" Madison said, eyeing Gaby's white ruffled blouse. "Did you just come from church? How was choir practice? Did you tell the monsignor I said hi?" she mocked.

Gaby glared at Madison as she undid one more button on her top.

"Gaby, it's gonna be hoppin'! We're gonna be eating finger sandwiches and playing bridge. Maybe even a little charades if things really get wild," Scarlett joked. Gaby stared ahead blankly. She wasn't amused.

While the three girls bantered, Jane checked over her outfit for the third time since Gaby had picked up her and Scarlett at their apartment. She found a long, loose string on the hem of her floral silk top and yanked hard. She smoothed it over her dark skinny jeans that had a small cuff just above her black stilettos. She was nervous about her ensemble, which she had spent about two hours trying to pick out. Was she too dressed up? Not dressed-up enough? She didn't know what was appropriate for a small house party in the Hills. She wanted to look nice, but not like she was trying too hard.

She was also nervous because Gaby had told Dana they were all going to a house party, and Dana had managed to track down Braden's number through his agent. As a result, the event was now being filmed. Jane hoped that Braden wasn't upset by it. She felt bad, like she had ruined his party.

"Oh, there's Dana," Gaby said, pulling her car to the side of the road. She rolled down her window as Dana approached them, talking rapidly into her Bluetooth.

"Let's get you all miked right away," Dana said without bothering to say hello first. "Yeah, they just pulled up," she said to the person on the other end of the phone.

One by one, each girl was miked outside. As usual,

Madison's outfit proved the most difficult.

"I'm a challenge tonight," Madison said, looking down at her skintight red minidress. She smiled charmingly at one of the sound guys.

"I have a lot of words I could use to describe Madison. But 'challenge' isn't one of them," Scarlett whispered to Jane.

"Play nice, Scarlett," Jane said. She was trying to be patient with Scarlett, but it wasn't easy. Her best friend was getting worse instead of better about hanging out with Madison and Gaby. Why couldn't she be a little more . . . cooperative? This was an important part of the show. Trevor expected the four of them to do stuff together once in a while.

After a few minutes and a few failed attempts at a leg strap, Madison reentered the car so they could park closer to the party and officially get out of the car. She had the mike pack sticking out of the back of her dress, resembling a large hump.

"They're gonna try and shoot around it," Madison explained, shrugging.

Gaby drove on for another minute until she reached Braden's house. Jane glanced out of the tinted window as they pulled up. She had never been to Braden's house before. It was pretty far up the twisted roads of Laurel Canyon. It looked big from the front. Braden had told her that he lived with his best friend, Jesse—the one he'd told her about at Cabo Cantina. It was a really nice house for an aspiring actor and a . . . what? Actually, Braden had never mentioned what Jesse did. But whatever it was, he didn't appear to be struggling.

Jane spotted two of the *L.A. Candy* camera guys near the front door, waiting to shoot the girls getting out of Gaby's car and going into the party.

"It's showtime, girls!" Madison said eagerly, checking her reflection in the overhead mirror one last time.

"Oh, goody." Scarlett rolled her eyes.

"Scar!" Jane snapped under her breath.

The girls climbed out of the car and made their way toward the front door. They knocked, and after a moment, Braden came to the door. Noise spilled out from behind him: loud music and voices and laughter.

"Hey!" he said happily when he saw Jane. "You made it!"

"Of course," Jane said, hugging him. He looked really good tonight, casually dressed in jeans and a soft blue T-shirt. "You know Scarlett. This is Madison and Gaby. Gaby and Madison, this is Braden."

Madison leaned over and kissed Braden on the cheek. "Thanks for inviting us," she said smoothly. Madison looked back at Jane and shot her an approving grin. Jane prayed Braden hadn't seen it.

"So where can we get drinks?" Gaby asked Braden.

"This way." Braden waved the girls inside. He touched Jane's arm. "Your show sent over a couple of camera guys, plus some girl named Alli," he said in a low voice. "But you probably already knew that, right?"

"Yeah. They told me. But they didn't ask my permission or anything. Sorry; they haven't been a pain, have they?"

"No. They're mellow. That girl Alli got a bunch of people to sign releases," Braden went on. Then he leaned in and whispered in Jane's ear, "Jesse and I said it was okay for the show to shoot here. But I didn't sign a release to let them film me, personally. Hope you don't mind."

"No, not at all." Ugh. She felt awful to have inflicted all this on him.

"Yeah," he said, moving his head away from hers, "my agent told me it wasn't a good idea. If I'm on any reality show, it'll be harder for me to get parts."

"No worries. So how *are* you?" Jane quickly changed the subject.

"Great! Come inside and say hi to my friends."

Braden led her down the hallway to a large living room that opened up to a beautifully landscaped patio and backyard. The place was nicely decorated. It looked like the ideal bachelor pad: brown leather couches, dark wood furniture, and several large pieces of artwork hanging on light-colored walls. They passed a couple of surfboards propped up in the corner of the living room. *Explains his beachy smell,* Jane thought.

The place was filled with guests—about fifty or sixty people, Jane guessed. If this was Braden's idea of a "small party," she'd hate to see what a blowout would look like.

Music blared through the speakers. Outside, some of the guests were splashing around in a pool that stretched across the backyard, with the Los Angeles city lights as the backdrop.

"Small party, huh?" Jane teased Braden.

"It was *supposed* to be small," Braden complained cheerfully. "It's Jesse's fault. He always does this."

"You two look like you need some drinks!" Jane heard from behind them.

She turned around to find a familiar-looking guy holding out a couple of frozen margaritas in plastic cups. Jane tried to hide her surprise. It was Jesse Edwards, the playboy she'd seen with the Victoria's Secret model at Area.

"Hey, man, we were just talking about you," Braden said, slapping Jesse on the back. "Jesse, this is my friend Jane. Jane, this is Jesse."

Jane smiled at him, trying to keep her composure and appear unmoved by his presence. *This* was the Jesse Braden lived with? Was she supposed to pretend like she didn't know who he was?

Jane was stunned that Braden—Mr. Anti-Hollywood—was best friends with someone like Jesse, who basically defined the lifestyle. On the other hand, Braden *had* told her that the two of them had been friends since childhood and that they were opposites. Still, it was kind of a shock.

Jesse handed Jane one of the plastic cups. "Braden told me about you."

"Did he?" Jane looked at Braden, a little surprised.

"Yeah. And I've seen you on *L.A. Candy*. Kind of a girly show, but it's cool. I was at Area for the premiere, but I didn't see you there. It was pretty crowded."

"Oh, you were there?" Jane said, pretending she hadn't seen him.

"Here, gimme that," Braden said, swiping the other drink from Jesse. "How're we doing on food?"

"Good, I guess. The pizza went fast, so I called for more," Jesse replied.

Braden's gaze bounced around the crowd. "Oh, God, there's Andrew. I gotta talk to him. Excuse me, Jane, I'll be right back."

"'Kay."

Jane sipped at her mixed drink and glanced around the room, wondering if she'd spot Willow. But the place was packed, and it was hard to make out everyone's faces. There was Scarlett, already swarmed by half a dozen cute guys. Madison and Gaby were at the bar, flirting with the bartender. Jane tried to think of a polite excuse to get away from Jesse. She didn't want to be rude or anything, especially since he was Braden's best friend. But judging from the tabloids, he probably hit on anything with a heartbeat, and she didn't really feel like waiting around for him to make his move. It was justifiable to blow him off.

"So, Jane. How are you liking L.A.?" Jesse said, cutting into her thoughts.

"I like it," Jane replied, trying to keep her voice on the cool, distant side. She didn't want to give him even the slightest impression that she was interested in him. "Scarlett—that's my best friend from Santa Barbara. She and I moved here a couple of months ago."

"Scarlett from the show, right?"

"Oh, right." Jane would never get used to strangers knowing about her life. "Yeah, she's the hot one with black hair."

"What are you talking about? You're *all* hot." Jesse smiled at her. "So you work for Fiona Chen. What's that like? I've heard she's nuts, but her events are awesome."

"Exactly!" Jane was impressed that Jesse actually remembered whom she worked for. "Right on both counts."

"Yeah? So what do you do for her?"

As Jane described her job to Jesse, she noticed one of the *L.A. Candy* cameras focusing in on them. She wondered if Jesse had signed a release. She tried to see if he was wearing a mike. If a guy was miked she could normally tell because the tape pulled from the underside of his shirt and made a mark. These days, she never knew who they were planning on miking.

Jesse told Jane some funny stories about a Fiona Chen party he had been to. Despite her resolve to get away from him, she found herself laughing and feeling entertained. He didn't seem like a player at all—just a nice, funny guy. She told him about Fiona asking her to help out with Anna Payne's New Year's Eve party, and how nervous she was about meeting with the actress on Tuesday.

"Don't stress, just make sure there's a lot of booze at the party," Jesse offered. "So when you're not working or filming, what are you doing?"

"Not too much, but the show keeps us pretty busy," Jane replied.

"Well, listen. If you think you could find an opening in your oh-so-busy schedule, we should have dinner sometime. Maybe away from your entourage?" Jesse motioned toward another camera pointing in their direction.

Jane stared at him. "Ummm . . ." She wasn't sure what to say. On one hand, she had zero interest in going out with the famous/infamous Jesse. On the other hand, he seemed like a sweet guy in person. Maybe his press image wasn't the real Jesse? If she'd learned one thing from being on TV, it was that things weren't always what they appeared.

Still, he was Braden's best friend. There was no way she was going to date Braden's best friend. Braden was the one she wanted to date. On the other hand, if Braden was interested in dating her, wouldn't he have told Jesse that? If he had, Jesse would *not* have asked her out. Which meant that Braden couldn't possibly be interested in her. Great.

She wished Braden would come back already. Jane's eyes flitted around the room and she spotted him on one of the couches. Willow was sitting on his lap, and they were . . . *making out*. Jane felt her stomach twist. So Willow was here. She hadn't dropped off the face of the earth. She was here, now, very much *with* Braden.

Jane blinked and forced herself to turn her attention

back to Jesse. He was still smiling at her . . . still waiting for her answer. He seemed oblivious to the disappointment that filled Jane's eyes.

"Sure, I'd love to have dinner with you sometime," Jane heard herself say. "But me and the cameras are kind of a package deal. I know it sucks, but it's what I signed up for."

"Well, if that's the only way, then I guess I'll just have to deal. Do I have to buy them all dinner too?" Jesse joked.

Jane was surprised at how easily he had agreed. "Nope. Just pretend that they don't make the whole first date thing that much more awkward."

As Jane punched her contact info into Jesse's Black-Berry, she saw out of the corner of her eye that Braden was no longer playing Couch Twister with Willow, but was sitting back with his drink. Willow was next to him, adjusting her neckline and checking messages on her cell. Braden had definitely noticed her and Jesse, and he had an intense expression on his face that she couldn't quite translate. If she had to guess, she'd say it was disapproval mixed with anger. But maybe she was reading too much into it. *Whatever*, Jane thought. *Braden has no right to care. He chose Willow, didn't he?*

30

HOLLYWOOD'S #1 PLAYBOY FALLS FOR THE GIRL NEXT DOOR

"Jesse Edwards?" Trevor said to Dana on the other end of the phone. "And he signed a release?"

Trevor listened for a few more minutes, thanked her, then hung up. He steepled his hands under his chin and gazed thoughtfully out his office window. The bright lights of downtown L.A. glittered like jewels against the dark sky. Jane Roberts and Jesse Edwards. Now, *that* was a relationship that would get ratings. Hollywood's number one playboy falls for the girl next door. It was one thing for Jane to be dating that wannabe-photographer. Granted, he had the looks, but they'd had to edit out about 90 percent of his sound. All the guy could talk about was his passion for Italian food. *Not* what the audience wanted. Not what *Jane* wanted. It had been nearly impossible to finesse those scenes to make it look like Jane was even remotely interested in him. The casual flirting at Les Deux and elsewhere didn't do much for story lines, either.

239

Trevor had been nervous that Jane might have been interested in her so-called "friend," Braden James. Braden was an actor, and actors usually refused to sign releases for reality shows. As it turned out, Braden was no exception. If Jane had decided to date him, Trevor would have had to put an end to it somehow. If someone couldn't be filmed, then that someone couldn't be part of Jane's reality. It was as simple as that.

But Jesse Edwards . . . that was a whole different story. Of course he signed the release; it meant getting two of the things he loved most—a pretty girl and attention.

Trevor picked up his phone again and punched a number. "Tonight's footage. I want to see it immediately. Have it sent to the edit studio."

Trevor could practically *see* the numbers going through the roof.

31

LOVE AT FIRST SIGHT

"Sam Roca Chica," Jesse said. He lifted his glass in a mock toast.

Jane pushed her salad around with her fork. "Huh? What's that?"

"My porn star name," he replied, his light eyes smiling. "It's your first pet combined with the street you grew up on. What's yours?"

Jane thought for a moment. "Fluffy Santa Cruz," she said, laughing. "Sexy, huh?" It was a weird conversation to be having with Jesse on their first date. She used to play this game in middle school with her friends.

"Was Fluffy a cat or a dog?" Jesse asked her.

"Umm, she was a hamster," Jane said, feeling a little embarrassed. "I couldn't have cats or dogs. My mom's allergic to them. What about Sam?"

"Sam was my dog," Jesse said with what seemed liked a sad smile. "She was part collie, part German shepherd, and part, like, twenty other breeds. My mom wanted me to get some foo-foo purebred or some genetically engineered freak dog like a puggle. But I found Sam when Braden and I went to the pound, and it was love at first sight. She was the best dog."

Jane hesitated. "Was?"

Jesse looked down. "Yeah. She died last year. She was fourteen. I was gonna get another dog. But I can't replace Sam, ya know?"

"Aw. I know."

Jane stared at Jesse for a moment, studying him as he busied himself cutting his Kobe rib eye steak. He was nothing like she expected him to be. But what had she expected? A smooth guy with a line for everything? A dysfunctional celebuspawn with issues? An egomaniac who couldn't stop talking about himself (aka Paolo 2.0)?

But Jesse was none of these things. He had been nothing but a gentleman since the moment he had called her two days ago, asking her out to dinner. He had picked her up in his black Range Rover, and as they drove he played her a mix he had recently made of songs by groups like Death Cab for Cutie and MGMT and Postal Service. He was still getting comfortable in front of the *L.A. Candy* cameras, which had followed them the entire time and were set up now in the far corners of the dining room of Geisha House. Jane loved the restaurant, which was filled with a glowing red light and had a dramatic square-pillared fire-place in the center of the room, rising to the second floor.

From time to time, Jesse typed funny notes on his phone and sent them to her, just to avoid the mikes and make her laugh.

Jesse was definitely a mystery. She couldn't quite read him. Was his nice-guy act a part of his player personality? Or was he simply a nice guy?

"So what are your parents like?" Jane asked him. "I think I've seen most of your mom's movies. She got an Oscar for Best Actress last year, right?"

As soon as she had spoken these words, she felt dumb. *Way to sound like a fan, Jane. You should ask him for an autograph while you're at it.* But Jesse didn't seem fazed at all. He just took another sip of his drink and smiled at her. "Yeah, she makes me sit through them all," he joked. "She's pretty great though. I remember she was always working so hard when I was growing up. Both of my parents were constantly on location somewhere."

"That's so neat. Did you get to travel a lot?" Jane asked.

"No, I had school, so I normally got left with nannies. Actually, it was pretty cool, being able to run around and do whatever I wanted without parents yelling at me or telling me what to do."

Jane raised her eyebrows. "*Nannies,* plural? How many nannies did you have?"

"I don't know. I think I went through like one every six months. I was, you know, what they call a 'challenge.'" Jesse grinned.

He finished off the last of his drink and signaled to the waiter for another one. "I'm getting you another one too," he said.

"Oh, I'm good," Jane protested, but Jesse just shook his head and smiled charmingly at her. "Fine, one more," she relented, smiling back.

Not that Jane was counting, but this would be his third drink in less than an hour. She was only halfway through her first. The guy could sure hold his liquor. He was drinking straight Jack Daniel's and wasn't acting drunk at all.

"So how'd your meeting with Anna Payne go?" Jesse asked her.

"Oh, she had to reschedule. Fiona's stressed about it, 'cause New Year's Eve is only a coupla months away, you know?"

"I'm sure you guys'll make it happen. I'll be expecting an invite," Jesse added with a grin.

"I'll see what I can do."

Once Jesse had paid the check, Dana came up to their table and told them they just needed a moment to reposition cameras outside for their exit. Jesse had been in the process of pulling out Jane's chair. He stopped and sat back down. "Ooookay. Jane and Jesse's First Date, Exit from Geisha House, Take Two," he joked.

Jane grinned. "Yeah, no date in L.A. is complete without awkwardly waiting for cameras to film you getting into a car."

"Hey, maybe we should pretend to have a fight on the way out. Fights are good for ratings, right?"

"Yeah, but maybe not on the *first* date."

"Good point. We can save that for our third or fourth date."

Jane smiled, not knowing what to say. Third or fourth date? Was it possible that he liked her as much as she liked him?

Dana texted Jane, indicating that they were ready. As Jesse escorted Jane outside to his car, she felt sufficiently buzzed from her two martinis and slipped her arm through his, for balance. "You tired?" Jesse asked her.

"Mmm. Long day," Jane replied. She rested her head against his shoulder.

Jane didn't notice that there was a photographer standing behind one of the *L.A. Candy* cameramen outside the restaurant. As soon as she and Jesse stepped onto the sidewalk, the photographer jetted in front of the camera guy and started snapping pictures. Jane instinctively shielded her face with her hand. She could barely see through the flashes.

Jesse appeared unaffected as he opened the car door for her, but Jane was freaked out. She could hear Dana yelling at the photographer as Jesse made his way around the car. Jane turned to him as he slid into the driver's seat and started the engine. This was the first time she had been ambushed by paparazzi. It was actually a little scary.

"Take me home?" she said, trying to shake her jitters.

"Of course."

Jesse pulled up in front of her apartment building. They hadn't spoken much on the drive over, and it was still quiet in the car as Jesse put it in park and turned to Jane. It wasn't one of those bad, awkward silences. It was one of those good, goose-bumpy silences, filled with romantic tension and the big unanswered question: Would there be a good-night kiss? Jane's heart was racing. She was glad the camera crew hadn't followed them home.

"I had fun. Cameras and all," Jesse said softly.

"Me too."

"So . . . what are the chances of you letting me take you out again?"

"I'd say they're looking pretty good."

"Really?"

Jane laughed. "Yes. Really."

"Well, how about next Saturday?"

Jane pretended to think about it. "Hmm. *Maybe*."

Jesse smiled, then put both his hands on her face and leaned over to kiss her. Her heart skipped. God, the guy knew how to kiss. Jane surrendered to the feeling of it, wishing it would last forever.

32

NUMBER ONE

Trevor leaned forward in his chair as he reviewed the night's footage. *Perfect,* he thought eagerly. He could not have predicted this pairing, but Jane and Jesse came alive on the screen. He could see the chemistry between them. This kind of romantic drama could make the ratings jump sky-high. They were already number one and with this, they would break records. Now, if only he could keep the relationship going long enough to hook viewers before things turned ugly. He knew Jesse Edwards's history all too well. Everyone in Hollywood did.

Although perhaps that inevitable ugliness could be managed, tempered somehow.

Mesmerized, he stared at the footage that continued to roll on his screen, of Jesse touching Jane's arm and whispering something to her (the mikes didn't catch it) as they left their table. The cameras then zoomed in on Jane's face. She had that sweet, wonderful, infatuated look that no amount of directing, editing, or retouching could fabricate. Trevor could already picture the episode in his mind . . . hear the music he would set in the background as Jesse and Jane gazed at each other (something by Eliott Smith, maybe "Say Yes") . . . see the fade to black as the end credits rolled . . . imagine audiences everywhere sitting at the edges of their seats and wanting more . . . feeling like having to wait an entire week to see what happened next to their favorite new reality couple would drive them crazy.

This couldn't have worked out better if he had written it himself.

33

WHO ARE THE HOT PROFESSORS HERE?

Scarlett hurried down the hall, her backpack slapping against her side as she tried to tune out the chattering voices of Madison and Gaby. Her phone vibrated in her pocket—*again*. She was 99.9 percent sure that it was Dana—*again*. The producer kept texting her and telling her to please slow down and *talk* to the two girls. Scarlett decided to ignore it. Just ahead, the cute camera guy—she thought his name was Liam—bumped into a student as he tried to walk backward to keep up with Scarlett's frenetic pace and film at the same time. Scarlett felt a little bad but kept walking as he was readjusting his equipment behind her. He and the rest of them would catch up later. And if they didn't? Well, they had enough footage.

"Hey, wait up, Scarlett! These Manolos aren't meant for jogging, ya know?" Madison complained cheerfully.

"I love U.S.C. I'm gonna sign up!" Gaby said. She

peered through an open doorway at a crowded biology lab and waved.

"Who are you waving to?" Madison asked her.

"I dunno. Someone waved at me." Gaby shrugged.

Scarlett sighed. Why had she agreed to give Madison and Gaby a tour of the campus for the show? Probably for the same reason she had "agreed" to wear a freaking bathing suit in that photo shoot: She didn't seem to have much choice in the matter. Whose stupid idea of "reality" had this been, anyway? Like Madison was really serious about going to college. Like Madison was really serious about *anything*. Gaby had no interest in college, but had come along "just for fun." Scarlett glanced impatiently at her watch, wondering how much longer she was going to have to drag these two around.

Madison pulled her phone out of her bag and stared at the screen. "So. Who are the hot professors here?" she asked Scarlett.

Scarlett stopped and gave Madison a withering look. "Seriously?"

"I saw a really cute guy giving a lecture in room one hundred something. I wanna take *his* class," Gaby said.

Madison looked down the hall at the crew, who hadn't started filming again.

"Sweetie, I don't think college is for you," Madison told Gaby. "You've gotta graduate from middle school first."

Gaby's eyes widened with hurt.

"Gaby, you'd love my photography class. The professor's cute—*and* he gives interesting assignments," Scarlett cut in. Why was she being nice to Gaby? She didn't even like her. Still, she liked Madison even less. Why did Madison have to be such a bitch to Gaby whenever the cameras weren't around? And often when Jane wasn't around, now that she thought about it.

Gaby smiled at Scarlett gratefully. "Really? I *love* photography. When I was little, I wanted to be a famous fashion photographer, like in *Vogue.*"

"That's funny, because—" Madison began.

"That's cool, Gaby," Scarlett interrupted. Seeing that Cute Camera Guy and crew had caught up with them and were filming from an angle behind Madison, Scarlett had an idea. Time to rein in the bleached blond bimbo. "So, Madison? Where did you go to high school?" Asking Madison about her childhood seemed to bring out the ultra-bitchy pretentious side of her.

Madison didn't disappoint. She tossed her hair over her shoulders. "I went to a private boarding school in Switzerland," she said huffily.

"Really? Which boarding school?"

"I'm sure you've never heard of it. You don't seem like the boarding school type."

"Oh, yeah? And just what *is* a boarding school type?"

"Well . . . not you, sweetie. No offense, but you and

Jane have got 'public school' written all over you—"
Madison stopped abruptly, noticing the cameras with a
worried expression.

Scarlett gave her an icy smile. Too late, bitch. They've
got you on tape. And it was just the kind of catty remark
she could see making the cut. She couldn't wait until Jane
saw this footage. Jane was in for a big surprise when she
witnessed Madison being a royal snob. A royal bitch *and* a
royal snob. Maybe then, Jane would stop talking about the
girl like she was the second coming.

When they reached the end of the hallway they
headed outside. Scarlett hoped this would signal the
end of her "tour," but the cameras followed. The early
November air was pleasantly cool, in the low sixties. Off
in the distance, Scarlett spotted Cammy—dressed in a
tank top and super-short shorts—talking to a couple of
guys. Uh-oh, better make a detour. After their initial
meeting in August (when Cammy had invited her to
rush), and right up until *L.A. Candy* started filming on
campus, the girl had been ice cold to her. But after that
first shoot in Professor Cahill's class, Cammy had started
hounding Scarlett nonstop, inviting her to parties and to
the movies and to study circles and everything else under
the sun. There were a few others like her too—classmates
who had never paid any attention to Scarlett before the
show, and who now swarmed around her every time she
walked into class and fought to sit next to her. Of course,
this was in stark contrast to the bunch who gave her the

evil eye every time the cameras were on-site.

But despite her new (admittedly small) fan club, Scarlett still hadn't made any real friends at U.S.C.—that is, friends who liked her for her and had no interest in being on TV. For one thing, she was too busy with other stuff, like classes, homework (which took up four to six hours a day), and dealing with Dana's annoying, OCD schedules. She had also started going to the gym every day—it was a good way to release her pent-up whatever—and rereading all of Gabriel García Márquez's novels, in the original Spanish. Just for fun.

But lack of time wasn't the real problem. The truth was that she didn't want to subject anyone worth being friends with to releases and cameras—i.e., the whole messed-up *L.A. Candy* package.

Scarlett had even slowed down in the hookup department. She'd originally thought she'd enjoy shocking TV viewers with the details of her active sex life. But she'd found that she didn't enjoy the invasion of her privacy. She didn't *want* America to see her hookups "as created and produced by Trevor Lord."

Her phone vibrated: *Bzzzzz!* Frowning, Scarlett peered at the screen. **CAN YOU PLZ TALK TO M AND G ABOUT THE SCHOOL? AND CAN YOU SMILE A LITTLE MORE?** Dana had written.

Whatever, Scarlett thought, annoyed. Plastering a bright, fake smile on her face, she first turned to the cameras, then to Madison and Gaby. "Soooo! You wanna go grab some lattes and maybe check out the library after? You could help me do some research for my paper on the Tokugawa period in Japanese history," she said in a bright, fake voice.

"Huh?" Madison and Gaby said at the same time.

Scarlett's phone vibrated again. Obviously she hadn't gotten it right.

But that was just it. She didn't *want* to get it right.

This time her smile was real.

34

SO YOU AND JESSE
ARE GOING OUT NOW?

Jane slipped her arm through Jesse's as they walked into the Arclight. They'd only been on a couple dates so far, but being with him felt so comfortable already. It was a Friday night, and the enormous, modern lobby was packed with people staring up at the big, lit-up "departure board" displaying movie titles and times. Out of the corner of her eye, she saw several *L.A. Candy* cameramen filming their entrance.

"You sure you're ready for this?" Jesse teased. "You can still bail, you know."

"I love scary movies," Jane replied. "I say, bring it on."

Jesse looked so handsome tonight, dressed in jeans and a gray cashmere sweater that accentuated his broad shoulders. Jane was wearing a white silk peasant top over skinny jeans and brown wedge shoes. As they made their way through the lobby, people pointed and whispered excitedly. Some of them even took pictures of her and Jesse with their cell phones. The show had been airing for about a month, but Jane still wasn't used to the attention she was getting from it. And walking in on the arm of Jesse Edwards—well, that meant *double* the attention.

She and Jesse got some popcorn and a soda to share, then headed for their theater. A young employee offered them each a pair of oversized yellow-framed glasses.

"It's in three-D?" Jane asked, surprised.

Jesse grinned. "Yeah. *Now* you wanna bail?"

"No way. I haven't seen a three-D movie since . . . I don't even remember when."

"This movie's gonna be amazing in three-D. The three other times I saw it, it was in a regular theater."

"You've seen this movie three times already?"

"Yeah. With Braden. It's tradition for us to see horror movies together." At Jane's expression of doubt, he laughed. "We watched them together growing up all the time. Whenever I'd crash at his house, we'd stay up super-late watching scary movies."

Jane smiled casually, trying not to react to the mention of Braden. She had spoken to him only once since the house party. He had called her the day after Jesse had taken her to Geisha House. Their conversation had been—well, *awkward* would be putting it mildly.

"So you and Jesse are going out now?" he'd said.

"Um, well, we went out last night." She hadn't told him about the date herself because the idea of calling him to say, "Jesse asked me out and I said yes," felt lame when chances were he wouldn't even care. It would be like holding a sign that read, "I like you and you don't like me back." *Liked*, she reminded herself. *Liked* him.

"He said you're going out again next weekend."

"Yeah," she said, noting an edge in Braden's voice she'd never heard before. "What's your point, Braden?"

He took a deep breath. "I know this is a strange thing to say about my best friend, but he's not your type. Don't get me wrong, I love Jesse like a brother. But I just don't see you guys together."

"What are you talking about?" She felt a little bubble of hope at what sounded like jealousy, which was kind of frustrating because she was *over* Braden. She liked Jesse.

"Look, you're my friend. I care about you. I don't want to see you get hurt."

Oh, of course. Your friend, Jane thought, and the little bubble of hope burst, leaving even more frustration in its place. "I'm a big girl," she said coldly. "I know how to take care of myself."

And that had been the end of it. He hadn't called or texted her since that conversation almost two weeks ago. Jane had wondered, more than once, why Braden had tried to talk her out of going out with Jesse. *Was* it jealousy? Or was it just Jesse's history with girls? Jesse had told her when they went out last Saturday night that that had been a stupid phase, a thing of the past. Jane didn't know him well enough to tell if he was being totally honest and sincere. But he had *seemed* totally honest and sincere. That was enough for her. Besides, they were just

257

dating. It's not like they were getting married or whatever.

Jane followed Jesse into the already-dark movie theater and sat down in their reserved seats. When she jumped and let out a quick scream at a particularly frightening part (thankfully, she wasn't the only one; everyone else in the audience screamed too), Jesse put his arm around her. His arm felt good: strong, warm, protective. Jane snuggled a little closer, and felt his face brushing against her hair, which made her shiver.

After the movie, Jesse led her to the Arclight Bar, which took up one half of the lobby. Three of the *L.A. Candy* cameramen were positioned in the corners, shooting continuously. Jane wondered what the crew had done while she was in the movie. Maybe they had gone to a crew meal?

Over martinis, Jane and Jesse talked for the next hour. He told her about how he had dropped out of U.C.L.A. to work in finance for a friend of his father's, but had quit that and was now thinking of going back to school, maybe to major in business. She said she hadn't totally ruled out college either. He talked about spending a lot of time at Braden's house when they were kids since his own parents traveled to be on location so much. He told some funny stories about all the trouble he and Braden used to get into, and she reciprocated with stories about her and Scarlett.

Over the course of their conversation, Jane found that the mention of Braden had less and less of an effect on her. Braden was her friend. He had never indicated to her that he wanted anything more than a friendship. But Jesse was right here, right now. He was handsome, he was sweet, he was fun. And he liked her as *more* than a friend. Jane realized it was time she truly let go of whatever feelings she'd harbored for Braden and move on to something *real*—Jesse and whatever tonight (and their next date and their next date beyond that) might hold for them.

Jesse's voice cut into her thoughts. "You ready to go home?"

Jane shrugged. She'd had two martinis—one fewer than he'd had—and she was starting to feel their effect. "Yeah, I'm a little tired. I spent the last few days driving all over L.A. doing stuff for Fiona. Things were kind of not-busy with her for a while, and now they're crazy-busy again. I knew the job was going to be a lot of work, but I was hoping I'd be more than a glorified errand girl, you know?"

"You just have to be patient," he counseled. "I'm sure Fiona will come to her senses eventually and realize that you're great and give you real stuff to do."

"I hope you're right."

"Oh, I'm right. You're definitely great." He flashed his big grin at her, while she willed herself not to blush. "So great that I've been talking about you to my friends for weeks. I really want you to meet them."

"Your friends?" Jane repeated. Her mind immediately flashed to Braden. She wondered if Jesse discussed her with him. She didn't dare ask.

"My birthday is in two weeks," Jesse went on.

Jane leaned over and kissed him lightly on the cheek. "Really? Happy birthday!"

Jesse smiled and pulled her in for another kiss. Jane smiled back.

Breaking from a kiss, Jesse continued, "So like I was saying, I'm gonna be twenty-one. I thought I'd get some friends together at Goa. 'Course you know Braden already, but there's a bunch of other people you haven't met. I'd love it if you could be there. You should invite your friends too. Like Scarlett. And Madison and Gaby and whoever else you want. It'd be nice for me to get to know them."

Jane wondered if Jesse knew what her friends thought about him. Scar giving him the cold shoulder whenever he picked Jane up at the apartment might have tipped him off.

"Absolutely," Jane said. "I'll text everyone as soon as you tell me the date and time." She stopped and studied him. He was staring at her with an expression she couldn't read. "What? Why are you looking at me like that?"

"Sorry. It's just that you're so beautiful."

"I am *not*."

"You are. You know I'm kinda crazy about you, don't you?"

"Hmmm . . . or maybe you're just crazy, period," Jane teased.

Jesse reached for her and kissed her again. *I'm kinda crazy about you too,* Jane thought as they kissed.

35.

MAYBE IT'LL BLOW OVER

Scarlett was in her room, watching *L.A. Candy* on TiVo. She and Jane had seen the first couple episodes together, Jane excited and laughing at how crazy it was to have their lives edited into perfect half-hour segments, and Scarlett cursing and horrified at how the producers chose to package them into pretty little clichés. But Scarlett was watching tonight with a purpose: to see if this might be the episode where she had tricked Madison into showing her true colors during her tour of U.S.C. She hoped it was, and she hoped the producers had the sense not to cut those scenes. She was trying to fast-forward when she heard Jane come through the front door. The clock on the DVD player said 1:14. Scarlett quickly stopped the show and switched to Comedy Central—she wanted to see it alone first before revealing Madison's true nature to Jane. She listened, making sure Jane was alone. Hearing only one set of footsteps, she called out, "Hey! Wanna come watch TV?"

No answer. A moment later, Jane walked by, digging through her purse. She glanced briefly in Scarlett's direction. Scarlett saw that her cheeks were flushed pink, and her eyes were . . . glowing. Dreamy. Scarlett stared at her for a minute, disoriented. She hadn't seen Jane look like that in ages. Not since Caleb, during their first blissed-out year before he took off for Yale and decided to redefine "monogamy." That was Scarlett's theory about him, anyway.

"Um . . . how was your date with the man-whore?" Scarlett yelled from her room. Jane had been dating Jesse Edwards for about two weeks now, and Scarlett had been giving her a hard time about it the whole time. She had seen all those tabloid articles featuring Jesse.

Jane took a few steps back and popped her head in the doorway. "His name's Jesse," she corrected her in a cool voice. "It was good."

"It was?"

"Yep." Jane smiled.

She walked into the room and slid into bed beside Scarlett, checking a text message. Scarlett leaned back to take a peek. It said: **I REALLY HAD A GREAT TIME TONIGHT. CANT WAIT 2 SEE U AGAIN.**

ME TOO, Jane typed.

Vomit, Scarlett thought. *Way to play it cool, Jesse.*

"Uh, Janie? Not to be a buzzkill, but we're talking about Jesse Edwards, right?" Scarlett said in as gentle a voice as possible. "How many times have we seen his picture in *Gossip* magazine? And how many different girls have we seen *next* to him in those pictures? I'm just saying . . ."

"He told me that was a stupid phase he went through, and he's trying to get away from all that now," Jane said defensively. "I guess one of his friends from high school died in a DUI a few months ago, and it really shook him up and changed his perspective on stuff."

"Seriously?"

"Yeah, seriously."

Jane turned her attention back to her phone, intently pressing buttons. Scarlett didn't know what to do. Her best friend had a bad history with boys, and bad judgment too. Caleb had burned her. Braden, with his nearly invisible but definitely very real girlfriend (she didn't care what Braden called her—she was a girlfriend), had *almost* been a huge mistake. Jane was probably still recovering from both Caleb and Braden on some level and was vulnerable to male attention of any kind—especially male attention from someone as hot as Jesse.

Maybe it'll blow over, Scarlett thought.

Then she watched Jane reading another text and smiling happily to herself. *Maybe not.*

"Well, just be careful," Scarlett said, feeling partly protective toward Jane, and partly annoyed that Jane was walking into another relationship with blinders on.

"What do you mean?"

"I mean, he's *Jesse Edwards*. You know he's probably

going out with like four other girls. He's a player."

Jane turned to face Scarlett. "You know what? I like him, and he's really sweet to me," she snapped. "New subject, okay? How's *your* love life?"

Scarlett didn't feel like answering the question. The truth was, she'd kind of been checking out Cute Camera Guy from the U.S.C. tour, Liam. He was not only hot, but he seemed smart, too. That day, she'd spotted him reading a copy of *One Hundred Years of Solitude*—one of her favorite novels—during a break.

She knew that the "talent" wasn't supposed to date the crew—Dana had gone over the ground rules in the beginning—but maybe there was a way around that?

Jane was staring at her, waiting for an answer to her question. Scarlett pretended not to hear and climbed off the bed. "I need a little TV-watching snack. Do you want anything from the kitchen?"

"I'll come with you," Jane replied, following behind Scarlett. "So how's your love life?" she repeated.

"Hmmm." Scarlett opened up the refrigerator. She gave it a moment, and then decided that even though she was kind of annoyed at Jane for not trusting her judgment about Jesse, she had to answer the question. She didn't want to say anything about her inappropriate crush on Liam, though. Not yet. "Nonexistent at the moment."

"Any cute guys at school?"

"Nah, not really."

"You're telling me that there are *no* cute guys at U.S.C.?"

Jane asked, teasing her. "There're, like, thousands of students there, right?"

"Yeah, well. I don't know. I've been kinda busy with papers and exams and stuff. And . . ." Scarlett hesitated, grabbing a bunch of grapes. "Don't you find it weird having the cameras around all the time? I don't want the entire country to see who I'm hooking up with, ya know?"

Jane shrugged. "I'm sort of getting used to it. Besides, it's not like they're with us twenty-four/seven."

"Sure feels like it sometimes."

Jane's phone buzzed on the counter just then, loudly. She glanced at the screen. "Oh, I gotta get that. Hello?" she said brightly. "Hey, Jesse!"

Jane listened for a moment, then laughed. "Yeah, I know. What? You want to take me *where* Monday night?" She laughed again.

Sighing, Scarlett walked back to her room and shut the door.

36

A NEW OFFICEMATE

On Monday morning, after getting miked, Jane had two surprises waiting for her at work. She had a new office *and* a new officemate.

"This is Hannah," TV Fiona said, introducing Jane to a tall, slim girl with a slick honey-blond ponytail and intelligent brown eyes. ("TV Fiona" is how Jane had started mentally referring to her boss when she could tell she had scheduled hair and makeup for the days the cameras were there.) Hannah was sitting at a desk across from where someone (little elves?) had moved Jane's desk during the weekend, along with her Mac, her disorganized filing cabinets, and her sad, half-dead plant. The two desks faced each other, with a wide aisle in between. The office was three times as big as her previous office/storage closet. Two *L.A. Candy* guys were shooting in the corners, their cameras arcing between Jane, Hannah, and Fiona. At least those guys would have a little more space now.

"Hey." Jane shook Hannah's hand as she surveyed her outfit: navy, high-waisted pants, a white silk blouse, and a single strand of long pearls. Hmm, conservative, but pretty.

"Hi, it's nice to meet you," Hannah said. She had a sweet, friendly smile.

"Hannah's going to be here part-time, helping me—and you—with some of our events," Fiona explained.

"Great!" Jane said enthusiastically even though she was wondering if it really took *two* people to pick up dry cleaning, lunch, raw honey, or whatever not-TV-Fiona wanted.

"I thought you could fill her in on our day-to-day schedule. Why don't you start her on the phones and filing system, and then I'll see you both in my office in an hour," Fiona said.

"Sure," Jane and Hannah said at the same time.

"And Jane? Don't forget, Anna Payne's going to be here at three."

"Yes, of course."

After Fiona left, Jane turned to Hannah. If the girl was impressed by the mention of Anna Payne's name, she didn't show it. "Sooo. Is this your first job in event planning?" Jane asked her.

"No. It's my second," Hannah said. She studied the Mac on her desk and switched it on. She picked up the phone on her desk, pressed some buttons, and nodded to herself. "I used to be an intern at David Sutton's."

Jane recognized the name immediately. David Sutton was probably Fiona's top competition in the L.A. market. "Why'd you leave?"

"I interned there for, like, a year. David was awesome, but he couldn't hire me. He warned me that working for Fiona could be rough, but this seemed like too good an opportunity to pass up. Might as well get out of my comfort zone and challenge myself. Know what I mean?"

Jane's eyes widened. Hannah's words reminded her of the things she had said to Wendell and Dana during her *L.A. Candy* interview. "Yeah, I know exactly what you mean," she said with genuine enthusiasm this time.

Jane spent the next half hour showing Hannah the phones and filing. But Hannah was a quick study, and she hardly needed to be trained. She was already familiar with most of the office systems.

She also seemed to be a quick study in front of the cameras. She didn't look nervous or self-conscious at all. *Some people are just naturals at this,* Jane decided.

"So. What part of L.A. do you live in?" Jane asked her, making conversation as they sat at their respective desks, sorting through piles of caterers' bills.

"Third Street by the Grove. How about you?"

"Oh, I live in West Hollywood, too. Right by there. At the Palazzo."

Hannah whistled. "Wow, I live in the Villas. We're neighbors. I love that area."

"Yeah, my roommate and I are pretty lucky to have

found it," Jane agreed, not mentioning that *Trevor* had found it—and that PopTV was paying for it.

Hannah stared at her computer screen. She was no doubt admiring the screensaver of the fat Buddha figure, Jane thought in amusement.

"So do you live with a boyfriend roommate or a *room-mate* roommate?" Hannah asked after a moment. "Sorry, is that personal?"

"No, not at all." Jane laughed, wondering if Hannah didn't really know or if she was just asking for the sake of the cameras. Not that Jane had started assuming everyone knew who she was, but she figured Hannah might know since she was being filmed and would likely show up on *L.A. Candy* soon enough. Signing a release may have even been part of the application process. "I live with my friend Scarlett. I don't have a boyfriend. There's a guy I'm kinda dating, but we're not, like, together." She blushed happily, thinking about Jesse.

Hannah grinned. "Ooh, you're all glowy. What's his name?"

"Jesse."

"How long have you guys been dating?"

"Just a couple of weeks," Jane replied. "The thing is . . ." She hesitated.

"Yeah?" Hannah leaned forward.

Jane shook her head. She didn't want to tell Hannah, whom she'd just met an hour ago, about the details of her relationship (could she even *call* it a relationship yet?)

with Jesse or about her friends' feelings about him. Sadly, Scarlett continued to have a bad attitude about him—and she had no problem expressing her criticisms whenever she was at the apartment. Which wasn't much, lately. (Was school really keeping her *that* busy?) Even Madison and Gaby seemed to be against him. Madison had called her a few days ago, telling her to "be careful." Gaby had texted her and said she personally knew five girls he'd gone out with and dumped within days. And of course, Braden had made his opinion of her and Jesse abundantly clear.

But Jane felt like her friends were dead wrong. So far, he was nothing like his old tabloid image. When they were together, his eyes never strayed from her. He treated her so well. And on Friday night after Arclight, when he'd dropped her off at her apartment, he'd whispered in her ear that she was different from any other girl he'd ever met. He'd said she was special.

Jane hadn't told anyone that yet, because she knew how everyone would react. But Hannah didn't know Jesse or Scarlett or Madison or Gaby. She was an outsider, which meant that she could be objective. Maybe Hannah was the perfect person to talk to about this.

"Anna, this is my assistant, Jane Roberts. Jane, this is Anna. Jane's going to be helping out with your New Year's Eve party," Fiona explained.

Jane stood in the doorway of the conference room, staring at the stunningly beautiful actress who was sitting across the table from Fiona. She wondered if Anna would remember their encounter at Les Deux. Or maybe she'd been too drunk that night to remember anything. On the other side of the room, a camera guy adjusted a knob before zooming in on Jane.

Anna smiled at Jane. The tabloids had dubbed it the "million-dollar smile" because of her full lips and perfect teeth. Jane couldn't help but be dazzled by it, even though the woman had been a total bitch to her at the club. "Pleasure to meet you, Jane," Anna said.

"Yes, it's a pleasure to meet you, too," Jane said, smiling back.

"Jane, why don't you sit down and talk to us about venues?" Fiona said.

"Sure." Jane took a seat next to Fiona, then pulled out her notebook and opened it to the first page.

"I did some research, and I came up with some possibilities," Jane began. "One idea is to have it on a boat." Neither Anna nor Fiona reacted at all, so Jane went on. "Or Rick's Place at the Hotel Figueroa downtown, which is a cool area." More blank stares. "Another idea is a rooftop at the SLS Hotel. I was thinking since we have nice weather in winter, might as well take advantage of it."

Anna's blue eyes lit up. "Love it! Jane, you're *good*."

Jane blushed. "Thanks."

"Maybe I should run it by Noah." Anna reached into her enormous silver Prada bag and pulled out her cell.

While Anna was busy with her call, Fiona turned to

Jane and gave her a thumbs-up sign. Huh? When did the boss lady start giving the thumbs-up sign? When the meeting was over, the camera guy took some quick shots of their good-byes and handshakes as they exited the conference room together.

As soon as the cameras were off, Anna glanced over her shoulder at Jane. She smiled and winked. "Just wanted to say—*love* your show," she gushed.

"That's nice of you, thanks! I'm a big fan of yours, too!" Jane replied. *Oh my God.* She couldn't wait to tell Lacie and Nora, who were both huge Anna Payne fans, about this meeting.

Anna waved good-bye and headed down the hall past dozens of cubicles, seemingly oblivious to the wake of worshiping stares she was leaving in her path. As Jane watched her go, she thought about the irony of it all. Just a few months ago, Anna Payne had blown her off big-time at Les Deux. Now she was one of Jane's fans. It seemed unbelievable to her.

37

A TIME BOMB WAITING TO GO OFF

Veronica thumbed through the photos that her favorite staff photographer, Manny, had just delivered. Jane Roberts getting into a Range Rover, Jesse Edwards grasping her arm protectively. The couple exiting Café Luxxe in Santa Monica, holding hands. Standing close together, buying popcorn at the Arclight.

Veronica went through the stack a second time. Excellent. She selected three from the pile. They would make a lovely spread. She made a note to reserve two full pages.

"Veronica?" It was her annoying little assistant, Diego. "Madison Parker here to see you."

Madison Parker? What did that publicity hound want now? Madison had approached Veronica at a movie premiere and introduced herself. Since then, she had been to the *Gossip* office a couple of times to see her, trying to peddle "juicy inside stories" in exchange for puff pieces about her own "rising career." Unfortunately, Madison's idea of "juicy" never amounted to much. And her "rising career"? Girls like her were a dime a dozen in L.A. She was lucky if she had a future selling Cellulite Busterz or organic cat food on the Home Shopping Network. Still, Veronica knew from experience that a good piece of info sometimes came from the unlikeliest of sources. *You never know what you'll find in the trash.*

"Fine. Send her in."

A moment later, Madison breezed through the door. As always, she was immaculately dressed—this time in a formfitting pearl gray dress with a plunging V neckline.

"Veronica," Madison said pleasantly as she slid smoothly into a leather chair. "Thanks so much for seeing me."

"I have a meeting in five minutes."

"No problem," Madison said. "I just wanted to pass on some information that you might find . . . interesting."

Veronica straightened some papers on her desk. "Yes? What?"

Madison leaned forward and lowered her voice conspiratorially. "It's about Gaby Garcia. She was at Les Deux last night for the *Dead at Dusk* video game launch party and she totally went home with Aaron Daly. I have pictures of them all over each other."

"Madison," Veronica said flatly. "Why you think I'd care about the questionable mating habits of Hollywood nothings is beyond me."

Veronica watched as Madison went through what looked like the five stages of grief before her beady little eyes landed on the spread of pictures on the desk—pictures of her costar Jane Roberts. Veronica noticed how the wannabe starlet's eyes narrowed. *Isn't that interesting?*

"You and Jane are good friends, right?" Veronica asked.

Madison looked up. She seemed to consider this, and then said, "You've seen the show. What do you think?"

Getting snippy with me isn't going to get you in the mag, honey. "Let me put it this way: How badly do you want to be profiled in *Gossip*?" Veronica asked. She knew she was taking a risk, but after years in Hollywood, she also knew how powerful a motivator jealousy was. And somewhere in the sweet little story about Jane and Jesse's sweet little romance, there was a time bomb waiting to go off. It was up to Veronica to be there at the very second it happened, so *Gossip* could be the first to run it—in full, fabulous, gory detail. And if by some chance there wasn't a time bomb after all . . . well, creating explosions was something Veronica was very, very good at.

Staying true to form, Madison barely hesitated before asking, "What do I have to do?"

"Find out what is really going on with Jesse and Jane," Veronica said. "There is no way he *isn't* cheating on her. I want names and I want photos."

Madison seemed to consider this. "I could do that."

"Good." Veronica glanced pointedly at her watch. "Don't come back until you have something."

"Fine."

Veronica waited until the girl was gone before allowing herself a slow, satisfied smile. She had an instinct that this arrangement just might yield results, and her instincts were usually dead-on. *That little nobody might be good for something.*

38

BIRTHDAY BOY

"I'm nervous," Jane whispered to Scarlett as they headed into Goa. One of the *L.A. Candy* cameramen was at the door, filming their entrance.

Scarlett looked her up and down. "Why? You look so pretty in that dress, and those peep-hole shoes are hot."

"Peep-*toe*," Jane corrected Scarlett, smoothing her black silk minidress. Scarlett prided herself on being igno- rant about fashion. On the other hand, ever since *L.A. Candy* had been on the air, Jane had gotten all sorts of free dresses and shoes to wear—including the ones she had on now—from publicists representing various designers. It was all so they could get that coveted line in a magazine, "Jane Roberts at Il Sole, wearing a black minidress by so-and-so designer." Jane had begun ripping the address sticker off the front of the boxes and saying they had been sent for *both* girls. It didn't really make a difference because most of the things that were sent, Scarlett was more likely to bury in her closet than actually wear. Tonight, Scar was dressed in her usual jeans paired with a black silk tee. "It's just that it's the first time my friends and Jesse are gonna hang out, you know?" Jane went on. "Not to mention we're totally late. *And* it's his birthday. So I want everyone to have a good time and get along."

Scarlett put her hands on her hips and cocked her head. "Translation: You don't want me to be a bitch to him."

Jane stared meaningfully at her friend. "Something like that."

"Got it."

Really? Jane thought. Lately Scar had been even more stubborn and difficult than usual. These days, Jane was having a hard time connecting with her best friend and confiding in her about stuff—especially her relationship with Jesse. They'd driven to Santa Barbara together last Thursday to have Thanksgiving dinner with their respective families. Scar had made so many sarcastic comments about Jesse on the way up that Jane felt like she had to say something. There was something about driving that made having difficult conversations easier.

"I know you don't trust Jesse because of his reputation," Jane had said to Scarlett. "But I'm the one who's been dating him for the last month. Don't you think I'd know better than the tabloids? Why can't you be happy for me?"

Scarlett had been quiet for a few moments, staring out the window, and Jane wasn't sure if she was going to respond. Then finally Scarlett turned to her and said, "Okay. You're right. I'll give him a chance. If he's the person you say he is, then I'm happy for you."

They had left it at that. And Scarlett hadn't made any nasty remarks about Jesse since. But she hadn't been particularly *warm* to him the few times he'd been over either. Jane could tell Scarlett hadn't changed her mind about Jesse, but she was trying to keep her criticisms to herself.

If Scarlett doesn't behave tonight . . . Jane didn't finish her thought. She wasn't sure where she was going with this. Would she give Scar an ultimatum, like start being nice to Jesse or we're not friends anymore? That seemed kind of extreme. Still, in more ways than one, it felt like she and Scarlett had been drifting apart lately. Was it just a phase they were going through or something more?

Once inside, Jane tucked her red clutch under her arm and glanced around, looking for Jesse's table.

"Can I help you?" a server dressed all in black asked her.

"I'm looking for Jesse Edwards's table."

"Right this way."

The waiter led Jane and Scarlett upstairs, to a more intimate room, where Jesse sat at a corner table covered with piles of presents and colorful cocktails. Two set lights hung overhead. Several *L.A. Candy* cameras were already there, shooting.

"Jane!" Jesse called out, waving. He quickly stood up, looking a little unstable, but still totally gorgeous in his black suit and white collared shirt with no tie.

Jane smiled uncertainly at him. She and Scarlett were only twenty minutes late, but in that time Jesse had clearly gotten a head start on the birthday cocktails. He seemed . . . drunk. She had seen him drink before. But they had spent most of their nights at quiet restaurants and movies, not clubs.

Jane went up to him and kissed him on the cheek. "Happy birthday," she whispered in his ear.

Jesse clasped her in a hug. It felt too tight, too intense. "I'm sooo fucking happy you're here," he whispered back, his words sounding slightly muffled. "It wasn't a party until you got here. Hey, let me introduce you to my friends."

"'Kay," Jane said. She wasn't sure what to make of Jesse's . . . *state.* On the other hand, it *was* his birthday. His twenty-first, in fact. Maybe the guy was entitled. It's just that she would have felt a little more comfortable if the whole thing wasn't being filmed. *Relax, Jane,* she told herself.

She turned and surveyed the table. Madison and Gaby were already there, sitting on the other end. Madison's magenta satin strapless sheath contrasted with the pale pink of Gaby's baby-doll dress. They both blew kisses at her, then returned to flirting with two cute guys with identical buzz haircuts.

On the other side of the two guys were D and Hannah, whom Jane had invited at the last minute. She was glad they'd made it.

"Hi, sweeties!" D called out, toasting Jane and Scarlett with his dirty martini. Was that a purple velvet smoking jacket he was sporting? "You are both to *die* for. And Jane? Your new friend Hannah here? Love!"

"Hi, Jane!" Hannah said, smiling shyly. She looked really pretty in a mocha shift dress with a loose bow accenting the V neckline.

"Hey, guys! Hannah, this is my friend Scarlett I told you about. Scar, this is Hannah, from the office," Jane said.

"Hi, Hannah-from-the-office. Nice to meet you," Scarlett said, waving.

Jane sucked in a breath when she spotted who was sitting across from D and Hannah. Braden. And next to him, Willow. Jane and Braden locked eyes for a moment. He smiled and gave her a little wave. She smiled back. Seeing Willow at his side, it occurred to Jane that maybe his silence or distance or absence or whatever had nothing to do with her and Jesse. Maybe he'd just been too busy with Willow.

". . . and these are my boys from high school, Antonio, Nelson, Howard, and Zach," Jesse was saying, pointing to the two guys with the same haircut and two other guys sitting near them. "And this is Tracey—"

"Trish," the girl—a striking blonde—corrected him with a giggle.

"Sorry, Trish, Winona, Ella, Starlie, and Lela," Jesse finished, going down a row of cute, mostly blond girls. "You already know Braden and Willow. Hey, everybody, this is Jane. And this is her friend Scarlett."

"Hey," Jane said, waving politely.

"So I'm gonna need a drink and a seat, birthday boy," Scarlett told Jesse. Jane smiled to herself. Good. At least Scar was trying.

"Straight to the point, huh? My kinda girl. Come, you sit next to me," Jesse said, taking Scarlett's hand and pulling her in his direction.

Jane frowned, confused. At that moment, Madison raised her cell phone in the air and snapped a quick picture of Jesse and Scarlett. "Scarlett, love your shirt!" Madison called out cheerfully.

Scarlett ignored Madison and glanced at Jane, then Jesse. "Uh . . . not that I want to deny you on your special day but that's Jane's seat. I'm gonna sit over there," she said, pointing to the end of the table where D was enthusiastically waving her over.

"Sure, whatever! Zach, I gotta go to the men's room. You gotta go to the men's room?"

"Yeah, man, I gotta go to the men's room." The guy named Zach rose from his seat and nodded his head in the direction of the bathrooms. He and Jesse disappeared before Jane had even had a chance to sit down.

Jane stared after them and took her seat. What the hell

was going on? Why had Jesse asked Scarlett to sit next to him? And since when did guys go to the bathroom together? She twisted a lock of her hair around her finger. This was *not* how she had imagined the evening. Not at all. She gripped her clutch nervously, and felt the outlines of her birthday present to Jesse inside.

Jane ordered a vodka soda from the server and sunk back into the couch. She watched one of the flickering lights on the table as the conversation and laughter rose and swelled around her. Five minutes passed, then ten. Various people asked her questions ("How long have you and Jesse been dating?" "Where'd you get that dress?" "Do you live in L.A.?"), and she was vaguely aware of answering them, but her mind was totally not present. Where was Jesse? He had been gone for almost fifteen minutes. Out of the corner of her eye, Jane noticed Braden watching her. He looked . . . worried. Sympathetic.

Feeling more uncomfortable by the minute, Jane started scanning the restaurant for Jesse. She spotted him from the balcony, weaving through the busy tables down below. He had his arm around some tall blond girl with serious boobs. Zach was following right behind, sandwiched between two tall, busty blondes of his own. Jane felt as though she had been kicked in the stomach. She bit her lip, trying not to cry. She turned her head to see if anyone else had noticed. She saw that Scarlett had spotted him as well. D and Hannah were both looking over at her with worried expressions. *Great, I have an audience for my humiliation,* she thought. Madison was pushing buttons on her cell phone and seemed oblivious.

Scarlett got up from her seat and rushed over to Jane. "Jane? You wanna go? This party's lame," she said in a low, angry voice.

Jane rose uncertainly to her feet. "I'm gonna go to the bathroom first," she mumbled. "Just wait for me here?" She took off just as Jesse and his entourage arrived at the table. She didn't want to be there for *that.*

When she got to the women's bathroom, there was a long line of pissed-off-looking girls. "This sucks. Why do clubs always have at least one broken stall?" one girl complained.

"If this keeps up, I'm gonna pee in that fancy potted plant over there," another girl piped up.

"Do your coke somewhere else!" a third girl shouted at the closed door marked *W.*

Ignoring the commotion, Jane crossed her arms over her chest and waited. She tried not to think about Jesse. In their few short weeks together, he had been practically perfect. She had come *this close* to falling for him. She knew he liked to drink. So did she. But she had never seen him drink this much. And she had never seen him even look at another girl, much less let one hang all over him. What had changed? Or was this the real Jesse?

Jane's head was spinning as she finally stepped inside the bathroom and shut the door. Once alone, she leaned over the cold, white porcelain toilet for several minutes, oblivious to the long line of impatient girls outside, oblivious to everything but the anxiety welling up inside her. Her face felt hot, sweaty. Her palms were shaking. *Deep breaths,* she told herself. But deep breathing did nothing to quell the rising tide of panic. She felt so sick. She felt a wave of nausea overtake her.

It was pitch-black outside when Jane woke up to the sound of her cell ringing on her nightstand. She groaned sleepily, reached over, and checked the number. Jesse. Again. He had been calling and texting her all night.

"Leave me alone," Jane mumbled at the phone, and tossed it on the floor.

Jane felt awful. She was so mad at Jesse for making her look pathetic in front of everyone. But she was even madder at herself. She had ignored what everyone had said and allowed Jesse to do the same thing to her that he had probably done to every other girl he'd dated.

What was so hard was that despite his behavior, she still cared about him. He had hurt her, but a part of her still wanted to see him again.

You idiot, Jane thought to herself as she looked at the wrapped present on the floor.

There was a framed picture of them inside. The picture was from one of those cheesy photo booths (she and Jesse had gone into one after seeing a movie together). The photo—four photos, actually—was a skinny strip of goofy black-and-whites: Jane and Jesse smiling; Jane and Jesse laughing; Jane and Jesse kissing; Jesse and Jane kissing some more and holding up their palms, as if to shield themselves from the paparazzi. The photos were so . . . *them*. Jane had framed the strip herself, wrapped the whole thing in pretty wrapping paper, and tucked it into her purse, to give to him after his birthday party, when they were alone.

It was her silly-shy-totally-awkward-Jane way of telling him how she felt about him. Because she was—or at least, she *had* been—pretty sure that he felt the same way about her.

Her phone started ringing again. Jane reached down and turned it off. Then threw it at the wall, hoping it would break into a million tiny pieces.

39

HOLLYWOOD'S NEWEST IT GIRL

"Do you think she's gonna break up with him?" Gaby asked Madison the next morning, over lattes at Starbucks. "I totally would. Or maybe she *already* broke up with him. Have you talked to her?"

"Hmmm," Madison said absentmindedly. She was too busy checking out the latest issue of *Talk* magazine. Inside was a photo of Jane with the blazing red headline: HOLLY-WOOD'S NEWEST IT GIRL!

WTF, Madison thought, irritated.

"On the other hand, he's super-hot, and he's super-rich, right?" Gaby went on, studying her nails. "So maybe with a guy like that, you let him get trashed and flirt with girls once in a while, as long as he makes it up to you later with nice presents. Like something that sparkles!" She giggled.

Madison turned the page, which featured a full-page spread about Jane and "her #1 new hit show, *L.A. Candy.*" *Her* show? When had it become *her* show? It was supposed to be a show starring all four girls. Of course, Scarlett's part was becoming more and more diminished as the season rolled on. The producers had to consistently cut out most of her footage because viewers didn't get her. Sure, she was gorgeous. But different. *Too* different. And kind of a loose cannon. On the show, she was meant to be seen, not heard. Madison wondered if she would even be on the next season. Well, if not—then good riddance.

Madison continued reading the article. It went on and on about how viewers related to Jane because, even though she lived a glamorous life, she still had that "every girl" quality.

"Every girl" quality? Gag.

And then the next line caught Madison's eye. "Jane is the breakout star on *L.A. Candy*."

Madison could feel the blood rushing to her head. *Calm down,* she told herself, feeling that she was about two seconds away from picking up her piping-hot latte and flinging it across the Starbucks patio at some poor, unsuspecting customer. Damn it. *Damn* it! How *dare* this so-called magazine treat her like this?

Madison forced herself to take a deep breath and read the rest of the article. It mentioned how Jane and Jesse's relationship was causing a major ratings spike. *Everyone* was tuning in to see America's favorite new TV couple. . . . It was really nauseating. Madison kept thinking back to that conversation she had with Veronica Bliss. Jesse was *not* a one-woman man, as he had demonstrated in spades at his party last night. Jane wasn't so innocent either. Madison saw the way Little Miss Every Girl kept glancing at her ex-crush Braden when she thought no one was looking. And Braden seemed more interested in staring at Jane than in entertaining his all-over-him girlfriend. He was practically craning his neck to see if Jane was okay when she caught Jesse with that other girl.

Madison sat up straighter. She might have just figured out the perfect way to dethrone Princess Jane. Because enough was enough. Jane *had* to go. And Madison had the perfect ally in Veronica, who was practically foaming at the mouth for a juicy scoop. Of course, Madison had those cell phone pictures from the party to share with the *Gossip* editor. But this could be even bigger . . . *way* bigger. And unlike the cell phone pictures, this would doubtless result in the sad, tragic downfall of poor Jane Roberts. Star today, slut tomorrow . . .

Gaby leaned forward, pouting. "Madison, what are you reading? You're not paying attention to a word I'm saying!"

Frowning at the interruption, Madison slid the *Talk* issue across the table. Gaby scanned the article, then scoffed. "Huh? That's annoying. Why do people keep calling her the star? Seriously, she's not even that pretty."

But Madison wasn't listening. She was plotting.

Madison watched as Braden walked into the bar of the Beverly Hills Hotel, aka Nineteen 12, which was relatively uncrowded for a Friday night. She was sitting in a structured brown leather loveseat, BlackBerry in hand, a single champagne glass shimmering in front of her.

She stared at him appreciatively. He was definitely cute. No wonder Jane liked him. She pretended to be over him, to have had eyes only for Jesse, but Madison knew that was bullshit, a lie Jane wished was true.

Braden saw Madison and waved. "Hey," he said, walking up to her table.

"Hey, Braden." Madison set her phone aside. "How are you?"

"I'm good," Braden replied, sliding into a smaller chair across from her.

There was a brief silence as he regarded her, his expression curious. Madison knew he must be wondering why she had called and asked him to meet with her, out of the blue.

"I know this is really random, but I wanted to talk to you about something, and I felt weird doing it over the phone," Madison began.

"Sure. What's up?"

"I'm just really worried about Jane right now. I'm not sure what to do. She's upset about what happened last Saturday at Jesse's birthday party, and I think they're kinda not seeing each other anymore, but she won't talk to any of us. I know you live with Jesse, and you and Jane had that little thing, so I just figured—"

"What *little thing*?" Braden cut her off.

290

"You know . . . I don't know if anything ever happened. But before Jesse, you two liked each other."

"Jane and I are just friends."

"Well, maybe you were just friends with her, but Jane was really into you. In fact, I remember her telling me all about you the first time we hung out off camera. She told me you gave her a teddy bear or something."

Braden frowned. "Wait, Jane liked me?" he murmured. He looked genuinely confused.

"Anyway, I just think she needs to talk to someone who she knows doesn't hate Jesse. She knows we all do. No offense."

"Um, yeah, okay. I'll talk to her," Braden agreed.

"Great!" Madison said with fake relief. "I think she's home right now. I'll text Scarlett and let her know you're coming. Seriously, she really needs you right now."

"Oh. Now? Okay," Braden said, getting up from his seat. "I'll head over now. Can you just text me her address?"

"Of course." Madison smiled at him as he left the table. As soon as he was gone, she turned and typed Jane's address into her phone, then she sent it . . . twice. The other person already had his instructions. Now with Braden on his way to Jane's, everything was going exactly according to plan.

40

WHY ARE YOU HERE?

It was Friday night, late, and Jane was alone in her bedroom. She could hear Scarlett in the living room watching TV, but Jane didn't want to talk to anyone, not even Scarlett. She wasn't in the mood for an "I told you so" lecture about Jesse.

The doorbell rang. Jane could hear Scarlett walk to the door and open it. There were quiet voices, then a light knock on her bedroom door.

"What?" Jane muttered under her breath.

"Jane? It's Braden." She heard Braden's familiar voice call out from the other side of the door.

Braden? Jane sat up and pulled her blanket around her shoulders, over her oversized white cotton V-neck.

"Come in," she said. He slowly opened the door, letting blue light from the television screen pour across her bedroom floor.

"So I guess you've finally come over to see my new

apartment?" she said. The joke sounded completely lame to her. She smiled apologetically.

Braden gazed at her without speaking. His eyes lingered for a split second on her thin tee before taking her in with a concerned expression. The only makeup on her face was a light trace of mascara under her slightly swollen eyes. Her complexion was pale and her hair hadn't been brushed. She knew she looked exhausted. Hannah had commented on it at work that day—not in a mean way, but in an "I'm concerned about you" way. Hannah had been the only person she felt she could really talk to all week. She'd missed a couple of days of work. Fortunately—if that was the right word?—Anna Payne had canceled the New Year's Eve party because her husband, Noah Moody, had gone off the deep end and almost OD'd in the bathroom of Hyde. *Another girl with relationship problems,* Jane thought bitterly.

"Hey," Braden said, standing in the doorway. "Can I come in?"

"Yeah. Sure." Jane glanced around her room. It was more of a mess than usual. There were clothes strewn across the floor.

Braden closed the door behind him and sunk onto the end of her bed. He sat there quietly for a moment.

"So how are you?" Jane asked, wondering what he was doing there. She didn't want to hear "I told you so" from him, either.

"Me? I'm good." He laughed kindly. "To be honest,

I'm kinda worried about you."

"Why? I'm fine," Jane said, sounding a little defensive.

"No, you're not. You haven't returned any of my calls or texts since . . . since last weekend."

"I haven't returned anybody's calls or texts since last weekend."

Braden reached over and smoothed a lock of her hair away from her face. His touch felt so nice. All of the feelings she had for him came rushing back. Her throat burned as she tried not to cry. Her lip trembled, and she felt a warm tear roll down her cheek.

"Jane." Braden reached over and wrapped her in his arms. She cried softly against his shoulder.

Jane shook her head and kept crying.

Braden hugged her tightly. "I'm so sorry. This is just what he does."

"It's f-fine," Jane stammered. "It's not like we were that serious, anyway," she lied.

"I tried to warn you about him, but I didn't want you to think . . ."

"Think what?"

Braden was silent. She pulled away and stared at him. He was looking at her with an intense expression in his eyes.

"Think what, Braden?" Jane repeated a little more firmly.

"God, Jane," Braden said, sounding frustrated with her.

"You know what. You knew I liked you."

What? "I did? So you're saying it's my fault that you didn't warn me?" she said angrily.

"No, that's not what—"

"Braden. You're dating Willow. Aren't you?"

"I just . . . ," he started.

"You just what? Why are you here?"

She put her hand over her eyes. Why was he doing this? He'd had his chance to be with her. Instead, he'd chosen to lead her on while he was seeing someone else— even if it *was* an on-again, off-again relationship. He knew she cared about him. When she was available he didn't want her. It took seeing her with his best friend for him to do something about it.

"I don't know, Jane. What am I supposed to do?" Jane had never seen him like this. "I've known Willow for, like, three years. It's complicated."

"That doesn't answer my question. Why are you here?" Jane snapped.

Before Jane knew what was happening, Braden leaned in and kissed her. She looked at him for a moment and said nothing. Then he kissed her again. She kissed him back. She wasn't sure if it was loneliness or desperation or what—but whatever it was, neither of them was stopping. She felt his hands sliding over her body and slipping the cotton tee over her head.

Soft light from the moon dimly lit Jane's bedroom. Her silk curtains rustled in the breeze that came in through her open window. She never closed the curtains because she was on the second floor, and there were no neighbors on that side of the property. She felt okay for the first time since last weekend. As she and Braden sank back onto her bed, she felt better than okay.

Jane was only half awake when she heard her phone. She reached over, eyes closed, and felt around for it. She heard a groan next to her and sat up immediately. She looked over to see Braden still asleep. Warm light filled her entire room. It was already morning? She didn't even remember falling asleep. Her phone beeped. She glanced at it to see that she had another message from Jesse. It read: JANE. I NEED TO TALK TO YOU. YOU WONT PICK UP MY CALLS SO IM ON MY WAY OVER.

"Shit!" Jane said out loud. Jesse was on his way over and Braden was still in her bed. He lived only fifteen minutes away. She glanced at Braden again. What had she done? Jesse would freak out if he found Braden here.

Jane shook Braden. "Hey, wake up!" He didn't move. She shook him again, harder. "Braden! I forgot I have to film this morning and the crew is almost here," she lied, sounding a little frantic. She felt bad about lying to him, but she *had* to get him out of the house before Jesse showed up. If she told him the truth, he might insist on staying, to protect her from Jesse.

"What?" Braden blinked at her, dazed, then glanced around her room. "When did we fall asleep?"

"I don't know, but the crew is on their way." Jane wrapped a blanket around herself and stood up. "They can't see you here."

"Okay." Braden sat up and reached for his jeans.

"I have to take a shower before they get here. Sorry." Jane rushed into her bathroom and locked the door behind her. She quickly twisted the shower handle, the water hissing as it began to run, but she didn't get in. Instead she slid down the wall and onto the floor with the blanket still wrapped around her, and pressed her ear against the door. She could hear Braden moving around in her room. "Leave," she whispered. A moment later, she heard her front door open and close. She sat on the cold bathroom floor praying that Braden didn't run into Jesse in the parking lot. Her heart was pounding. She shut off the shower and just sat against the wall, listening. She grabbed her bathrobe off the floor next to her and slipped it on.

About five minutes later, she heard a knock on the front door, then someone opening it. There were muffled, angry voices . . . Scar and Jesse. Was she trying to get rid of him? A moment later, she heard knocking on her bedroom door, and Jesse calling out her name. Jane prayed that he and Braden hadn't crossed paths.

She opened her bathroom door and peered out. Jesse was standing in her doorway. He looked as awful as she did. He stepped in, shutting the door behind him. The room was silent. He just stared at her. Her heart melted a little. He looked so broken. Without a word, he walked toward her and hugged her.

"I'm so sorry, Jane," he whispered.

"I know," Jane said, hugging him back. She was so confused. She had just been with Braden. And now she was with Jesse. She had feelings for both of them. *You're a mess,* Jane scolded herself.

Then Jane's blood went cold. As she looked over his shoulder she saw a note, taped to her bedroom door. It said:

JANE, I DON'T KNOW WHAT LAST NIGHT MEANT,
BUT I'M NOT SORRY. PLEASE CALL ME LATER.
BRADEN

Jane hugged Jesse tightly. What was she going to do? She couldn't let him see that note. He would know what she had done.

Jesse started to pull away and she hugged him harder, trying to find a way to keep his back to the door. After a moment he slipped out of her arms and turned to sit on her bed, where her door was in plain sight. Jane panicked. She grabbed his face and kissed him. "You taste like cigarettes," she improvised. It was the best she could do. "I didn't know you smoked."

"Oh, sorry," Jesse apologized. "I quit before, but then I started again a few days ago."

"I have mouthwash," Jane said, pointing in the direction of her bathroom.

Jesse stood up quickly and headed toward the bathroom. The moment he was out of sight, Jane ripped the piece of paper off her door and quickly shoved it into her laundry hamper. *What the hell am I doing?*

There was another knock on her bedroom door. "Janie, you okay in there?"

"I'm fine, Scar," Jane lied. "I'm totally fine."

41

THE *REAL* STAR OF *L.A. CANDY*

Madison lay back on her leather couch, the one that had cost more than a year's rent at her last apartment, and surveyed the photos. Despite the photographer's constraints—he'd had to take them from a distance, in the dark, and from the top of a tree branch—they were good. *Really* good. Thankfully, Jane didn't believe in closing her curtains. The guy had captured her and Braden making out, with her in nothing but her bra and panties, and him in his boxer briefs. *Hmm, he's definitely hot.* As an extra bonus, Jane looked awful, even though she was probably just tired and stressed out over what happened at Jesse's birthday party. That should make for a killer headline. HOLLYWOOD'S NEWEST IT GIRL HOOKS UP WITH BOYFRIEND'S BFF.

Oh, Jane, Madison thought. *You are so history after these photos are published.* And Jane deserved it. Didn't she?

Madison picked up her glass of wine and took a long sip as she went through the rest of the photos. She was so tired of hearing about Jane. Miss It Girl. America's Sweet-heart. Rising Star. *Gag.* She, Madison Parker, was the *real* star of *L.A. Candy.* And after everyone saw these photos of their precious princess behaving like a total slut, they would elevate Madison to her proper status.

When Madison reached the last photo in the pile, she hesitated, then held it up to the light. In it, she could see Jane's face clearly. She looked confused and lost. Like a little girl. For a moment, Madison felt a pang of some-thing. Guilt? Regret?

She glanced at the photo again. She knew that if she went through with this, she'd be crossing a line she wasn't sure she was ready to cross. She wanted to be number one. She *deserved* to be number one. But these photos would destroy Jane's reputation, her career, her life. Did she really want to be responsible for that kind of devastation? Jane, sadly, thought of Madison as her friend. Did she want to be the kind of person who could betray her friends? It's one thing to trade harmless gossip, like the item she'd given to Veronica Bliss about Gaby hooking up with that C-list actor at Goa. It's another to ruin someone.

Sighing, she rose to her feet, accidentally knocking over her wineglass, barely hearing the crash as the fine crystal hit the floor and shattered. She scooped up the photos and stuffed them back into the brown manila envelope.

I can always save them for later, she thought. *In case of an emergency.*

In the meantime, she would just have to keep trying

to persuade Veronica Bliss to write flattering pieces about her for *Gossip* in exchange for dishy little items about Jane, Gaby, Scarlett—or herself. Plus, she still had those cell phone pictures from Jesse's party. Madison smiled serenely. She was on the right track. The more publicity about herself, the better. People would eventually begin to notice her incredible beauty, her charm, her style, her . . . star quality. And they would clamor to see more of her on *L.A. Candy,* and less of boring little Jane.

Patience, Madison, she told herself.

42

I NEED SOME TIME TO THINK

Jane lay in bed, her room dark except for images that flashed across her muted TV. No Braden, no Jesse. She had told them both, separately, that she wasn't feeling well and needed to stay in tonight.

After Jesse had left that morning, she had taken a long shower, then spent the afternoon trying to figure out what to do. Should she be with Braden? Or Jesse? Or neither? What had she been thinking, hooking up with Jesse's best friend last night? This wasn't a game. This wasn't television. This was life—*her* life, and the lives of two guys she really, really cared about.

She'd gone out for a walk around the neighborhood, to clear her head, and returned an hour later with her decision. She needed time off from both Braden and Jesse. She wanted to be alone for a while, to think things through. And in the meantime, she needed to have zero contact with either of them. It was the only way.

An image of a couple kissing filled her TV screen. Jane winced, then picked up the remote and started clicking. News. Good. Nothing romantic about that. Keeping the volume off, she watched a story about a California wildfire, then another about a bank robbery, followed by the weather . . . and then she forced herself to turn her attention to her phone and do what had to be done. Her phone was on her nightstand next to B, the stuffed toy puppy Braden had given her on the night of the *L.A. Candy* premiere. She opened her nightstand drawer and placed B inside. She didn't need reminders.

She texted Braden first. HEY, I NEED SOME TIME 2 THINK, she composed carefully. PLEASE WAIT FOR ME 2 CALL U, OKAY? DON'T CALL ME. IF U CARE ABOUT ME, PLEASE RESPECT THAT. THIS IS ALL SO COMPLICATED. LOVE, JANE.

Before hitting the Send button she copied the message and sent it to Jesse.

43

SHE'S NOT WHO YOU THINK SHE IS

Veronica Bliss was in her office, trying to finalize the upcoming issue of *Gossip*. She had to go to press by the end of business. Should she go with one young actress who might or might not be addicted to diet pills, or another who had returned to rehab yet again? *God, I'm scraping the bottom of the barrel,* she thought, just as her intercom buzzed.

"Veronica? Madison Parker here to see you," Diego announced.

"Send her in."

For once, Veronica actually didn't mind the little fame-whore dropping by to see her. She had given her an assignment to dig up dirt on Jane Roberts and Jesse Edwards. She'd heard through other sources that the loving couple had had some sort of fight during his birthday party at Goa. What she needed now was details . . . and more important, pictures. Unfortunately, she'd found out about the party too late to send her own people.

Madison walked into the room, grinning from ear to ear like she owned the place. Veronica took a deep breath, quelling the impulse to take the girl down a notch. Maybe she had something. It was worth being polite, at least for the next forty-five seconds.

"Hi, Veronica," Madison said smoothly.

"Madison. What do you have for me?"

Madison reached into her bag and pulled out her cell phone. She handed it to Veronica. "You're gonna love these pictures," she said smugly. "Just click on the arrow—there are six of them, total."

Veronica took the phone and began scanning through Madison's photo gallery. The first picture showed a guy who looked like Jesse Edwards, sitting at a table, grabbing the hand of some girl who was standing with her back to the camera. Was that Scarlett Harp? It was hard to tell.

The second picture was almost impossible to make out too: a guy with his arm around a blond girl, taken from a distance. The other pictures were equally blurry, grainy . . . useless.

Veronica shook her head and tossed the phone back to Madison. It fell near her feet, and the battery popped out, clattering loudly across the floor.

"Shit, what are you doing?" Madison said angrily, bending down to pick everything up.

"What are *you* doing is a better question," Veronica said curtly. "I can't use these pictures. Next time, use a real camera, with a flash."

"But these are hot! They're from Jesse's birthday party at Goa. He was flirting like crazy with Scarlett—as in Jane's best friend? And the other pictures? He was practically making out with this random blonde with thirty-eight double D—"

"What random blonde? Do you have a name?" Veronica interrupted.

Madison frowned. "Um . . . no. But maybe I could ask around." Her face lighting up, she added, "Oh, and I have something else, too. I'm ninety-nine percent sure Jane has an eating disorder. She's lost weight. And at Jesse's party, she threw up in the bathroom. She forgot to turn off her mike, and the whole crew heard—"

Veronica raised her hand, silencing Madison. Enough. "That's not an eating disorder, Madison, that's a diet," she snapped. "One of my photographers saw Jane on the street yesterday. She looks better than ever. Seriously, unless you give me something worth printing, I'm not wasting any more time or magazine space with your coattail-riding ass. Now, give me something good, with pictures I can actually use, or you'll be lucky to make the 'Stars Are Just Like Us!' section showing you buying zit cream at CVS." She glanced impatiently at her watch. "Your time's up. And I'm not just referring to your fifteen minutes."

Madison's eyes blazed with cold fury. She seemed to be considering something.

"Fine," she said after a long moment. "You want pictures? I have pictures. Clear your next cover."

"*Excuse* me?"

"I said, clear your next cover. Believe me, it'll be worth it."

Veronica glanced at her watch again. But she wasn't actually looking at it. It was just an excuse to think. She had to admit that she was a little intrigued. "What pictures? Let me see them."

"I'll have them sent to you this afternoon—by a special messenger. He'll make your story even hotter."

"He? Who's *he*?"

"You'll see."

He was waiting for her at a corner table, nursing a watered-down-looking scotch and smoking a cigarette. It was two in the afternoon, and the bar was almost deserted. The only other occupants were a couple arguing in a corner booth. The place was a little depressing. But it was private.

"Hey, Jesse." Madison slid into the chair opposite him. "Thanks for meeting me."

The guy looked like crap. He had stubble on his face; his eyes were bloodshot. He'd either been drinking too much, not sleeping enough, or both. His two-hundred-dollar Thomas Pink shirt was badly wrinkled and untucked carelessly over his jeans.

Jesse sat up a little straighter. "How's Jane?" he said, without even bothering to say hello or how are you or any of the other usual niceties. Rude. "Have you seen her? Do you know if she's ready to talk to me? She said she needs her space, and I'm trying to respect that, but it's making me a little crazy." He sounded miserable, desperate. "I don't understand what's going on with her. I went to her apartment on Saturday morning, and I thought everything was cool between us. Then I got that text from her on Saturday night. Has she said anything to you?"

The bartender caught Madison's eye, but she shook her head, indicating that she wasn't drinking today. She had to stay clear-headed for what she was about to do. For a brief second, she thought about backing out. After all, what she was about to do would humiliate Jane. And Jane trusted her.

No, she told herself firmly. *You've gotta stay strong.* It was all Veronica Bliss's fault, anyway. If she hadn't been such a smug, awful bitch that morning, Madison wouldn't have changed her mind about using the photos.

"Jesse, you've gotta give up on her. She's not good enough for you."

"What are you talking about? Of course she is. *I'm* the asshole, not her."

Madison leaned forward and placed her perfectly manicured nails on his arm, silencing him. She let her lips curl into a meticulously calibrated smile: a little bit sympathetic, a little bit flirty. He glanced at her in surprise, then smiled back. It was a ghost of a smile, but it was definitely a smile. God. *Men.* They were so easy sometimes.

"She's not good enough for you," Madison repeated, keeping her hand on his arm. "You've seen the show. She exudes this image like she's this perfect little princess. But I know her. She puts on a good act. Deep down, she's not who you think she is. Who *anyone* thinks she is. She's just as messed up as the rest of us."

Jesse picked up his drink and took a long swig, his eyes never leaving her face. "What are you talking about?"

"So you wanted to have a little fun on your twenty-first birthday. So what?" Madison breezed on. "It's totally understandable. Everyone does it. Why did she make such a huge deal out of it?"

Jesse shrugged and took another swig of his drink. He looked thoughtful. *Good.* He was starting to come around.

"Jane, on the other hand, didn't have an excuse for what she did," Madison continued.

Jesse frowned. "What *she* did? What are you talking about?"

Madison reached into her bag and pulled out the brown manila envelope. She hesitated a moment before sliding the envelope across the table. "I'm sorry, Jesse," she said gently. "I really am. But I didn't want you to see these somewhere else first."

"What's this?"

"Just look inside."

Jesse stared at the envelope for a long second before picking it up and opening it. He pulled out the pile of photographs and tipped them up to see them in the dim light.

The first one was enough. The one of Jane lying on her bed dressed in nothing but her underwear, with an almost-naked Braden next to her, his hands all over her. Jesse's face tightened—first with shock, then hurt, then pure, hot rage.

"What . . . the . . . fuck?" he spat out.

"I know, I know. I'm sorry," Madison whispered, squeezing his arm. "It happened last Friday night."

"Friday night?"

Jesse went through all the photos again—twice, three times, four times. They were all variations on the same sordid theme: his girlfriend cheating on him with his best friend. It couldn't get worse (or, from Madison's perspective, better) than that.

"What . . . the . . . fuck?" he said again. He looked mad enough to kill someone. "Where did you get these?"

"From a reliable source. But that's not important right now," Madison said. "What's important is . . . *this* is the real Jane."

Jesse sat there for a long moment, saying nothing. He lit another cigarette and began smoking again. She waited a moment to let him digest everything. Then she made her next move. If nothing else, she was the queen of timing.

"She's been lying to all of us. America's Sweetheart isn't so sweet." Jesse looked up and Madison worried that he'd detected anger in her voice. Quickly recovering, she said, "I just hate what she did to you. You're a good guy. You deserve better." Madison moved even closer to him so that he could see her perfectly molded cleavage, smell her warm perfume, sense just how deeply, deeply sorry she was for his heartbreak. "There's someone you need to take these photos to. Someone who will know exactly what to do with them."

"Who?" Jesse asked her.

Madison told him.

44

OH . . . MY . . . GOD . . .

Jane sank back against the pillows, watching the morning sun streaming through the window and making lazy patterns on the cream walls. She glanced at her clock. It was a few minutes after seven. She remembered that it was Friday. Their weekly staff meeting had been rescheduled this week because Fiona had three important meetings lined up with clients. Anna Payne was one of them; the New Year's Eve party was still off, but she and Noah were back on, and she was hiring Fiona to plan their Valentine's Day recommitment ceremony. Anna was pretty sure he'd be out of rehab by then. Dana had scheduled cameras to be at two of the three meetings. It was going to be a busy day.

But first . . . shower. She rose out of bed and started for the bathroom when her cell phone rang, stopping her in her tracks. Phone. Where was her phone? She spo'
it on her floor, half-hidden underneath a white silk

She picked it up and smiled when she saw the name on the screen: Diego Neri. She hadn't seen him since the awful night of Jesse's birthday party. Now that she was taking a break from Jesse (and Braden, too), she had more time on her hands. She reminded herself to make a date to go out with D, maybe to a club. She should ask Scar to come with them too. They'd spent so little time together lately. She missed her friend.

Scar had been in a really good mood all week, ever since Jane had told her about taking a break from Jesse. She hadn't even given Jane an "I told you so" lecture. Jane hadn't told her about hooking up with Braden, though. Thankfully, Scar hadn't heard him sneak out of the apartment on Saturday morning. She hadn't told *anyone* that— not even Hannah.

"Hey, D," Jane said into the phone. "You're up early! Or have you been up all—"

"Jane!" D sounded semi-hysterical. "Oh God! I'm so, so, *so* sorry!"

Jane frowned at the phone. What was he talking about? "Sorry for what, sweetie?"

"Veronica gave me a few days off, so I had no idea what was going on. She knows you and I are friends."

"D, what are you talking about?"

There was a pause. "You haven't seen the new issue of *Gossip*?"

"No. Why?"

"These photos of you . . . someone leaked them to the

magazine. It's the cover, with a four-page spread. Ohmigod, Jane, I feel like jumping off a bridge! I should have prevented this somehow! I should have seen this coming and protected you and—"

Jane's blood ran cold. *What* photos of her? "Lemme call you back," she said, hanging up without waiting for D's response.

She jumped out of bed and ran over to her laptop. She could barely think straight as she Googled her name. What was going on? What were these photos that had freaked D out so much?

And then she saw.

They were not only on the *Gossip* website, but they were all over the Internet. Photos of her wearing nothing but underwear, looking awful . . . and in a very, very compromising position with Braden. Several positions, actually.

She felt as though she were watching a slow, hideous car wreck as she scrolled through the photos . . . and then the full story of how she had allegedly hooked up with her boyfriend Jesse's best friend just nights after Jesse's twenty-first birthday party, completely breaking Jesse's heart. (There was no mention of Jesse's own terrible behavior at Goa.) The story hinted—using the flimsiest bits of so-called evidence (Jesse had been spotted in the jewelry store Fourteen Karats . . . people at Fiona Chen Events had been speculating . . .)—that Jesse had been on the verge of giving her a promise ring to seal their "whirlwind romance" when Jane had done this to him. The story even hinted at other possible infidelities by Jane—nothing substantive, just wisps of ugly rumors.

"Oh . . . my . . . God," Jane whispered, unable to take her eyes off the screen. She couldn't breathe. "Oh my God . . . oh my God . . . oh my God!"

Jane clamped a hand over her mouth and shook her head. She felt numb. She was in absolute shock. It wasn't really happening. This couldn't be real.

But it *was* real. Everyone in the world, including her friends, her coworkers, the people at *L.A. Candy,* her little sisters, her parents . . . and *Jesse*, were going to see these photos. If they hadn't already.

Her cell started buzzing again. At the same time, the landline started ringing. "Just . . . go . . . away," she murmured. She collapsed onto the bed, slid under the covers, and began sobbing quietly into her pillows.

45

THAT'S WHAT FRIENDS ARE FOR

Scarlett pressed Redial for the hundredth time while pulling into the underground parking garage of her and Jane's apartment building. "Damn it, Janie. Answer your fucking phone!" she said, frustrated. She had been trying to call Jane ever since Cammy had come up to her in the library and shown her the *Gossip* website's pictures of Jane and Braden on her iPhone. *O-M-G! Is she okay? She didn't seem like such a slut on the show! But I guess you never know about people, right?*

Scarlett ran toward the elevators, her backpack slapping against her side. She'd left the apartment at 6 a.m., heading for the library to study for final exams. She should have stayed home. Why hadn't she stayed home?

Hurry. She had to hurry. Then again, what if Jane wasn't home? What if she was at work, hiding in the bathroom and freaking out? But she couldn't think about that now.

She noticed two paparazzi staked out near the elevators.

She stifled her shock. She had never seen them around the apartment building before.

As soon as they saw Scarlett, they rushed toward her. One of them began snapping pictures of her, and the other one attempted to balance a camcorder as he ran. Their voices tumbled over each other:

"Scarlett!"

"Hey, Scarlett!"

"Any comment on today's story?"

"Is this the first time Jane's cheated on Jesse?"

"How do you feel about Jane's pictures?"

"Move!" Scarlett snarled at them as she pushed her way to the elevator door, got in, and punched the number of their floor. Parasites. These paparazzi were the most awful people. *They* were responsible for all this. They had somehow Photoshopped pictures of Jane to make her look half-naked, and like she and Braden had hooked up. Jane and Braden had definitely *not* hooked up. Jane would have told her if they had. And now Jane was probably having a total breakdown. Scarlett knew her best friend did *not* deal with crises very well.

Just as the elevator doors slid open, Scarlett spotted someone coming up the stairs and heading toward her and Jane's apartment door. It was Madison. What was *she* doing here?

Scarlett strode quickly toward the apartment door, digging through her pockets for her keys. "Hey, Madison?

Jane's not really in the mood for company right now. Could you come back later? Like maybe next week?"

Madison turned around. Relief lit up her face. "Scarlett! I'm sooo glad you're here! I came up the back way so I could lose those photographers. We've gotta get in there and make sure Jane's okay!"

"Oh, I'm on it, thanks." Scarlett stepped past Madison and shoved her key in the lock. "Bye now."

"Scar? Is that you?"

It was Jane's voice, coming from inside. It sounded thin and hoarse, as though she had been crying. Scarlett pushed open the door and rushed in. Madison was at her heels. Fine, so she wouldn't be able to lose the bitch just this second. She would get rid of her after she'd checked on Jane.

Jane was curled up on the living room couch, still wearing her pajamas, her laptop propped on her knees. Her hair was tied back in a messy knot and her face was splotchy with tears. She didn't look up at Scarlett and Madison, but instead kept her eyes glued to her computer screen. She was clicking from website to website, her fingers listlessly punching keys.

"Janie?" Scarlett bent down and put her hands on Jane's shoulders. She glanced quickly at the screen, at one of Jane's photos accompanied by the blazing headline: L.A. CANDY STAR HAS SWEET TOOTH FOR HOOKING UP. "Janie, are you okay?"

"It's everywhere." Jane's blue eyes welled up with tears.

"I can't believe . . . Did you see?" She could barely get the words out.

Scarlett gave Jane a fierce, protective hug. "This is all bullshit, Jane, and you know it. It's gonna blow over. In the meantime, I'm gonna find out who faked those photos and—"

"Scarlett, they're not fake," Jane cut her off. She began crying again.

"What do you mean? They're real? You and Braden didn't—"

"We did. Just once. I didn't mean for it to happen. But when he came over that night . . ." Jane covered her face with her hands and began crying harder.

Scarlett's mind was reeling. Jane and Braden had hooked up? Why hadn't Jane told her this before? She and Jane had always told each other *everything*. Although Scarlett was keeping a few secrets of her own these days. She vowed to come clean with Jane soon—to be as close as they used to be before *L.A. Candy* came along.

And then something else—something more disturbing—occurred to her. "If these photos aren't fake, then who took them?" she asked Jane sharply.

Scarlett felt a hand on her shoulder. Madison leaned over and gestured to her, indicating that she wanted to talk to her privately. Scarlett moved back until she and Madison were standing a little ways away from Jane. "What *is* it?" Scarlett snapped. "Can't it wait?"

"Listen, this is important." Madison lowered her voice so Jane couldn't hear. "I didn't want to say anything before. But I have a couple of friends at *Star* and *In Touch*. Both of them told me that Jesse's been shopping these photos around at all the tabloids. I don't know how he got them, but—I guess he's pretty pissed about Jane cheating on him with his best friend. He felt humiliated. And he wanted to humiliate her back." Madison gazed worriedly at Jane. "Guess it worked."

Scarlett stared at Madison, trying to process what she was saying. "Jesse? *He* did this?"

"That's the word."

Scarlett sucked in a deep breath. Then she turned to Madison. "Can you stay with Jane for a little while? Don't answer the phone, and don't let anyone in the door. Get her off that damned computer, and no TV, either. I have something I have to take care of."

"No problem," Madison promised. "I'll stay here all day and night if you need me to. That's what friends are for."

Scarlett went back to Jane and gave her friend another hug. She could feel her trembling. "I'll be right back, okay? Madison's gonna stay with you. I promise everything is gonna be fine. This is all gonna go away."

Jane hugged her back and nodded without saying anything.

Scarlett scooped up her keys and rushed out the door.

★ ★ ★

"Open the door, Jesse!" Scarlett yelled.

No answer. Scarlett had been ringing the doorbell, shouting and pounding her fists against the front door for the last five minutes—but no answer. She had a strong suspicion that Jesse was home. His Range Rover was in the driveway, and she could see lights on inside. She wasn't sure about Braden. She didn't see his car. But she assumed he was probably at the closest coffee shop searching for apartments in the paper.

"Open up!" Scarlett shouted. The door opened a crack, and she saw Jesse standing there.

He looked like shit, as though he had been drinking and not sleeping for several nights. He was dressed in a pair of navy cotton pajama bottoms and nothing else. Scarlett shoved her way inside, smelling stale vodka on his breath as she got close to his unshaven face. "Listen, you asshole," she said, not bothering with any sort of greeting. "You're such a worthless piece of shit. Do you have any idea how low you are?"

Jesse rubbed his eyes and regarded her with a sad, tired expression. "I think you've got the wrong guy, Scarlett. Braden's out."

"Yeah, I'll take care of him next. How *dare* you? Jane *dumps* your pathetic ass, and instead of sucking it up like a man you go to the fucking tabloids and try to sell those sleazy photos of her and Braden? What makes you think you—"

"Whoa, whoa, whoa!" Jesse held up his palms. "Wait a

322

second. You think *I* gave those photos to the magazine?"

"Yeah, deny it and act innocent all you want. I know the truth."

"No, you *don't* know the truth. It was Madison."

"Madison?" Scarlett said, surprised. "Wait. What?"

"She asked me to meet with her a few days ago in some dive bar. I agreed, 'cause I thought maybe Jane had sent her to talk to me or something," Jesse explained. "That's when she showed me the photos. I have no idea where she got them. She told me I should get even with Jane by taking them to Veronica Bliss at *Gossip*."

"She . . . did . . . *what*?" The volume of Scarlett's voice quickly rose.

Jesse grabbed her arm. "Listen to me. Those photos made me sick to my stomach. I wanted to kill them both. I still do, to be honest. But there was no way I was gonna do that to Jane. I still care about her. I couldn't do that to her." He added, "I guess I shoulda warned Jane about what Madison was up to. I didn't think about that until it was too late."

Scarlett stared at Jesse for a long moment. She could see it in his eyes. He was telling the truth. He was still the same screwed-up, arrogant asshole who wasn't good enough for Jane. But in this horrible, awful instant, he *was* telling the truth.

Which meant that Madison—that psychotic bitch— had orchestrated all of this.

And Scarlett had left Jane alone with her.

Scarlett was completely out of breath when she burst into her and Jane's apartment. She looked around. Madison and Jane were gone.

"What the hell?" Scarlett muttered, stomping around the apartment. She checked Jane's bedroom. There was no sign of them anywhere. "What did you do with her, you crazy bitch?" Her chest swelled with anxiety and worry.

And then she saw. There was a note taped up on the refrigerator. Jane had scribbled it hastily on the back of a Chinese carry-out bill. It read:

SCARLETT: I'M SORRY, I HAD TO GET OUT OF HERE. MADISON IS SNEAKING ME OUT AND WE'RE GOING TO HER PARENTS' CONDO IN MEXICO FOR A FEW DAYS. I NEED TO GET AWAY FROM EVERY-ONE AND EVERYTHING. MADISON SAYS THERE'S NO CELL RECEPTION AT HER PLACE, WHICH IS PROBABLY A GOOD THING. I LOVE YOU! SEE YOU WHEN I GET BACK. XOXO JANE

ACKNOWLEDGMENTS

To Max Stubblefield who has helped me achieve every goal I've set and become a very good friend along the way. To Nicole Perez who has done so much for me and has always made sure I had good posture. To Kristin Putt-kamer for everything she does, including saving my book when I forgot to back up my hard drive before accidentally downloading a computer virus.

To P.J. Shapiro for always looking out for my best interests. To Dave Del Sesto for helping me keep my life together. To Adam DiVello for finding me in a parking lot at Laguna Beach High School and sticking with me ever since. To Sophia Rossi for being the big sister I never had. To Tony DiSanto, Liz Gateley, and everyone at MTV, without whom this book would not be possible.

To HarperCollins for giving me this opportunity, and specifically Zareen Jaffery and Farrin Jacobs for guiding me through the world of publishing. To Matthew Elblonk who helped in obtaining this opportunity for me and assisted in making my dream come true. To Nancy Ohlin, my collaborator, for helping me every step of the way while I navigated the writing process—I couldn't have done it without you.

Also I would like to thank Maura, Lo, Jillian, Natania, and Britton because they are the most amazing people I know and I am lucky to call them my best friends. And of course my family, whose support has been essential in helping me achieve my goals.

Turn the page for a

behind-the-scenes look at

Lauren's book tour. . . .

I can't wait to start my book tour. It's my first one so I don't really know what to expect but I'm really excited. I have spent the last week putting together all my outfits for the tour. Two weeks . . . a new outfit every day. It was a challenge!

June 5, 2009

Time to sign some books . . .
1:02 PM Jun 5th from TwitPic

A table at my book launch party—with my book and my *Cosmo* cover!
photo credit: HarperCollins

At my book launch party!!
8:48 PM Jun 10th from TwitterBerry

Gooooood morning! My book goes into stores today! So exciting :-) and tonight is my first signing . . . 7pm at the Grove in L.A.
8:43 AM Jun 16th from TwitterBerry

I can't believe how many people showed up to my signing! It's crazy. This is such a great way to start my tour. Hope my hand doesn't get sore from signing.

Just left the Grove . . . Thank you to everyone who came!!
You guys made my first signing great! Next stop . . . NYC :-)
9:44 PM Jun 16th from TwitterBerry

Jimmy Fallon!!
2:36 PM Jun 18th from TwitPic

Just finished filming Jimmy Fallon and now I'm heading to my
book signing in NYC! PS Jimmy was so cool . . . Just became
an even bigger fan :-)
3:48 PM Jun 18th from TwitterBerry

About to go to bed after a long day. The book signing was amazing! Thank you so much to everyone who was there. Your support means so much.

8:40 PM Jun 18th from TwitterBerry

About to take off for Chicago for a signing at Anderson's Bookshop in Naperville.

7:13 AM Jun 20th from TwitterBerry

On our way to the Mall of America for today's signing . . .

11:20 AM Jun 21st from TwitterBerry

The crowd at the Mall of America signing. photo credit: HarperCollins

Went to Mall of America and made a new friend.

With the Mall of America
bomb-sniffing dog. photo
credit: HarperCollins

Houston, we have arrived :-)
9:33 AM Jun 26th from TwitterBerry

We're heading to Blue Willow for tonight's signing. It's my
second to last one. I can't believe the tour's almost done!
4:33 PM Jun 26th from TwitterBerry

I just got to my hotel room and they had a mini "L.A.
Candy" book made of chocolate for me. It's really cool!
Get it? It's candy . . . Haha
10:21 PM Jun 26th from TwitterBerry

This is printed on choc-
olate . . . So cool
10:21 PM Jun 26th from TwitPic

Heading to our last signing in Austin
11:45 AM Jun 27th from TwitterBerry

L.A. Candy event in Dallas.
photo credit: HarperCollins

My book tour is officially
done . . .
1:26 PM Jun 27th from TwitPic

After 2 weeks, 8 hotels, 10 flights, 11 signings, 3,000 side braids, 10,000 books signed . . . I'm done :-) I'm coming home!!!!
1:49 PM Jun 27th from TwitterBerry

I'm wearing all the friendship bracelets I got on my book tour on Chelsea Lately tonight. Fancy!!
2:41 PM Jun 30th from TwitterBerry

Backstage at Chelsea Lately . . .
2:41 PM Jun 30th from TwitPic

Well, my first book tour is officially over. It was such a good experience. I got to travel all over the country and meet so many people. Thank you to everyone who came out to support me. I enjoyed meeting each and every one of you! Can't wait til my next one!

Now that I'm back at home, I'm hard at work on *Sweet Little Lies*, the sequel to *L.A. Candy*. There's a lot more drama in store for Jane and her friends and I wanted to share a special sneak peek with all my fans! So, turn the page for an excerpt . . .

Sweet Little Lies

IS THAT THE GIRL FROM THAT SHOW?

Jane hurried toward baggage claim, eager to get out of LAX as quickly as possible. With Christmas only two days away, the place was packed. Good—she would be able to slip in and out without anyone bothering her. Her baseball cap and oversized Chanel sunglasses would keep her anonymous. Or scream, "I'm a celebrity in hiding." Jane never thought she would actually *crave* anonymity, but she did. Now more than ever.

She felt her bikini bottoms chafing against her hips. In her rush to leave the Parkers' condo, she had slipped her jeans on over her bathing suit, practically running out the door with her hastily packed suitcase into the waiting cab. She glanced at the clock on the departures-and-arrivals board: 4:15. If she had stayed in Cabo, she and Madison would be catching the sunset on the beach . . . or mixing margaritas in the kitchen . . . or making plans for the evening. Jane had grown accustomed to the slow, lazy rhythm of their days, their carefree routine. The way Madison made Jane's breakfast every morning (coffee, yogurt, and fresh fruit arranged in the shape of a smiley face), talked her down whenever she was in one of her funks, entertained her, distracted her, comforted her. Madison had been a perfect friend.

Jane passed an airport newsstand and turned her head to avoid catching a glimpse of the tabloids. She hoped her face was no longer plastered on any of them, but she didn't want to risk looking. For a brief second, she had the impulse to turn around and get on the next flight back to Cabo. But she knew she couldn't, and besides, Madison had probably taken off herself to meet her parents for the holidays in . . . Where exactly did Madison say she was going? Jane had asked her several times, and Madison had been vague about it. New York? Boston? London? Some island somewhere? But that was Madison: always full of fun, fabulous, half-formed plans.

As for Jane, it was time to face the music. Hopefully not all at once. Her immediate goal was to get to the apartment, unpack, repack, grab the Christmas presents she'd bought for her family, then jump into her car and drive up the coast to Santa Barbara. And at some point she might have to listen to the thirty-one messages that were waiting for her on her phone. She assumed it hadn't taken long for her voice mailbox to fill up.

If she was lucky, maybe Scar would still be in their apartment, and they could talk in person. She knew that the Harps were headed to Aspen at some point, but she wasn't sure exactly when.

Rounding the corner, Jane passed another magazine stand—and stopped in her tracks. There was her face, up and down one of the racks, on the cover of *Talk* magazine. It featured a photo of her with the cover line: L.A. CANDY STAR CAUGHT IN LOVE TRIANGLE.

Jane bit her lip, trying not to freak out.

Just days ago, she had been a rising star, "America's sweetheart," a normal girl with normal problems whom everyone could relate to and wanted to see on TV week after week. A few issues ago, *Talk* had dubbed her "Hollywood's Newest It Girl." And *now* what was she? A slut who cheated on her boyfriend with his best friend? It didn't get much worse.

How had her image gone from good to terrible in such a short time?

Jane had to get out of LAX, ASAP. She saw the sign that said, BAGGAGE CLAIM, and hurried toward it. Once there, she scanned the crowded carousels, trying to figure out which one would have her bag. Within a few minutes, she spotted her baby blue rolling suitcase rounding the nearest carousel. She picked it up and turned to go. *That was easy,* she thought.

She heard them before she saw them.

"Jane!"

"Over here, Jane!"

Jane whirled around, knocking her suitcase over.

There were four of them in all: three photographers and a fourth guy with a handheld camcorder. They must not have noticed her at first.

"Jane, have you talked to Jesse?"

"How do you feel about the photos being released?"

"Is it true that you leaked your own photos?"

"Jane, why did you cheat on Jesse?"

They were shouting at her, their voices so much louder than the background noise of flight announcements and crying toddlers. Everyone around them turned to stare at her. She heard nearby murmurs—"Who is she?" "Ohmigod, is that the girl from that show?" "Janie! Isn't she that actress?"—and saw people pulling out their cells and snapping pictures of her. Jane felt frozen in place—trapped.

Then she took a deep breath and remembered what to do. She picked up her suitcase, walked briskly past the shouting photographers and ogling crowd, and headed through the sliding glass doors in the direction of the taxi stand. With her hat over her eyes, her sunglasses in place, and her head held high . . . *ish*.

Sweet Little Lies

An L.A. Candy Novel

Fame
comes with perks—
and problems.

L.A. Candy, the hit reality show, has
made Jane Roberts a full-fledged celebrity. But a
tabloid scandal has her escaping to Cabo with Madison,
who almost has Jane convinced that her BFF, Scarlett,
is responsible for her media troubles. In *Sweet Little Lies*,
Jane is learning that some lies are only as sweet as
the people telling them.

www.harperteen.com

HARPER

An Imprint of HarperCollinsPublishers

GOSSIP

YOUR #1 SOURCE FOR ALL THE HOLLYWOOD DIRT THAT'S FIT TO SLING

Jane Roberts may be a star on PopTV's new hit show, *L.A. Candy*, but she's finding that fame isn't always as sweet as it seems! In this city a photo can make or break a career, and our darling Jane just found out the hard way, with a quick snap of the shutter. Use your phone to take a picture of the code below to satisfy your craving for gossip, videos, and exclusive series secrets!

- With your phone download the 2D bar code reader software at **http://lacandy.mobi/reader**
- Take a photo of the code using your phone's camera.
- Be the first to know about the sweet trouble that lies ahead for Jane and the cast of *L.A. Candy*.

www.harperteen.com

HARPER
An Imprint of HarperCollinsPublishers